THE
CRASH
PALACE

ANDREW
WEDDERBURN

COACH HOUSE BOOKS, TORONTO

first edition

Published with the generous assistance of the Canada Council for the Arts and the Ontario Arts Council. Coach House Books also acknowledges the support of the Government of Canada through the Canada Book Fund and the Government of Ontario through the Ontario Book Publishing Tax Credit.

LIBRARY AND ARCHIVES CANADA CATALOGUING IN PUBLICATION

Title: The Crash Palace / Andrew Wedderburn.
Names: Wedderburn, Andrew, 1977- author.
Identifiers: Canadiana (print) 20200156489 | Canadiana (ebook) 20200156500 | ISBN 9781552454053 (softcover) | ISBN 9781770566255 (EPUB) | ISBN 9781770566347 (PDF)
Classification: LCC PS8645.E27 C73 2020 | DDC C813/.6—DC23

The Crash Palace is available as an ebook: ISBN 978 1 77056 625 2 (EPUB) 978 1 77056 634 7 (PDF)

Purchase of the print version of this book entitles you to a free digital copy. To claim your ebook of this title, please email sales@chbooks.com with proof of purchase. (Coach House Books reserves the right to terminate the free digital download offer at any time.)

for Mom and Dad

'It seems thematic that (Faerie) is all about following permissible paths, not about travelling freely in any direction. You can't really map Fairyland. It resists definition, and directions and distances are mutable. The way to get somewhere is not to follow a map but to follow instructions: "Follow the setting sun until you get to the Glass Hill, then throw a straw in the air and travel in the direction it points, until you reach the Oracle, who …" etc.'

— Paul Hughes, *Paul's Dungeon Master Notebook*

Spin that wheel, spin little girl,
Spin away that grain.
Cart that gold right out the door,
Dig that royal name.

Little Rattle, Little Rattle,
Little Rattle Stilt!
No-name No-name
No-win game.
Little Rattle Stilt!

Pound that stilt, pound little man.
Pound that stilt and grab.
Grab a handful, yank it up,
Rip yourself in half.

(Solo, 4 bars)

Little Rattle, Little Rattle,
Little Rattle Stilt!
(Repeat & fade out)

The Fish Cans, 'Little Rattle Stilt,'
from *Nail My Heart to the High Level Bridge*
A&M Records, 1986

Years later, Audrey Cole bumped into a van on Centre Street, just up from Cash Corner, and thought, This is just like Wrists' van.

She bumped into the van's passenger-side mirror walking head down against the wind, a mid-December wheezing wind blowing over Calgary off the eastern faces of the Rockies. The Beltline street lights glowed orange in the brittle sky, and Audrey, shoulder forward against the cold with both fists in the pockets of her too-thin-for-walking-around jacket, knocked her arm against the glass.

She shouldn't have been walking south down Centre Street on a Friday night at ten o'clock. Home was west, the other way along 12th Avenue. At home Shelly was in bed, hopefully had been for hours, herded up the stairs by her grandmother, who would have come back downstairs to put all the colouring books, bead-eyed stuffed bears, plush hedgehogs, and stringy-haired plastic princesses left in front of the television into their Rubbermaid tub.

Audrey should have been at home, on the couch with her mother for the late cycle of the local news while her daughter slept upstairs, except that she'd seen the Skinny Cowboy.

She'd got a clear look and she was sure.

Her first feeling was to run. Turn around and run in the other direction, who cares what anyone looking thought. For two months she'd been telling herself that of course she would never see the Skinny Cowboy, even if she'd wanted to find him, and there he was plain as day, and her stomach dropped and she wanted to run.

She spotted that worn leather jacket with the flowers stitched on the shoulders and the long silver hair under the wide-brimmed black hat on the other side of 8th Avenue. Her stomach wanted to run.

I want to talk to him, she reminded herself. I want to talk to him and get it out of the way.

She stuffed that fear down and didn't run away. She started to cross 8th, to follow him, but a crowd of partygoers just emptied from the Palliser Hotel flagged down a cab in the intersection, snarling traffic while they haggled with the cabbie, and by the time she'd shoulder-cut her way through the throng, he was disappearing under the train bridge southward on 1st Street.

You should have shouted at him, Audrey told herself, standing on the sidewalk of 12th Avenue and Centre Street – Cash Corner. The wrong way from the late evening news and her mother and daughter and all the toys in the Rubbermaid tub. *Hey, hold up*, you should have shouted. Before he disappeared into an alley or down a manhole, into the night.

She didn't shout at him but by Cash Corner she'd lost him.

They called it Cash Corner because in the morning men would lean on the fence and wait for trucks to stop with work. They would hang their tool belts and backpacks from the chain-link. A truck would stop and the driver would say, 'I need two drywallers,' and some of the men would pick up their tools, put out their cigarettes, and crowd around the window, and the rest would sit back down.

You should have shouted at him, Audrey told herself. She walked south down Centre Street, farther the wrong way from home. Then she bumped into the van mirror.

She jumped, startled at the contact, spun sideways by the lever of her pocketed arm. She put a hand on the van's window frame to straighten herself out.

Maybe not like Wrists' van, she decided after a more thorough look. This was newer. She cupped a hand on the glass to see into the cab through the street-light glare. This van had a proper modern plastic dashboard and a full complement of rear-view mirrors. Seats you'd last in for longer than an hour without losing feeling below your waist. Without thinking, Audrey pulled on the handle. The door didn't open and she let go of it like a hot pot lid, realizing what she had done. But no alarm sounded.

Of course it's locked, Audrey. Every car door is always locked. Some things people aren't careless about.

Audrey Cole walked up Centre Street pulling on door handles. Just to be right about the always-lockedness of car doors. She pulled handles and the locked car doors did not open. Sedans and hatchbacks and bulbous, oversized utility trucks all sealed securely. Red lights blinked behind the glass on some dashboards and these she avoided. A station wagon with a ski rack beeped at her when her fingers touched the handle. A boxy old Impala honked once when she was six inches away. Two strikes, Audrey, she told herself, and skipped the next two cars.

The last car on the street was a sleek grey Audi sedan, washed that day and not yet recoated in winter road salt. A car that lives in a garage, she thought, that never gets snowed on. She pulled the handle and the door opened.

Audrey stood on the sidewalk looking down into the open door, at the leather seat inside. Cars like this have little fobs with remote lock buttons. People get in the habit of shutting them off, walking away, and then thinking later, *Did I lock the car?* They press the button that locks the door with a short, sharp click. One day they ask themselves, *Did I lock the car?* and as a test of trust they say *Yes, of course, I always lock the car*, and put the keys back in their pocket without touching the button. *I always lock the car, it's silly to think otherwise.*

She shut the passenger door. Walked around to the driver's side and climbed into the seat. Wrapped her hands around the steering wheel. Ran a palm along the dashboard. The car smelled like eucalyptus shampoo and shea butter. Everything felt the right size and scale. Her feet and hands could easily reach everything they needed to. In Wrists' van, or Joe Wahl's van, or even her father's pickup truck years and years ago, she always had to stretch, extend a leg to push a clutch, lean up and ahead, even with the seat pulled all the way forward. She was always two sizes too small for anything she ever drove. But the Audi was all the proper proportions, everything right where she would want it. As if she'd been there in Munich and the robot arms had assembled it around her, fitting each piece to her body.

Audrey pulled down the sun visor. In the movies when they're in a hurry to escape the scene of the crime they look under the sun visor, where the car owner has left their keys, because apparently that is where people in movies leave their keys. She opened the glovebox: AMA maps, registration.

The elbow rest had a flip-up lid, which she opened. She picked through CD cases and a packet of tissue paper, and at the bottom was a set of keys.

They put out bait cars, Audrey. She'd seen the newscasts: desirable makes and models left by the police in tempting places for someone to come and yank. The cops follow at an easy pace, the work all done. They put cameras in these cars. They run the footage on the six o'clock news. Teenage joyriders smoking joints at eighty kilometres an hour through school zones in the middle of the afternoon.

'Car,' said Audrey out loud, 'are you a trap? Or just a what-do-you-call-it. Statistical happenstance?'

That wide-brimmed, beat-up black cowboy hat: she didn't know anything about hats but she knew that hat from across a street. People think when they buy a cowboy hat that they're going to look like Clint Eastwood in Italy, but once it's on their head it's too stiff and doesn't fit right, and they wear it once a year for the Calgary Stampede with boots they can't walk in and a boxy, wrongly proportioned Navajo print shirt, and they are poorly prepared for Cowboy Hallowe'en. The Skinny Cowboy was not these people. The Skinny Cowboy was Clint Eastwood in Italy.

First she wanted to run away, flush with that old fear, but she told herself, Track him down and tell him what you want to tell him. And she followed him up Centre Street, the wrong way from her house, until he disappeared.

She put the keys in the ignition and started the car. Trying to picture that hat from across the street, trying to picture the silver hair and the stitched roses underneath it. The engine made a barely there purring sound. There were only thirty thousand kilometres on the odometer. The street was dark, just Audrey in the car. She felt with her feet and there was a clutch and she gasped with abrupt joy. Pushed in the clutch, put it in gear, and drove away from the curb.

§

She drove around the Beltline, looking for the Skinny Cowboy. Up and down tight streets, driving slowly to watch for cowboy hats on the sidewalk. She crossed McLeod Trail into Victoria Park and didn't see the Skinny Cowboy hanging around any of the self-storage garage doors or lurking in one of the vast Stampede grounds parking lots.

Up 9th Avenue, the grid city of two-storey houses and four-storey walk-ups thinned and ended. She drove between dark lots and open construction holes rung in rebar-tipped concrete posts, into the irregular east city of oddly angled roads and rail yards. Trains rolled past, flashes of graffiti colour in the occasional light. In Inglewood and then Ramsay the tracks converged into wide switch yards, and the city turned and snaked along these vectors. She opened the window with a button and let in the Ramsay Inglewood smells: the chicken plant up 11th, just-washed cement trucks, idling diesel engines. Flickering gas flares hung in the air above Fleischman's Yeast, blue candles diffusing the gas of billions of living and dying things, thick and dense, stronger than any morning bakery or skunky beer bottle. She drove past the vacant brewery, through a set of switchbacks out onto Ogden Road, empty in the night, and picked up speed on the long straightaway. Seed-cleaning plants. Western and Chinese Diner. Calgary Metal, huge and red, oversized letters hung on a rusty red fence. Sunday Special All You Can Carry $20. She saw headlights ahead and slowed down, and sped when they passed.

She didn't see the Skinny Cowboy. She was a long way past the roaming range of a pedestrian now. She closed the window and sealed herself back inside the eucalyptus-butter engineered air of the sedan cab.

She followed Ogden south and it was empty for a long way, blocks and blocks of just her headlights in the dark, south and east and south again, and then up ahead lights moved above her in the dark: traffic on Deerfoot Trail over the Calf Robe Bridge. On Deerfoot she could go north or south and be anywhere. Anywhere in Calgary, or anywhere else for that matter.

The road curved and lights blinked, ahead under the overpass: yellow tow-truck lights and blue and red police lights. She let her foot off the gas. Some kind of accident, thought Audrey. Police cars parked lengthwise across the road made a fence. Must have been serious, she thought. She slowed, staring into the blue and red.

Audrey, you stole a car, she told herself.

Formed the words in her mind and blinked, while the car closed toward those red and blue lights. Her foot drove hard into the brake and she lurched forward in a hard stop.

She put the car in reverse and made a fast three-point turn, then back in a hurry the way she'd come. The tires squealed and the sound startled her and she pushed her foot to the floor, shifting upward quickly. The night yards rushed past: she looked down at the speedometer: eighty-five, ninety kilometres. She took a few long Ogden Road curves at high speed, pushed like salad in a spinner against the car door. Ahead of her, headlights came around a curve and she shifted down again, crunching back toward at least legalish speeds until a yellow cab drove past. She saw the green exit sign up ahead for 25th Avenue, which would get her back to the Beltline. The Skinny Cowboy was long gone, but she should get home anyway.

Don't panic, Audrey. Just get home.

§

Later she sat parked on 12th Avenue across from her little mustard-yellow house, where the porch light was still on above her door. Her tangle of winter-bare caragana hedge and her brown winter-dead lawn. Technically not hers, but her name was on the lease and she was never late with the rent.

The car wasn't hers and she sat inside it feeling the steering wheel.

You have to get it someplace, Audrey. Take it up a few blocks and leave. Get it away from here. They don't dust a car for prints and they don't interview witnesses when it turns up damage-free, keys back in the elbow rest. Drive it a block, lock the keys inside, and then go home. Hurry back and quietly open your door. Take off your coat and climb the stairs without creaking too much. They are asleep and it's late so do your best not to wake them when you go in. It's eleven o'clock: Shelly's been asleep for hours. Get inside and forget you did this crazy thing and think back months from now and laugh.

She took the key out of the ignition and put it in her pocket.

Audrey Cole opened the door and stood inside her little entryway in the dark. Jackets hung from wooden pegs: mother and daughter and grandmother jackets, a denim jacket and raincoat and puffy winter parka, a little red ski jacket and canvas coat, toddler-sized. A pair of red mittens tied together with a length of yarn hung over the doorknob.

She pulled off her boots and stepped into the living room. Her mother was breathing heavily in the darkness, on the fold-out sofa bed, under just a couple of bedsheets.

While Shelly was still a baby, Madeline Cole used to sleep in the spare upstairs bedroom. She would come down into the city from her home in Canmore and stay for a week at a time. When Shelly turned two, she said to Audrey, 'She's a big girl and she needs her own room. Move her in here and I'll stay downstairs in the living room.'

Audrey found the sofa bed in the *Bargain Finder*. Talked the just-graduating university student down to half the price and even got him to borrow a pickup truck to drop it off. She moved the little wooden bassinet that the baby girl had always slept in down into the basement and covered the spare upstairs bed with all of the stuffed animals her grandparents had given her over three Christmases and two birthdays. Audrey took the spare bed frame apart so that the box spring could lie on the floor. If she rolls out, she'll be closer to the ground, she told herself.

Tonight Madeline breathed thickly and regular in the dark on the folded-out bed. Audrey watched her mother sleep for a while and then walked quietly as she could past her and up the stairs.

She opened her daughter's door. Shelly Cole slept still and quiet in her little corner bed, just her face above the covers, surrounded by her stuffed bunnies and bears and ducks. Her nose was clogged and she snoozed thickly in the room, and Audrey leaned on the door frame listening to her daughter's noisy breathing.

It's not so late, thought Audrey. Everyone asleep, pulled under for the night, tucked in, safe. But it's not so late. There are more hours in a night if you're awake.

'I just need a little time, baby,' she said very quietly. 'I need to go up there and see it so I can stop thinking about it. So I don't go crazy.'

She went into the kitchen. Reached up and took a glass jar down from above the refrigerator. Inside was a single key. She tipped the key out into her hand. Held it for a moment, then pushed it into her jacket pocket.

Audrey Cole went back downstairs and out into the night.

PART ONE

THE LEGENDARY LEVER MEN

1

2001

CANMORE, ALBERTA

Audrey Cole passed her driver's test the day after her sixteenth birthday. One hundred per cent from the Rundle Mountain Driving Academy in Canmore, Alberta, all checkmarks, thanks to two years of constant practise in her father's old Dodge pickup. Any chance she had, after school, after washing dinner dishes in the sink and stacking them to dry, she would practise putting the truck in gear, shifting the long stick in and out of neutral, though she had to slide down and almost off the seat, leg all the way straightened, to find the tension point on the clutch. She drove up and down their alley, all the way to the end, then in reverse, looking backward over her shoulder, and once the sun was down she ventured out into the neighbourhood, long loops and figure eights through the closest-to-home intersections, excited to be alone.

Sometimes on weekends she and her father would drive to Calgary without her mother: he might need to go to the garden centre or she might send them in to the T&T Supermarket in the northeast for some kind of dried Chinese mushrooms, unavailable at any grocery store in town, that she needed for a recipe she'd seen on TV. Her father would pull off onto the shoulder just past Dead Man's Flats. They would switch seats, and once she was driving on the highway he'd try not to give too much advice. 'Listen to your engine and watch the RPM needle on these hills here. Don't push it too much. Don't spend so much time looking in your mirrors. It's the road up ahead you have to pay attention to.' She would move the seat forward and he'd dig through the glovebox for the right cassette. He liked instrumental surf music: Link Wray, Dick Dale, the Ventures, and she knew every curve and sign on Highway 1 and 1A between Canmore and Calgary in time to reverb-heavy, tremolo-arm chords and space-echo arpeggios. He'd usually flip sides midway up the long, gear-rattling drive up Scott Lake Hill, and at the top he'd always say, 'This is the highest point on the highway, you know, the whole country, highest point right here.' Sometimes she would say, 'Dad, the Kicking Horse Pass sign says 1,600 metres and this is only 1,400,' but mostly she didn't bother. 'Could've sworn someone told me this here is the peak of the road, sure of it,' he'd say, and then he would turn the stereo up and hum along to the riff under his breath, because they were passing Jumpingpound Creek, and 'Rumble' was his favourite.

He taught her to drive, mostly out of town, sometimes on the highway but more often turning down side roads – rural routes, dirt access roads for campgrounds and gravel pits, old two-lane highways that people stopped using after they brought the Trans-Canada through. Roads that you wouldn't notice going by at highway speed, roads that opened up into a secret alternate grid of pathways, that put you into different landscapes, where the mountains looked a little different, or you saw a river valley that would be hidden from the highway. Just in the space between Canmore and Calgary there were hundreds of these routes and she realized that most people just drove by and never knew any of it existed. He taught her to drive and she found a whole alternate series of overlay worlds, little gravel-covered portals like from science fiction or comic books, trapdoors into secret places that vanished forever if you forgot the specific, unmarked intersection that had brought you there.

She turned sixteen in July. The week before school started, her mother gave her $200. 'I know when I was your age, a little spending money sure made all the difference. That should last you a little while.'

Audrey flipped through the *Bargain Finder*, finger-scanning prices, ready with a pen, and there it was: 1982 Volvo Station Wagon, Needs Work: $400. She walked across town to see it the next day. A flap of cardboard covered a hole in the passenger-side floor. Yellow was more conjectural than descriptive. 'You have to be careful,' said the owner, 'because the whole electrical system shuts off if you touch the turn signal.'

'I'll give you $150 for it,' she said, and drove her new car home.

'No,' said her mother, standing on the front step, arms crossed, staring at the car in the driveway. 'No, Audrey.'

'Now you don't have to drive me around everywhere.'

The fuel gauge dropped on every hill and the empty light didn't work. She took experimental drives to learn the range of different gasoline quantities: five dollars took her across the river and up the hill to the new Nordic Centre entrance and back. Ten dollars would get her to Banff, just into town, where she'd turn and head back, draining the last of the tank just past the Welcome to Canmore sign and coasting into the first gas station.

On weekends she drove up the Spray Lakes Road and practised throwing it into neutral and pulling the handbrake to skid around in the gravel lot above the reservoir. She made full-speed grinding stalls that spun her out in choking clouds of dust, frightening grasshoppers, sparrows, and faraway back-country campers who couldn't see her and only heard the metal stress and four-cylinder cough echoing, magnified and strange, off the high, sheer Mount Rundle south face.

The Volvo had a tape deck and she pillaged the cabinet drawers beside the living room stereo for cassettes. She didn't know which group names went with any given song or sound, and anyway, most of them didn't have singing, so she chose them based on the covers: irregular slab fonts in vivid colours, purples and turquoises, coral pinks and sunset golds, the letterform serifs zigging and zagging off into arrows and tangents, laid over lurid tiki masks, hourglass-hipped cartoon girls go-go dancing on the hoods of red convertibles, apple-cheeked blond men in red suits posing with their guitars and drumsticks. She filled the glovebox and played the tapes loud, the baritone-saxophone honks and lowest notes in every bass walk crackling and buzzing out of the pushed-past-their-breaking-point speakers.

Sometimes she drove east toward Calgary, but mainly so that she could turn around and drive back into the mountains, the full view of the front range laid out in front of her windshield. Eastward, as the foothills softened and flattened into uninterrupted prairie, the roads lost their shape and straightened, stiffened into a flat grid of range roads and township roads, the dead edges of long-ago surveying. Impossible to get lost in or surprised by. But westward: heading up and in toward the mountains, zooming up the slow incline of the foothills, into the wide funnel of the Bow Valley, the highway curved and meandered more and more the farther you went, swooping with the contours of the river valley, rippling from the topographical gestures of the mountainsides. You took an exit into Kananaskis or Bow Valley Provincial Park and the road twisted and shook free, gave you switchbacks and hairpins, abrupt drops into meltwater canyons, steep climbs past gravel pits and limestone quarries lurking hidden in the pine forests. She did her best to get lost, looking for forestry roads, laneways for campgrounds and hiking trails. At worst she'd reach a dead end and have to five- or six-point-turn her way around, head back the way she came.

On one trip back from Banff, she stepped into the clutch and felt it snap. She ground it into first gear with a violent lurch and drove fifteen kilometres an hour the rest of the way into town. Traffic roared past her on the left, windows open for fingers, fists, angry shouts. On the long single-lane off-ramp from Highway 1, a furious slow-moving caravan formed behind her. Drivers veered side to side for a glimpse at whoever was going so goddamn slow. She shuddered into the first truck-stop parking lot. Took everything out of the glovebox, her registration and insurance and her dad's cassettes, unbolted her licence plate with the tip of her pocket knife, threw it all in her backpack, and left the car there.

'So long, Car,' she said. 'It's been a slice, I guess.'

She found a Toyota hatchback on three stripped-bald winter tires and a doughnut spare, as is, ninety-five dollars. 'It was my son's and he left on his Mormon mission and never came back,' explained the frizzy-haired woman who took the crinkled bills from her and gave her the keys. 'I mean, I'm sure he's fine, he's just out there somewhere not calling me, too busy knocking on strangers' doors, I guess, so damned if I'm going to keep his crummy old car around anymore. I just want to make the money back I spent renewing his stupid registration.' Audrey found a fourth tire in the classifieds and started driving the ten blocks to school every morning, window down if it wasn't too cold so that the Deltones and Wraymen could spill out into the neighbourhood. On Thursday afternoons she had an hour between afternoon classes. Would put five dollars in the tank and drive to Lac des Arcs. She would sit on top of a picnic table eating her lunch sandwich, bundled up in her jacket and toque for the deepening autumn weather, staring at the flat lake top while she chewed.

When she wasn't driving she went to school, where she did algebra and quadratic equations and wrote a group social-studies report about the history of Czechoslovakia. Algebra and quadratic equations were the easy part, and she mostly zoomed through these classes with plenty of time to doodle or stare out the window. When she was younger she always got the top marks in math. She'd loved the word problems and factors. She'd loved the little thrill of solving the puzzle and getting the answer right.

When she was sixteen, Audrey didn't get the top marks or win awards. She put in enough effort to get mostly good marks, and a right answer wasn't any particular kind of pleasure anymore. When a teacher said, 'Audrey, you'd do better if you tried harder,' she'd feel peevish and grouchy for a little while. She'd flush with hot anger, which faded quickly, and then she'd go back to staring out the window.

She did group projects in social studies with other girls, girls she'd mostly known since kindergarten, girls she'd taken swimming lessons with and ridden bikes after school with when they were eight. Now they were all taller young women who liked to grouse and gossip, and some of them were already planning for university. They'd all survived puberty with varying degrees of acne and awkwardness. Audrey ended up skinny and gangly and not as tall as some of the other girls. 'Hey, Earth to Audrey,' one of the other girls said as they sat around the table working on the Czechoslovakia report. 'Are you going to help with this or what?' And Audrey felt snappish and mad, but it faded quickly. Most of the feelings faded quickly, and she'd be out of the classroom soon enough anyway.

On a Saturday morning in November she drove the Toyota east up Highway 1, out of the mountain funnel, the glovebox freshly filled with Thee

Midnighters, the Chantays, and Link Wray, who she always brought now that she was familiar enough with the tapes to have favourites. She had a pencil map scribbled on a piece of notebook paper. At fifteen kilometres over the speed limit, it took fifty-five minutes to get to Calgary. In the city she slowed down and kept to the right lane, held her breath every hill that the Toyota struggled to climb, but they made it, up and down Sarcee Trail, then into the heart of the city along the vectors of her map to the graphite star at the end of the last line: MODEL KINGDOM.

Inside, a grey-bearded man wearing an embroidered sailor's hat listened to her question and brought different boxes: sailing ships with cloth sails and string rigging, full-colour photographs of the finished models. She pondered the pictures with her tongue between her teeth, and when she eventually put her index finger on the *Merchant Royal, El Dorado of the Seas*, he nodded in approval. Brought her tubes of glue and tiny jars of enamel paint, each with a two-word name: Sunflower Yellow, Panzer Grey, Raw Umber, Rust Red.

She gave her father the ship for Christmas. He sat in his armchair Christmas morning and peeled the green-and-red paper off the large box. He held it up and smiled, then turned the box so Audrey's mother could see it.

'We'll build it together,' he said to Audrey.

In the basement he laid an unused door across two sawhorses underneath a single bulb hung out of the exposed ceiling joists. He brought two stools downstairs and set them on either side of the new table. A desk lamp for more light. She sat on her stool, holding the box. He spread out the instructions and the pieces. All the pieces either beige or brown, linked together in racks by plastic piping, a plastic tab with a letter pressed in to identify them. He had a pad of paper and a pen and made a list while he read the instructions.

He had tools: sandpaper squares and blocks, a plastic-topped case with a knife handle and different-sized blades, paintbrushes.

Audrey read the instructions. The pieces had names that she could not recognize or connect to the small plastic shapes. There were belaying pins and bollards, pin rails and topgallant sails. Stanchions, yardarms. She folded the white page up to isolate Step One.

'So we glue these together first?'

'We're a long way from gluing anything together.' He reached over and pointed to the page. 'See this little code here? That's the colour we paint that piece. We have to paint them before we can glue them.'

'So we're going to paint them tonight? Did I get all the right paint?'

'Not yet.'

'What are we doing tonight then?'

'Preparing.'

He twisted pieces off the plastic rack and held them under the lamp. Then he fit the knife with a small triangle blade and carefully sliced away the little stub of plastic left from the connection. He sanded it smooth, then wiped it off with a damp cloth.

Audrey looked at all the pieces spread out on the table. 'This is going to take a while, isn't it?'

'Sure is,' said her father.

§

'Is it all right if I take your truck?' she asked him sometimes.

'What, you buy and sell your own used car lot and you've got to borrow my truck?' he might answer. 'Take your own heap if you think it will stay on the road for you.' Or sometimes he said, 'Sure, the keys are in my jacket pocket.' She took her mom's grocery list down off the fridge and drove his truck across town to pick up sandwich meat and canned tomatoes and peanut butter. His truck was too big and the transmission wasn't the easiest, a four-on-the-floor shifter that wanted to stick in neutral and actively fought back moving second to third. But it ran great otherwise and she liked the low gear power and the way it growled and grunted leaving a stop sign or climbing an off-ramp. The factory stereo sounded clear and held together at high volumes. Sometimes she took it out of town, on her own routes, down to the Rafter Six Ranch road, or over to highway 1A, past Seebe underneath the flat stone face of Yamnuska, and she passed slower drivers, roaring out into the oncoming lane, enough horsepower in the truck to pass eighteen-wheelers or camper vans and then zip back into her own lane, and each time she grinned knowing that in the Toyota she'd have been flattened by oncoming traffic. Back in town she always stopped and put a few dollars of gas into her dad's tank, and if he ever noticed the extra time it took her to get two litres of milk and dish detergent, he never said anything.

They gave her an allowance, a hundred dollars a month, and she mostly put it into her gas tank five and ten dollars at a time. Put aside what she could in an envelope in her dresser drawer. On a Sunday in February after a week of soft weather had cleared the snow off the highway, she took a $20 bill out of the envelope and filled her gas tank all the way. Then she headed north. Took the Icefields highway exit toward Jasper and climbed up into the sky. Up and up, hugging the mountainsides, the young Bow River running the other way between altitude-thinning, shortening pine trees. Close to the treeline, the hatchback chugged and slowed. Audrey dropped a gear to try and get up the last stretch of hill, and thick black smoke coughed out from all the inside vents. She pulled over onto the shoulder, yanked the handbrake, and jumped out of the car.

She watched it from a few metres back and it didn't explode, just groaned and smoked. She sighed, took her keys, took everything out of the glovebox. Unscrewed her licence plate, put everything in her backpack.

'Well, Car, I guess this is it. You've got a good view up here at least.'

She ran across the highway so she could face southbound oncoming traffic with her thumb out, shivering in the high mountain mid-winter wind. Eventually an empty Greyhound bus slowed and stopped.

'Should we call a tow truck?' asked the driver.

'I'll do it once I'm home,' said Audrey.

'It was my grandfather's. It's fifteen years old but it has hardly any kilometres on it, mostly it stayed in the garage. I don't think he did much beyond drive it to the landfill and back every few weeks.' A grey Nissan four-cylinder pickup truck, automatic, an old canopy back over the box. No tape deck, not even a radio, but it was the only thing for sale in her price range. He opened up the hood and showed her the little engine, and the air filter was piled with old leaves from some previous autumn. She gave him a hundred dollars and he signed the back of the registration for her. She drove it back in the strange silence, listening to the little engine rattle and putter, wondering if it was meant to sound that way.

§

'I got a phone call about your car,' her father said. He held a fragile plastic model ship mast. 'The RCMP called and said they had to tow it down the 93.'

Audrey put a tiny piece of model glue onto the middle of a yardarm with the tip of a toothpick and pressed it carefully into the centre of his mast.

'I had some problems with the transmission,' she said, not looking up from the model.

'They sent me a bill,' he said.

'They probably should have left it there,' she said. 'It's pretty much scrap.' She set down the pieces and picked up the instructions. Scanned through the diagrams to find the pieces they'd need next.

'Abandoned vehicle removal and disposal. Two hundred and thirty dollars. Give that more time to dry,' he said. 'These are pretty brittle.'

'The car isn't even worth that – how can they charge you more than the car is worth?'

'I think what you mean is "Gee, Dad, thanks for bailing me out and not asking to be reimbursed for my teenage misadventures."'

'Sorry, Dad.'

They spent a few nights a week in the basement sanding and cutting and gluing. They painted the two halves of the hull and he showed her how to wipe off the still-wet paint with a solvent-soaked cloth to make the surface look old. She painted stanchions and bollards and they glued them into little holes on the flat deck pieces.

'Look, your mother gets that same phone call, it's a whole different story, right? "Mrs. Cole, we found your daughter's car empty on the side of a mountain an hour north of Lake Louise." She'd lose her mind. Right?'

Audrey put another bead of glue on the mast and laid the next of the finished yardarms carefully onto the bead. He reached across and put his finger on the plastic, like a Christmas bow, and she fiddled with either side to get the pieces square.

'Anyway, you told me you traded it in for that new heap out there.'

'I guess *traded* isn't really the right word.'

§

She was somewhere south and west. She climbed hills and had views of the easternmost Rockies, close enough that the individual peaks stood out from each other, the raw granite crags and cirques distinct enough that, if she'd known their names, she could have spoken to them.

She saw a handmade sign on a fence and slowed down to read:

ELBOW FALLS RALLY RACE

She followed a washboard gravel road up and down a ridge of hills. A long line of parked vehicles ran up the edge of the road. She parked at the end and got out. Old pickup trucks, little hatchbacks, old station wagons with ski racks. After a while she started passing orange traffic pylons. She smelled grilling meat.

In a gravel parking lot, people in orange vests stood around a propane BBQ. A man in a cowboy hat was grilling burgers. Audrey saw a knot of people standing up at the top of a little ridge above them.

She hiked up through the brush. People were standing behind a line of orange fluorescent tape, in a clearing between pine trees. Just past them was a stretch of gravel road. An S-curve switchback, a short straightaway, and then a final curve before disappearing back into the woods. The gravel was brown and fresh, deep and scored with tire marks.

She stood in the small crowd and was going to ask someone when she heard the engine.

She heard the engine and the conversation died down. Everyone stood quietly and then the car came around the corner. Taking the curve hard, back end drifting out in the soft gravel, kicking up a great cloud of dust. The driver shifted down through the S-curve, then revved up to pick up speed through the straightaway. Came close enough that Audrey could see the two of them in the car: two motorcycle helmets, a driver and a passenger, their heads bobbing back and forth through the curves. The car roared past, picking up speed, a Japanese sport sedan with a big spoiler, bright blue, the windshield, doors, hood, fenders all covered in stickers. It roared past and everyone cheered and they heard it shift again for the last curve and then it was gone, around the corner into the trees, the engine noise fading.

The cars came one after the other, a few minutes apart. All of them tackling the S-curve and then the short straightaway before the tight turn disappearing into the trees. Each of them a little different. They attacked the first curve aggressively or cautiously. They didn't all drift out on the first curve. She saw them pick different spots to shift and rev.

The cars, the Subarus and Hondas and Ford Fiestas, got close enough each time for Audrey to catch a quick glimpse of the drivers and co-drivers in their matching helmets.

She watched twenty cars go by and at a certain point started cheering with the rest of the crowd. Cheered when the cars came into the curve, when they came by close enough to see the helmets, when they sped up through the straightaway and then disappeared around the other curve.

A big man in a denim jacket turned around and beamed at her.

'That was a good day of racing,' he said.

'Yeah,' said Audrey. 'Absolutely.'

§

On cold mornings she revved the engine of the Nissan to get it started and sat waiting for the temperature needle to rise off the bottom before putting it into drive. The steering was stiff and the truck would lurch and choke in first and second gear. On an afternoon spare she drove to the self-serve Fas Gas station and opened the hood. A man with a moustache filling his diesel half-ton wrinkled his nose.

'That radiator is just about to go, kid,' he said. 'Can't you smell that?'

She checked the oil and it seemed fine, and when the man with the moustache went inside to pay, she closed the hood and patted it.

'You're fine, Truck. Doing fine. You just like to warm up a bit more first thing in the morning.'

A few blocks from the school, the temperature needle floated up to the red H line, and a smell like a melting plastic bottle thrown into a campfire filled her nose. She braked for a yield sign and the truck lurched and shuddered. She turned the key to restart it and it coughed and stayed still. Behind her someone honked. Audrey sighed and put on the hazard lights.

'Truck,' she said, 'come on, Truck. You can do it.'

She twisted the key and revved the gas pedal and the truck sat still, stinking like burnt plastic.

A few days later she found the invoice pinned to the fridge under a magnet: Abandoned vehicle removal, $120. She put it in her purse. Sat down at the kitchen table and sorted through the pile of junk mail: Safeway and Home Hardware fliers, a leaflet from their Member of Parliament, and at the bottom, the new *Bargain Finder*.

Nothing under $2,000. After paying the truck removal bill, she didn't even have twenty in her envelope. She walked to school the next morning, hands in her pockets. They published the *Bargain Finder* once a week. But even a week from now she wasn't going to have enough in the envelope. At school she tapped her pencil and imagined an unloved two-seater that just needed a new fan belt, a little rusty and peeling but five-speed with good tires. A little rust and they'd knock that much off the asking price. Maybe in a few weeks there would be a pickup truck or a Jeep. Just something that she could drive.

2

2005

MOOSE LEG – FORT SASKATCHEWAN – EDMONTON – NANAIMO –
VANCOUVER – KELOWNA – KAMLOOPS – REVELSTOKE – NAKUSP –
CRANBROOK – GOLDEN – LETHBRIDGE

The truck driver had finally stopped his rig when she pulled the screwdriver from her purse. She was backed against the passenger-side door of the truck cab, pointing the screwdriver at him, shouting. It takes a long time to stop a truck like this, she thought while she shouted. The driver geared down and stopped on the shoulder in front of a green highway sign that read FORT SASKATCHEWAN 12 KM. She opened the door and dropped out of the truck.

The wind and snow blew hard against her and she ran up the highway shoulder in just a T-shirt and jeans. Your jacket is still back there in the truck, Audrey thought. Your jacket and your bag.

She ran out into the highway and a horn blasted, brakes squealed, white headlights blinded her.

She stood in the snow shielding her eyes with one hand, the screwdriver still tight in the other, and behind the white light a van had stopped on the shoulder ten yards in front of her. She ran to the van and slapped her free palm hard on the window.

'Hold on a second, hold on,' the van driver said through the glass. He fumbled with his locked-up-from-hard-braking seat belt. She heard the man in the passenger seat say, 'She's got a screwdriver, Wrists. She's got a screwdriver, watch out.'

She pulled open the driver door. A horn honked and she ducked as a car screeched past just behind her and carried on into the night.

Audrey shook in the cold. Four men got out of the van. Behind her a door shut and she turned to watch the truck driver climb down out of his cab, a barrel-big man in a work shirt and down-filled vest. He shielded his eyes against the van headlights.

'She tried to stab me,' he shouted over the noise of his idling engine.

'I'm still going to stab you,' shouted Audrey. She walked toward him. The man from the passenger side of the van ran around to get between them. Held his arms out, palms toward either of them.

'Well, having parachuted in here devoid of context, it's clear there's a grievance that's not settling of its own accord, and isn't likely to be settled on the side of a highway in a blizzard either,' he said. 'I imagine a little time and space would put everybody back in their proper mood. Time and space off the road and out of the snow.' He was tall and rail-thin and moved gingerly, each step and motion careful and planned to avoid strain. His voice projected out from the bottom of his narrow chest with little effort and carried clearly over the engines and traffic and wind.

'You're welcome to her,' said the truck driver. 'I'd frisk her before you let her in that van though.'

Audrey lunged and the van driver was in front of her with his arms spread. She juke-stepped; he made to block her and she kicked him in the shin.

The truck driver climbed back up into his cab. 'See you later, sweetie,' he shouted. The engine revved and lurched into gear. The window rolled down and her canvas duffle bag, purse, and jacket flew out one after the other down onto the slushy asphalt.

The thin man waited for the truck to slowly lurch back out onto the highway, then walked over and picked up Audrey's things.

'I got the plates,' said one of the other men from the van. 'We can phone it in. Make a proper complaint.'

'He's lucky this isn't sticking out of his neck,' said Audrey. She stepped back from them with the screwdriver at arm's length, pointing from man to man.

'Just take a few steps back this way,' said the thin man with her belongings under his arm.

'Out of his neck,' said Audrey.

'Just a few steps this way off the highway.'

'Get the cellphone, we'll call the RCMP. Before I forget the plate number.'

'How about she starts by putting that thing away,' said the van driver.

'People are supposed to conduct themselves a certain way,' she said.

'Just put the –'

'Off the highway. Off the lane.'

A car drove past, and the wind it made shook her at a violent angle. She felt paper thin, like she might blow and spin away. She stared at her hands ahead of her in the white van headlights: they shook and shook. Audrey, it is freezing cold, she told herself. The four men stared silently with their arms half outstretched, maybe to catch her if the wind blew her suddenly in their direction. All of their eyes wide and frightened.

She pointed the screwdriver at the passenger-side thin man.

'"Devoid of context"? Really? You need it spelled out?'

'Just put that away,' said the driver. 'We're all going to freeze out here, but you aren't getting in the van pointing that thing at anyone.'

'Anybody touches me, I don't need a screwdriver to make him regret it. Got it? I will … I will …'

'Absolutely.'

'Loud and clear.'

'I will make a bloody mess of you.'

'Absolutely.'

She looked back and forth at them. 'Everybody else just picked me up and drove me as far as they could. I said I'm just looking for a ride and they said sure and drove me as far as they could. No trouble.'

'We know,' said the thin man. 'Hey, sure, we know that.'

'I got his plates, we'll call him in. Bastard.'

'Nobody wants to freeze in a blizzard. We've got a spare seat. We'll take you as far as we can. What's your name?'

He held her bag and jacket out. She took them and dropped the screwdriver into the bag. She hugged her shaking arms around the fabric.

'Audrey Cole.'

'Audrey Cole, I'm Rodney Levermann,' he said, and held out a hand to shake. 'These are the Lever Men: Wrists McClung, Dick Move, and Hector Highwater. We're on our way to Edmonton, and you can sit up front there.'

'Those aren't names,' said Audrey.

'Where we're from they're names. Come on, get in. Where are you headed?'

'Edmonton.'

'Well then, we're all in it together. In the van, everybody, before a snowplow runs us down. Make room, everybody in.'

§

She was twenty years old and had been working up north as a crew driver, taking rig workers back and forth from the Moose Leg work lodge, before she ran away and met the Lever Men. At Moose Leg, the rig workers she drove around called her Easy Money.

'Hey, Easy Money,' they said to her in the morning, 'why the long face?'

'Why the red eyes, Easy Money? Late night?'

'You want a late night you should come with us, Easy Money. We'll show you a good time.'

'Get in the truck,' said Audrey Cole.

The truck was an enormous white Chevy Suburban that sat warming up in the parking lot outside Moose Leg, exhaust rising behind it in the 5:00 a.m. murk of a winter morning. Audrey would start the truck and walk around it scraping frost off the windows while her crew stumbled out of the grey dormitories one after the other, a metal lunch box in one hand and a hard hat in the other, the untied laces of their workboots snapping on the gravel. They wore fluorescent green vests lined with reflective tape over the chests of their grey overalls. They coughed and spat on the ground and smoked their first cigarettes of the day. There might be six or seven of them on her route any given day squeezing into the three benches of the huge truck, and if any of them was more than five minutes late she would honk the horn exactly once.

'Hey, Easy Money, Larry is still coming. Hold up a minute.'

'Larry's got a minute,' Audrey would say, and watch the clock.

'Don't be such a hard-ass, Easy Money, give him a minute.'

'That's what I said,' said Audrey, 'one minute.'

Every morning Audrey drove the full Suburban out of the parking lot and through the long warren of washboarded gravel roads toward one of the half-dozen drilling leases crewed out of Moose Leg. The roads were thick with the previous night's untouched snow and layers of older ice, but the truck was new and huge and she carved through the weather easily enough. Each drilling lease was just a few acres of raw mud cut into the scrubby pine forest, spiked in the centre by a red-and-white-latticed derrick, maybe sitting straight up or maybe cocked at an angle, depending on how the geologists in Calgary had decided to best pierce the bedrock. She parked and the crew tumbled out, lit new cigarettes, and walked across the still-dark snow-packed ground to a company shed sitting up on cinder block feet for their morning safety meeting.

Sometimes a supervisor in a heavy parka would ask for a ride to another lease, or maybe a company consultant in a white shirt and tie under his not-heavy-enough jacket would need a drive down to Cold Lake or back to Fort McMurray. Otherwise she'd wait in the idling truck, watch the riggers climb up into the shed, and if no one needed driving anywhere else she'd drive back to camp for breakfast.

Later in the day she'd make other runs: take a surveyor out to a site circled on a map, or taxi an Edmonton safety inspector from one lease to another. Then, after the sun was down, she'd head back to gather her crew up, all of them groggy and surly after a twelve-hour shift, and bring them back. All of this at twenty dollars an hour. Easy money.

§

'Audrey, why?' her father had asked, reading over the paperwork they'd given her to sign. 'Why do you even want to do this?'

She shrugged, sitting across the kitchen table in her parents' house in Canmore. 'You've been on me to go to school. "Go to school, Audrey," you keep telling me. I can make some money and apply to one of those schools out east. I could go to Halifax or, what's it called, the school in Montreal.'

'McGill,' he said.

'Sure. It's twenty bucks an hour, Dad. For driving around. I can spend some time up there and go to any school I want.'

You should go to school, Audrey, they'd been telling her ever since she graduated from high school. Audrey was bussing tables in a hotel restaurant out by the highway. She walked around the big timber-framed restaurant with her grey bus bin picking up plates and glasses and empty beer bottles. The staff were all other twenty-year-olds, kids she'd grown up with, or Australians who worked summers so that they could ski all winter.

She'd work Sunday brunches and a few weekday nights, and she and the other twenty-year-olds would hang around afterward, sitting at the bar, sipping highballs. Audrey wasn't crazy about drinking – it made her stomach hurt and she didn't like the flushed, buzzed feeling. She'd buy a highball or usually just a ginger ale and sit nursing it while the other staff got drunk and loud. They'd put on their jackets and head up the road to one of the other hotels, where other twenty-year-olds she'd grown up with worked, and they'd sit at that bar for a while doing more or less the same things.

She did this for nearly a year, feeling more and more agitated.

'It's hard up there, Audrey,' said her father. 'The people are… It's hard.'

'They've got Human Resources and mandatory drug testing and they keep you so busy you can hardly get into trouble.'

'It's not that, kiddo, it's…'

'I'll be two weeks up, one week back. They fly us in and out, Calgary to Fort McMurray. So I'll be around. I'll be out of your hair two weeks at a time. You're always on me to get going with life. I'll put some money away and I can get going anyway I like.'

Her mother looked over the pamphlets and didn't say anything. Brightly lit photographs of young men and women in hard hats against white backgrounds. 'Building Canada's Energy Future,' said the pamphlet. She flipped through them, not really reading, and then set them down and looked at Audrey's father.

'It's a dry camp,' Audrey said. 'No trouble to get into.'

'Dry camp, with a curfew, all these rules – it's like you're signing up to go to prison.'

'Two weeks on, one week off. You'll hardly know I'm gone,' said Audrey.

She didn't sign up for the two weeks on, one week off though. She checked the box for twenty-four days on, four days off, which was the longest rotation available. As long as you're going up there, Audrey, she told herself, you might as well go up there. You know, stick it out for the long haul.

§

The first time she saw Moose Leg she just stood and stared. The van from the Fort McMurray airport dropped her off along with a half-dozen other workers, everyone stiff and groggy from the bumpy small-plane flight from Calgary, and then the long van ride. She stood with her big hiking backpack beside her on the icy gravel, full of everything she'd thought she'd need for a month-long stay. The camp was a warren of aluminium-sided trailers pushed together into a single complex, grey with yellow trim, snaking lines of low flat-roofed work sheds, white vapour puffing from sheet-metal chimneys. Everything sour-smelling from the propane heaters struggling to keep the complex warm. The pamphlet had said there were two hundred rooms. Audrey tried to imagine two hundred people living in those corrugated sheds. Eating and showering and sleeping in there all together. It seemed impossibly huge and not nearly big enough.

There were bigger camps, people told her. Huge, sprawling complexes housing hundreds and hundreds of oil-sands workers. They were building camps on the Firebag River that would house over a thousand workers each for the new steam-assisted operations there. She saw pictures of vast industrial tangles of pipes and smokestacks that would pump steam deep into the ground and liquify the hard tar down there into something they could pump out of the ground. She tried to imagine the amount of steam that would need a thousand workers to create.

Parked all around the camp were rows and rows of trucks. Identical white three-quarter-ton trucks, white Suburbans, cargo vans, each with a long aerial with an orange flag on top.

'This flag is your life,' Valerie told her the first week. 'The guys in the big rigs hauling the really heavy gear, that flag is all they'll see of you out on Highway 63. You haven't seen trucks this size, kid. No flag and you're going to get run off the road or run under, and they won't notice or even slow down.'

The company flew the crews in and out of the Fort Mac airport and delivered them by the vanful to Moose Leg. Drug dogs sniffed the new hires and inside they submitted urine samples, and if they came up positive they were put right back on the van that had just brought them. Valerie told Audrey that once a whole vanful of new recruits had all tested positive and been shipped back, leaving them short an entire crew until the next cycle.

'Jesus,' Valerie Murphy said the first time Audrey sat down across the cafeteria table from her. 'Jesus, you're just a baby. You're going to get eaten alive out here. Kid, you do exactly what I tell you and you might get out all right.' She was a short, ruddy woman with a wind-burned face and strawberry-blond hair chopped into a drill-sergeant crewcut. She ate her way through a plateful of mashed potatoes with gravy and drank chocolate milk through a straw.

'First, you follow all the rules to the letter. We're a dry camp, so you're dry. You're going to figure out fast that it's "dry" in quotation marks, but it doesn't matter. You see them boozing, you stay out of it. Smoking only by the blue flags, so that's the only place you smoke. You smoke, kid?'

'I don't smoke,' said Audrey.

'Don't start.' Valerie fiddled with the straw in her chocolate-milk carton. 'You take your boots off when you go to the boots-off lounge and you keep your room clean so when they do the spot searches it's easy for them to find nothing, 'cause you've got nothing in there for them to find. Right? You follow all the rules and if you see any of those other shit-balls not following them, you ignore them. You do your own thing, which is only the thing you're supposed to be doing.'

'My own thing.'

'And the absolute most important thing, the rule you follow religiously like your life depends on it, is you're never out of your room after lights-out. Never for a minute, regardless of the circumstances. Lights out, you're in your room with the door locked. Got me?'

"Cause they'll send me back.'

'Well, sure, they'll send you back, kid, but the reason you stay in there with your door locked is to keep everybody else out.'

§

Audrey spent a few days in a small room with the other newbies watching safety videos. You could fall off a ladder, or drop a pipe end onto your boot and crush all the toes inside. You could touch a live electrical panel and fry yourself, or fall off a scaffold, or crash your truck. They made a point of stressing how much easier all of these things were to do when you were drunk or high on cocaine.

'The one thing you've got to never do,' said the safety consultant, 'is drop anything in the drilling shaft. You'll wreck the bit. That drilling bit costs way more than you do.'

She took tests and signed forms and they finally gave her the keys to the truck.

She waited a few days, to get the feel of the routine, and then one morning, once she'd dropped off her crew, she took a different turn. Turned onto a crossroad on a whim and followed it just to follow it, through a long alley of featureless pine trees.

'Let's see what's out here, Truck,' she said.

She took side roads when they came up, watching the clock and the digital compass in the console, to not get too lost. Every ten or twenty kilometres she hit a featureless, unmarked intersection, and at first she picked a turn at random, and when none of the choices gave her roads that were any different and the clock had gone on a while, she made her way back toward Moose Leg.

At the lot, the supervisor checked the odometer.

'Where have you been?'

'Wrong turn, I just got a bit lost.'

'Wait here,' he said, frowning. She waited while he pulled up the floor mats and looked under the seats with a flashlight. Felt inside the glovebox, in the armrest, behind the sun visors. He got out and lay on the ground and ran his hands around the insides of the wheel wells and under the bumper.

'You've got a map,' he said eventually, after failing to find any booze or hard drugs or hidden prostitutes. 'Follow it,' he said.

§

There were a few other women in the camp. Valerie and a few other tough old crew drivers, who liked to sit together for lunch and complain about the ventilation in their rooms, the water pressure in their showers, the weather, how much they were paid, the length of their shifts. A few of the roughnecks were big-shouldered blond women with tattoos on their forearms, who came down to the boots-off lounge in their white tank tops to play video games or yell at hockey games. A safety analyst from Calgary appeared for a few days at a time, carrying a heavy binder with her everywhere she went. Audrey would see her hunched over paperwork in the farthest-away corner of the camp cafeteria in the afternoon, and when she drove her to a lease to go over the incident reports she liked to sit up in the front and listen to the FM CBC station that played classical music.

Mostly there were men. Everywhere she went – driving her truck, sitting in the van, sitting in the cafeteria – she was surrounded by men.

Big, thick-necked, heavy-bellied men, with ball caps and tattooed forearms, with barbell earrings, with tobacco-stained teeth and bloodshot eyes. They had names that she did her best not to learn, and the best practice for this was not saying anything to them or paying any notice to anything they did.

In the boots-off lounge there were a couple of TVs, one for hockey and one for video games. On any given night there'd be men from Cornerbrook, Newfoundland; North Bay, Ontario; Sydney, Nova Scotia; Shawinigan, Quebec, so Saturday nights, to avoid conflict, they put the names of any hockey game the satellite could pick up into a jar and drew for it. You got an extra slip in the jar if it was your actual hometown team playing, to increase your odds. Mostly they played video games on the other TV, first-person shooter games with space marines, hunting each other four at a time, yelling at the quartered screen, shooting each other with digital space rifles. There was a little bar fridge that the company kept stocked with Pepsi and Sprite, and a vending machine with potato chips and chocolate bars. They poured the Pepsi and Sprite into plastic cups and then topped it up with liquor from the mickeys they kept inside their jackets, and the room stank like a boozy gym locker.

Water dripped from the not-tight-enough seams in the ceiling into buckets around the room. There was a pool table and a few dumpy couches, and in the other corner, against the wall, the pinball machine.

PINOCCHIO, said the back glass in bright red letters. A cartoon of the little wooden boy, mouth agape, eyes crossed at his nose, extended several fibs. Above the score counter, Jiminy Cricket had his arms stretched outward, like he was trying to get the puppet's attention, to warn him about something.

There were three ramps, one making a long loop around the whole playfield, another that led up to a plastic whale, with a hinged jaw that opened up to swallow the ball. The third ramp ran up to a raised platform with three bumpers, on top of which donkeys wearing baseball caps stood on their front legs, their back legs raised up. When the ball hit the bumpers, the legs kicked and the donkeys brayed electronically out of little speakers.

Audrey came in every night to play pinball. She did her best to come either early or late enough to mostly avoid other people.

They hadn't had pinball back at home in Canmore, and outside of a few times on trips to Calgary bowling alleys, she'd never really played. The first few weeks she lost loonie after loonie on low, unmemorable scores, as the bumpers dropped the ball down the gutter after a few weak bounces around the inside of the playfield. She tried to shoot the ramps and missed, and tried to catch the ball on the way back down and lost it down the gutter.

'Geez, Easy Money, look at you work that thing. Look at you work those balls around.'

She watched an older roughneck from Moncton with a scruffy grey beard hit a high score, and how he squared his shoulders to the machine and kept his fingers on the paddle buttons all the time. She watched one of the cafeteria cooks gently nudge the old machine with the front of his pelvis, not exactly rocking it, just applying a bit of pressure here and there.

'Hit it hard, Easy Money! The balls want it hard!'

She played pinball, staring down at the machine, and when she was out of loonies she went back to her room.

If she timed it right, she'd get the washroom with the lock. All the bathrooms were communal: a few urinals and toilet stalls around a gang shower and a trio of small sinks. All except for one, a little water closet at the far end of camp with a toilet and a shower stall, and a door that locked. There was always someone inside. She'd wait in the hall with her backpack over her shoulder, everything she needed inside. Eventually they'd come out, one of the other women staying in the camp, or more likely one of the men, grinning about the stink they'd left behind, or maybe they'd make a point of rolling up the girlie magazine they'd had in there with them. 'Enjoy it, sweetie.'

She'd lock herself in and stand in the little shower, hoping she'd get more than a few minutes of hot water.

Back in her room, locked inside, she had a single bed, a little desk with a chair, a lamp, and a clock radio. It was barely big enough to spread her arms out, but she didn't have to share it, like most of the men who slept two or four in bunk beds in not much bigger rooms. Audrey would lie on the bed, staring up at the acoustic-tiled drop ceiling, and put on her headphones. She had brought a little portable CD player, and a sleeve with a dozen compact discs. She lay on the bed on top of the sheets for a while listening to the Ventures. Loud enough that she didn't have to listen to the men come back down the hallway later, fumbling with their room keys, or through the thin walls talking on their cellphones, watching TV, listening to the radio. Grunting in the thin-walled bathrooms or panting on their squeaking bedsprings.

§

'What are you doing here anyway?' Valerie asked her over a spoonful of instant mashed potatoes.

Audrey thought about the question. Not the question so much as whether or not to really answer it. Then she carefully reached into her little leather purse and pulled out a small wallet. She laid this down on the table in front of her plate of macaroni and cheese and opened it up. She pulled out a folded piece of paper. With two hands she unfolded it and pressed it flat.

Valerie leaned over to look at the picture. 'It's a car,' she said.

'It's a 1996 Mitsubishi Lancer,' Audrey said carefully. 'This is the Evo III. See that moulding in the front? You get more air into the radiator than in previous models. Look at that big spoiler.'

'It's a … race car?'

Audrey leaned toward the photograph, which she had cut out of a magazine. The ink had faded to white along the fold lines, like window mullions.

'Tommi Mäkinen won four straight World Rally Championships driving Lancers.'

'Is that where you've got the co-pilot who sits there shouting when to turn?'

[43]

'A co-driver. Sometimes. You can do those races, yeah. And there's races where you're driving on your own.'

'Which kind of races do you drive in?'

'Well, none yet,' said Audrey Cole. 'I mean, I've gone out to some drifting days with my old Honda Civic. But it won't work for a real stage-rally race. I'd have to get it rebuilt from the ground up. I might as well get out and push. I need the real thing.'

'So you're going to buy a race car.'

Audrey pushed the picture into the middle of the table and had a spoonful of macaroni. 'There's a shop in Calgary that's selling a '96 for $16,000.'

'That doesn't seem like so much,' said Valerie through a mouthful of potatoes.

'That's crazy cheap. Crazy cheap but I need cash upfront. But,' said Audrey, leaning into the photograph again, 'but there's a lot you've got to do to get it race-ready.'

Valerie chewed her potatoes.

'You've got to have a roll cage. It's a safety thing. So that it holds together if you roll it off the road or flip it in the ditch. And tires.'

'Gotta have tires,' agreed Valerie.

'You have to have all the tires. For every situation. Tires and extra wheels. They make the courses multi-surface and who knows what the weather is going to be, so you've got to have tires for everything. That's a few grand right there.'

'You've gotta have a helmet,' said Valerie.

'Yes,' agreed Audrey, nodding seriously. 'Yes, you've got to have a helmet.'

'Fuzzy dice. Pine-tree air fresheners.'

Audrey set down her fork. Picked up the picture and carefully folded it back up. Slid the paper into the wallet and the wallet into the purse.

'I might be able to do it all for $25K,' said Audrey, 'maybe. Maybe more. So I guess the thing is to sock away as much as I can, as quickly as I can.'

'Well,' said Valerie, pausing for a slurp of chocolate milk, 'I guess you've come to the right place for that.'

'I guess so,' said Audrey.

§

She spent her four days off at the Four Eagles Motel on the southeast
edge of Fort McMurray, a long, low, single-storey strip of rooms sand-
wiched in between two car dealerships, their vast lots full of row after
row of oversized pickup trucks.

'Take the charter back to Calgary,' Valerie told her before she left.
'Don't spend your off days in Fort Mac. What are you going to do, hit the
karaoke bars? Go to the strippers? Go home, kid.'

Audrey shrugged. 'I'll probably just sleep the whole time,' she said.

She'd thought about going back. Mostly to check on her car. Her
baby. Her baby was a cherry-red '88 Honda Civic and it was parked at the
company lot back at the Calgary airport. Sitting under who knows how
much snow. She'd spent $4,000 on it, saved carefully from bagging
groceries and bussing tables. She thought about flying down to Calgary
to clean the snow off her baby. Imagined sitting in her car while it warmed
up. Driving up the highway toward the mountains. And turning off
anywhere she liked. No one was going to check the odometer when she
brought it back to the parking lot four days later for her return flight. She
could start it up and be anywhere, any road, just her and her baby.

In the end, though, she was more worried that she'd lose her nerve.
That she'd get back to Canmore and would lose her nerve, wouldn't be
able to get it back to face the men in the boots-off lounge again. That
she wouldn't turn up for the return flight at all. Just go back to the
timber-framed hotel restaurant and start filling up the bus bin with
empty bottles again.

She thought about all the hours of filling up the bus bin that $25,000
was going to take. And so she booked four days off in Fort McMurray
instead.

At the Four Eagles Motel she lay in a giant bath and let her legs float,
suspended in the hot water, free above the tub bottom. Steam condensed
on her face and in her hair. She lay for a long time, letting the steam

soften twenty-four days of clenching tension and break down the oily smells built up in her skin: five men in a tight truck, their sweat, cigarettes, and night-before liquor. The sour smell of propane heaters. Never enough hot water in the tiny shower at Moose Leg to cut through it all. The tub water cooled off and she drained it and refilled it and lay awhile longer, until she was pink and pruned all over.

Audrey sat on top of the bedsheets and squeezed moisturizer out of the little motel-room bottles from beside the tub. Rubbed it into her legs and shoulders. Then she wrapped herself in a towel. Unpacked her little portable CD player and put on Shadowy Men from a Shadowy Planet.

She flipped through the stack of driving magazines she kept in her bag, propped up on an elbow in the little bed. The pages marked with little sticky flags, so that she could flip to specific photographs and interviews.

She opened to a flag on a four-page spread from 2000 about Tommi Mäkinen's new Evo 6.5. Close-up photographs of the engine, all the tightly packed black hoses and bright steel and red metal. Mäkinen himself in his red jumpsuit and helmet, emblazoned all over in Marlboro and Mitsubishi and Micheline logos. A tight portrait of Mäkinen behind the wheel, frowning seriously before his red microphone headset, lantern jaw set in determination.

'Right now, preparing for 2001, it is mostly preparation,' Tommi Mäkinen told the magazine. 'Analyzing different things. Make our car faster, faster. Of course, we are looking for good results soon as possible. But we are realistic. It's important to prepare.'

She fell asleep on top of the sheets, wrapped in her fluffy bath towel.

§

By her second rotation, she was playing Pinocchio with her hips forward against the machine. Stood straight or put a foot behind herself to lean down closer to the field top. Index and middle finger on either flipper. She fired the ball and made loops and ramps and then shot the ball into the whale's throat. The red LED display rolled her score. She fed balls into the whale, and when it had swallowed three it spat them back out, the display lighting up for PLEASURE ISLAND MULTIBALL. She worked three balls at once up the ramps and through the loops. She put the balls up into the donkey bumpers, and they kicked it back and forth. A digitized donkey bray from the little speakers with each bumper bounce. The donkeys kicked the balls back and forth and the red lights on the screen animated the little wooden boy himself, growing red-pixel donkey ears.

In between pinball games, she drove the big white truck from the camp to the lease to the other lease on the routes that they outlined for her. They checked the odometer every day and brought a Labrador retriever to sniff around the seats and tires a few times a week. She called it the truck but it wasn't one truck, it was whichever of the fleet of a dozen different identical Suburbans was parked in her spot that day. She got to know individual members of the fleet by signature chips and pockmarks in the windshields, by the model year differences in the stereos, by the floor mats and upholstery.

'Hey, Easy Money,' they'd say on the drive back, piled into the back seats, stinking like engine grease and propane and sweat. 'Easy Money, hurry it up. Don't waste our downtime driving like an old lady.'

'Easy Money, let us drive, we'll show you.'

'Easy Money, you're a hundred-dollar-a-barrel luxury around here. You're an OPEC production increase away from being the first pink slip.'

'You just keep ignoring them,' Valerie told her at lunch. 'Just like you're doing.

'Stick around, Easy Money,' they said when her last ball drained down the gutter at the bottom of the Pinocchio machine.

'Yeah, Easy Money, don't split. Hang out and work those balls a little longer.'

'Of course, there have been setbacks,' Tommi Mäkinen reassured her later. 'Not all results have favoured us. But we persevere. And of course we learn. Persevere and learn as a team. We have a good relationship with the manufacturer. They hear our suggestions and we have a dialogue. So the setbacks will all enable what we are really after: faster and faster times.'

§

She drove a crew back from the lease down the empty road, the truck's high beams flashing against the black trees. Behind her she felt the crew alert and watching, all of them worked up in a state. She watched them in the rear-view mirror, her stomach tight. They craned their necks to see out the window, staring ahead.

'Up there, there it is,' someone said.

Ahead of her a pair of red hazard lights blinked on the road shoulder. 'Pull over, Easy Money. Right up there where they're stopped.'

'What are you guys up to?' she asked.

'Just pull over, nothing to worry about.'

She thought about stepping on the gas, passing the car wide, but instead she braked. She came to a stop ten yards from a parked truck, the bed covered in a canopy.

A woman got out of the truck cab and walked around toward them, shielding her eyes against the headlights. She had teased-up dyed-black hair and long jangly earrings, with raccoon makeup and bright lips. She hugged a heavy parka around herself, underneath which her legs were in sheer black tights and patent leather boots. She squinted at the truck, then pulled a bottle of brown liquor out from the inside of her jacket and waved it at them.

'What the hell have you done?' asked Audrey.

'Easy Money, listen. We're going to get out and party here for a little while. Just a little while, see? You're going to hang out in the truck and wait for us.'

The woman opened up the truck tailgate and there was a mattress underneath the truck canopy, wrapped in blinking pink and blue Christmas tree lights.

'Jesus Christ, you guys.'

'You're going to hang out and wait for us and you're not going to say anything when we get back.'

'No one needs a spoilsport and no one needs a snitch. Right?'

'Right, Easy Money?'

She didn't want to turn around, and just looked at them in the rear-view mirror. All of their faces hot and their eyes glistening. They clenched their teeth, staring at her in the mirror.

'You've got half an hour,' she said eventually.

'Come on, Easy Money.'

'I can come up with a story for being half an hour late but not any longer. Everybody out and I'll honk the horn when you've got five minutes.'

When they'd piled out of the truck, she pulled around and parked thirty yards farther up the road. Face hot, heart racing, stomach still in her throat. She kept the truck running and watched the time. Stared ahead out the window, doing what she could to not look in the rear-view. She turned on the radio and hunted around the dial. After a while she found the classical music station that the safety analyst from Calgary liked. She sat listening to strings and pianos, watching the minutes tick by on the clock. Doing her best to keep breathing evenly.

She watched the clock, and when enough minutes had ticked by she honked the horn.

They took their time piling back in, stinking like whisky and sweat and perfume, something with vanilla and chocolate. They didn't say anything and one of them giggled and another laughed and then they all laughed as she put it in drive and pulled away. One of them rolled down a window. Hung his head outside and howled like a dog in the night. He howled and they laughed and she pushed the accelerator to the floor.

She made it two days into her third rotation and then she ran away.

§

In Edmonton, Audrey sat by herself in a booth, sipping ginger ale, watching the men onstage. She drank four glasses of ginger ale while they loaded scuffed amplifiers and black guitar cases, coated in peeling old stickers, into the cold, sparse Jasper Avenue bar. The hot yellow stage lights were on, and she could see the grey in their hair, the deep crow's feet in their sun-leather faces. Wrists and Rodney wore old cowboy shirts, the stitched designs worn out and faded. Worn-down boot heels that clopped and snapped on the wooden stage.

'Give me that kick,' said the soundman from the back of the room.

Dallas 'Wrists' McClung thump-thump-thumped beats on the bass drum. Wrists had the second-whitest hair, after Rodney. Grey-and-white-peppered hair buzzed down to a World War II crewcut, and heavy black-rimmed glasses that sat on swollen, scarred ears. He kicked the bass drum with his arms crossed, a stick in either hand, while the sound man at the back of the room turned dials. Across the floor a few people leaned on the bar and ordered more rye-and-gingers. Then boom-boom-boom, the drum was in the big main speakers.

'It's too loud,' yelled someone in a cowboy hat.

'I love this song,' yelled a girl in a denim jacket smoking at the bar.

Hector Highwater wore a black-and-red Hawaiian shirt, with hibiscus leaves and silhouetted hula girls, and faded green tattoo ink swirled up the back of his neck from under the collar. He pulled two bar stools up onto the stage and set an old suitcase organ across them. He stood with one hand on the organ keys and pulled cables in and out of different jacks until a grinding organ chord whined across the room.

Richard 'Dick' Move slung a heavy bass guitar over his shoulders, hung down below his belt at the end of a leather strap. He was stocky and short with big shoulders, and wore a faded black T-shirt with little holes around the collar and hem. MARS IS HEAVEN, said the T-shirt in white block letters.

Rodney Levermann sat on a chair, watching. He had clipper-buzzed white hair that was a week or two grown out from his last shave. He watched them move gear and then stood up carefully and walked toward a big tweed-covered speaker cabinet. Dick dropped his bass and intercepted him.

'Whoa, boss, let me get that.'

'I've got it,' said Rodney.

'Sure you do, sure you do,' said Dick, pushing himself between Rodney and the cabinet. He hoisted it up with a grunt and pulled it up onto the stage. Rodney followed, pulling himself up gingerly.

'Put it there, closer to Wrists,' said Rodney, pointing. 'No, closer.'

He waited for Dick to position the cabinet properly, then set an old amplifier head, no front faceplate, the tubes and wires naked in the undercarriage, on top. He knelt in the middle of the stage and opened a red tool box. He pulled out a set of pea-green plastic shell rifle-range ear protectors and snapped them over his narrow head. Knocked on either shell with a fist and wiggled them tightly over his ears. Then he knelt again and took an ash half-hollow Telecaster out of its case. The wood around the single f-hole was worn down through the finish by years of pick strokes. He plugged the guitar in and flipped off the standby. Waited while the lights on the front of the head lit up red. He stood up, twisted the microphone in its stand, and sucked in his cheeks.

'Check check. And forgive us our trespasses. Check. One two. As we forgive those huh. One yeah. Trespass. Daily bread. We're ready when you are.'

The bar was quiet.

'I guess we're ready any time, sure,' said the man at the back of the room.

And then instead of whatever she'd expected, they played reverb-heavy, tremolo-arm surf chords and space-echo arpeggios – exactly something her father would have had on a cassette, that eyes closed she'd have known in time with fifty-five minutes worth of Highway 1 landmarks – the Exshaw cement plant, the Kananaskis park off-ramp, the all-alone lights of the all-by-themselves reservation houses out on the Morley Flats, the trucker weigh-in station, and in a few minutes the Cochrane overpass Petro-Canada – and then it's just down one hill and up another into the city limits. None of them sang or spoke into the microphones, they just played fuzzy, echoing surf-rock riffs and vibrato country chords for an hour and a half, by the end of which Audrey was alone in the bar with the band and the staff.

She sipped her ginger ale and closed her eyes and let the music pour over and into her.

Afterward, Rodney slumped in the booth, panting, sweat on his lined face and in the clipper-length bristles of his scalp. His washing-machine-thin shirt stuck translucently to his pigeon chest. Dick Move came back to the table with two closed hands full of beer necks, a shot glass of bourbon clasped and spilling between his two upright thumbs.

'Domestic bottles is all they'd give me without paying,' he said. He stood trying to solve the problem of how to let go of the beer bottles without probably dropping the bourbon. No one at the table made any move to help him out.

Hector came back from the bar with a bottle of beer and two glasses of whisky. He put one of the glasses in front of Rodney.

'What's the plan tomorrow?' asked Hector.

'Tomorrow? You mean tonight. We have to play in Nanaimo tomorrow.'

'So we'll drive to Nanaimo tomorrow.' Hector drank a shot of whisky and tilted back his beer.

'We have to be there at seven,' said Dick Move. 'It's what, ten hours?' He put the beer bottoms flat on the tabletop and focused hard on his fingers, working on which ones needed to release the bottle necks and which needed to stay tight around the shot glass.

'When I was in the Plunging Necklines we used to play in a bar in Nanaimo called the Log Driver. Is that still there?'

'It's ten hours from Calgary to Vancouver and we're in Edmonton. There's a ferry to Nanaimo that's two hours on its own. We have to drive tonight.'

'Wrists has to drive tonight, you mean,' said Hector. 'I'm drinking.'

Wrists came to the table with two hands full of beer bottles. 'Don't get too comfortable,' he said, 'we have to drive tonight. Load-in for Nanaimo is seven o'clock. We have to take the ferry.'

'You have to drive to Nanaimo, we're drinking,' said Dick Move.

'I'm not driving, I'm drinking. Hector's driving.'

They sat around the table looking at each other.

'I mean, I guess I could sober up a bit after I finish these,' said Hector. Wrists sighed, twisted in his seat. Rummaged in the jean jacket hung over the back of his chair. 'I write all this down for you dough heads. Don't you read the printouts?' He pulled out a padded manilla envelope, heavily creased. From this he produced a folded piece of paper, the printer sprocket-reel holes still attached to either side.

'Day Four – Saskatoon to Edmonton. Trap & Grizzly, Jasper Avenue. Load in 6:00 Set Time 10:00 90 minutes.' He jabbed a finger on the sheet and read slowly, exaggerating each syllable. '*Leave early drive overnight to make Day Five Nanaimo load-in at 7:00 PM.*'

Hector and Dick both took long pulls at their beer bottles.

'What if we got up, like, really early,' asked Dick.

'It's eight hours just to Kamloops from here. Three more past that to Vancouver. Then however much time you wait at the ferry terminal. Even if we left at six we might not make it.'

'If we're getting up before six we might as well drive tonight.'

'I'm not driving anywhere tonight.'

'I'm going to be too drunk to drive anywhere tonight in about ten minutes.'

'I'm not going to Edmonton,' said Audrey Cole.

The men all looked at her.

'I wasn't going to Edmonton.'

'Where are you going?' asked Rodney.

'It doesn't much matter,' she said. She pushed her ginger-ale glass into the middle of the table.

They looked at each other and Rodney grinned. He took the shot glass from between Dick's thumbs and drank it.

'Hey,' said Dick, 'that was …'

'What time do you want to get going?' Rodney asked.

'Once you're all finished with those,' said Audrey. 'We'll have time.'

'Hold on,' said Wrists.

Hector clanked his bottle against one of Dick's and drained it down. 'Pass me another one of those,' he said.

'Hold on. Hold on,' said Wrists. 'We're not taking on a teen runaway.'

'I'm not a teenager. I'm twenty.'

'You look like a teenager.'

'You look like a grandfather,' said Audrey, and Dick and Hector both laughed.

'We're not popular,' said Wrists. 'We're not popular and we don't draw and there isn't going to be any money. We're not giving you any money.'

'I've got money,' said Audrey.

'Tomorrow at this time you're going to be a thousand kilometres away in some other shithole that looks more or less like this one. And whether or not you're going to Edmonton, you're not going to be anyplace in particular.'

'And that will be just perfect,' said Audrey. 'No place in particular.'

'Jesus, Wrists, now you're talking me out of going,' said Rodney. 'Just drink up.'

'Drink up and give me the keys,' said Audrey Cole.

§

On the highway, Wrists flipped through the radio dial from the passenger seat, and songs and voices, waves of guitar clatter and pitchman babble approached and receded in and out of atmospheric fuzz, in occasional time with the oncoming traffic. He found a scratchy country-and-western oldies station playing a George Jones song that sank into hornet buzz under every power line.

A pine-tree air freshener hung off the rear-view mirror, which had a photograph of a little girl stuck to it with a paper clip. She was outside in a yard, standing barefoot in grass in a little sundress, smiling.

'Whose daughter?' asked Audrey.

'Mine,' said Wrists. 'Take it easy on hills. You aren't winning any races in this thing.'

Audrey drove fifteen kilometres over the speed limit, her foot always a little up or down over that dashboard hashmark, pulling into the other lane to pass slower traffic. White lights flared up and faded behind like the radio swell, old men in long cars, pickup trucks full of teenagers, double trailer trucks that rattled the van and blotted out the radio, spitting mud and gravel against her windshield as she pulled ahead and drifted back right. She drove into the night and the traffic thinned farther from the city, until she was alone rushing into the dark.

The radio slide guitar took an upswing in a clear reception pocket and the faraway band moved into the middle eight while the band in the yeasty, damp-smelling van with her snored and snorted. She looked down at the speedometer, gave it more gas, held the wheel tight, and passed another transport truck while the radio plunged back to static.

§

Wrists' van was a 1987 Chevy Beauville, 391,000 kilometres, powder blue for the most part, spare tire mounted on one of the outswinging back doors. No passenger-side mirror, no power steering, no shocks, loud as a school bus. Audrey fought it up and down Highway 16, heaving along the alpine roads between Jasper and Kamloops in the early-morning dark. Drove through the night while the Lever Men slept boozy in their seats. The sky turned deep blue, then grey and then pink. Low banks of cloud hung floating between the mountains, just above the treeline. She stopped at a rest stop just out of Tête Jaune Cache at sunrise to stretch her arms and roll her shoulders. Everything was damp and cold. Wrists got out of the van and had a cigarette.

'Spell you off for a while?'

'I'm still good for it,' she said.

'You're no good to anybody if you fall asleep on the highway.'

'Another few hours.'

On the plateau highway past Merritt, the mid-morning sky turned black and a high mountain storm fell on the van. Snow tore against them and she turned on the headlights. Audrey sat up as straight as she could, elbows out, fingers drumming on the wheel. She stared into the swirl ahead for red brake lights or headlight glow, for some sign of another driver. She felt the men, awake, quiet, watching her. The road wound down, twisting through the Coquihalla Pass. They passed a lonely transport truck on a tight corkscrew turn, the headlights blinding, and she squinted and pulled them as close to the right shoulder as she could.

'We could pull over ...'

'Just a little wind.'

They dropped underneath the storm ceiling on the last highway turnout into the Fraser Canyon, plunging into stillness like a child doing a cannonball into a lake. She took the exit into Hope and pulled into a supermarket parking lot. Parked and dropped out of the van. The Lever Men had cigarettes and Dick Move got in the driver's seat. Audrey curled up in the back and tried to sleep with her head rested on the cold glass, but the bouncing van kept her awake.

§

In Nanaimo, there was already a band on the stage at the end of the long, narrow, red-walled pub. Thin young men in tight-fitting black jean jackets over pressed black-collared shirts, with keys and wallet chains hung on the outside of their tight black denim pants. All of them with salon-fresh black haircuts, the slightly different angles of which presumably made them distinct from each other. They ran through a long sound check, testing the echo length of their digital delay pedals and the reverb depth of their vocal microphones, and then eventually full songs, pausing every few bars to complain about the monitor mix to the increasingly bored sound man at the back.

When they were finished, they made a show of placing their expensive guitars in stands and leaving them on the stage. They stood looking around the room, deep in concentration, then selected a bar table near the front, which they angled a bit toward the stage, and then unpacked a suitcase full of T-shirts, compact discs, and stickers. They set up a framed sign, surrounded with white Christmas lights, listing the prices of all the merchandise.

'Do you have stuff for sale? I could sell it,' said Audrey.

'Dick forgot the merch box in Regina,' said Wrists.

'Kid,' said Dick, 'in my own defence, all that was left in the merch box were the same twelve copies of *Most Records Are Too Long* by the Lever Men that no one was interested in buying the last time we came through here, or in Regina, Saskatoon, Winnipeg, or Altona, Manitoba, for that matter.'

'No T-shirts?'

'Wrists, she's right, we should make some new T-shirts,' said Hector. 'We should dip into the old bank account and get some made. Find someone in Victoria with a silkscreen set-up in their garage. Get a new income stream.'

'We should remember to make girls' sizes this time. Diversify our fan base.'

'Move beyond the men's double-extra-large demographic.'

'Hey, what's the beer situation, Wrists?' asked Dick.

Wrists dug into a pocket and pulled out a reel of paper tickets. Handed two each to Dick and Hector.

'Two beers apiece? Wrists, this is bad news. We've got to sit through the local trust-fund rock act *and* play a set of our own on just two beers apiece?'

'Come on,' said Hector, slapping him on the shoulder, 'we'll break into the emergency supply.'

'Good thinking, Heck. Come on, kid,' Dick said to Audrey.

In the parking lot Hector opened up the back doors of the van. Rummaged through the suitcases and sleeping bags until he uncovered a camping cooler. Pulled off the plastic lid and produced a six-pack of wet beer cans. He cracked a couple for himself and Dick and held another out for Audrey, but she shook her head. They sat down on the concrete parking blocks.

'Expecting a better crowd tonight?' she asked.

'The haircut band looks like they might draw,' said Dick.

'Young people like haircuts,' agreed Hector.

'What about your fans?'

They looked at each other and laughed. They knocked their beer cans together.

'Here's to our fans!' said Dick.

'Our dozens of fans, spread across the country,' said Hector.

'Dozens with an S might be a stretch,' said Dick.

Hector raised his beer up above his head. 'To our nearly one dozen fans!'

They laughed and drank and Dick got up to get two more cans of beer out of the cooler.

Audrey felt a hot surge of irritation rise up, which she choked down. Eventually she just asked, 'So if you're that popular, why drive all the way out to Nanaimo? Aren't any of your dozen fans easier to get to than this?'

Dick had a long sip of beer, only to have the can foam up and overflow when he stopped. He slurped up the foam and wiped his face with the back of his forearm. He caught his breath and then furrowed his brow and pointed toward the building.

'Kid,' he said seriously, 'that is Rodney Levermann in there.'

'*The* Rodney Levermann,' said Hector.

'When I was a kid, like a fifteen-year-old kid in middle-of-nowhere suburban Calgary, the first real rock'n'roll band I ever saw was Onion Bomb. This'd be 1983. No, 1984. What year is it now?'

'It's 2003,' said Hector.

'No, it's 2005,' said Audrey.

'Holy shit, 2005, no kidding,' said Dick. He put his tongue into the side of his cheek and concentrated for a while, counting on his fingers. 'Right, so 1984. How old were you in 1984, kid?'

'I was born in 1985.'

'I was fifteen and I went to a community hall to see a rock'n'roll show. This being the early eighties, you had a bunch of hardcore punk rock and skateboarder thrash metal. I remember SNFU was the headliner. But before they went on, there was this band, Onion Bomb. Heck, get me another beer. You want a beer, Audrey?'

She shook her head.

'In 1984, before you were born, you went to see rock'n'roll at community halls in the suburbs and it was hardcore punk rock. It was a lot of dumb young men with shaved heads missing teeth running around in circles crashing into each other. *A gugga a gugga gack gack gack KRAANG* and the singer who was the angriest, dumbest young man yelled something about Margaret Thatcher at you.'

'Margaret Thatcher or Ronald Reagan,' said Hector, handing Dick a beer. 'It was very important that you were properly angry at Margaret Thatcher and Ronald Reagan all the time.'

'All the time. We were there to see SNFU,' said Dick, 'which is a punk rock acronym for Society's No Fucking Use.'

'No,' said Hector, 'it's an old military acronym for Situation Needs Further Unfucking.'

'It's an acroynm with a curse word in it which is what mattered at the time. And then this band Onion Bomb came on. And they were all wearing scuba masks with snorkels and they wore water wings and those big plastic flippers on their feet. Kid, you have to understand, this was not done at this time.'

'It was not done,' agreed Hector. 'People would have thought you weren't sufficiently angry at Margaret Thatcher if you did that kind of thing.'

'And so between angry hardcore punk rock this band gets up wearing scuba masks and flippers like a bunch of clowns. And then they started playing ...'

He had a long drink of beer and then set the can down carefully on the gravel beside the block. Folded his arms and stared up at the street light.

'There were all these other feelings,' he said eventually. 'Feelings outside the what-do-you-call-it. Previously allowed range. Complicated feelings, you know? Like complicated feelings that you wouldn't expect from clowns in scuba gear opening for SNFU. Not clown feelings, not angry feelings.' He had a long drink and sighed. 'It's hard to explain, kid. You were fifteen once.'

'Yes,' said Audrey, 'more recently than 1984.'

'Those fifteen-year-old feelings are important, and they're hard to express properly, which is what Onion Bomb on a good night did better than any other band. They instantly became my favourite ever band, and their guitar player was this older guy named Rod Levers, and I found out reading a photocopied fanzine that before *that* he'd been in one of the first punk rock bands in Edmonton, Sue Father's band the Fathers. You ever hear of Sue Father, kid?'

Audrey shook her head.

'That's a whole other story. Anyway, I was a big fan, for a long time. Just a big, big fan, for years and years. And then one day, Wrists phones me. This was back when I was playing in the Hidden Fees.'

'What did the Hidden Fees play?' asked Audrey.

'Hardcore punk rock about Ronald Reagan,' said Hector.

Dick nodded in agreement. 'Yep. *A gugga a gugga gack gack gack KRAANG*. We were pretty good. Toured all over the ski resorts, playing for snowboarders whose older siblings were SNFU fans. Anyway, Wrists phones me up. "Hey, Dick," he says, "you still in that Hidden Fees group?" And I said, "Yep, sure am." "They pay you all right?" he asked me. And I said, "All right, Wrists. We've got a good thing with these snowboard towns. It's worth a few hundred bucks a week." And he said, "Dick, you want to quit that and be in Rodney Levermann's band? It won't pay a few hundred bucks a week. It won't pay much of anything and we won't play that often." And I said, "You got it, Wrists." Didn't even think about it. No need. Quit the Hidden Fees that day. "Rodney Levermann," I told them. Which was sufficient reason.'

They drank their beer and then stood up and stretched and belched. Hector lined up the empty beer cans and crushed each with a single stomp of his boot heel.

'You feeling better?' Dick asked Hector.

'Better enough.'

'Well, let's go show those kids the real thing,' said Dick.

'You're in Nanaimo now,' Wrists said to her later, after they had finished their set and the last of the the crowd left, the few of them that hadn't left right away once the younger band had finally cleared off the stage, after the bartender finished paying them out in not very many five- and ten-dollar bills. 'You said you weren't going to Edmonton, so now you're in Nanaimo.'

'She's not going to Nanaimo,' said Rodney.

'I'm not going to Nanaimo,' said Audrey. 'Where am I going?'

'Vancouver,' said Rodney. Wrists shrugged. The Lever Men all downed their whisky and went back to the bar.

She found a motel near the ferry terminal and backed the van in as tight as she could against the back wall, easing on and off the gas until the rear bumper nudged the faded cedar siding wall, tight enough that no one would be able to open the back doors. They piled into the lobby and Wrists pulled cash out of an envelope in his jacket.

'Give us something with two double beds and a cot.'

'I'll get my own room,' said Audrey.

'I'm not paying for you to have your own room,'

'No, I'm paying for me to have my room,' she said.

Later she stood in the shower, stretching. Tried to work out the new knots that had found their way under her shoulder blade. Too-far-to-shoulder-check-properly knots. She stood on one wobbly leg and pulled her knee up into her chest to stretch a tight knot in her hip flexor joint, stiff as a lacrosse ball from twisting her foot between the gas and brake. She shaved under her arms and brushed her teeth. Cut her toenails.

She took her little portable CD player out of the bottom of the backpack. It didn't seem worse for wear from being thrown out of the truck window back in Fort Saskatchewan, and the Dick Dale CD spun up when she pressed play. Dick Dale's guitar sprang to life and she flopped back on the bed. Biggest bed since the Four Eagles Motel. Flapped her arms and legs like she was making a snow angel on the sheets.

'We are still hungry,' said Tommi Mäkinen to the magazine interviewer. 'We are proud but we are hungry to continue. We want to go faster and faster. We know we can have better times. So we are proud but know we can go further. Faster and faster.'

She lay back and did her best to sleep.

§

Wrists sat beside her with a map of British Columbia, back-folded to just the four panels of Greater Vancouver, and they slowly made their way through gridlocked traffic to a three-storey hundred-year-old hotel a few blocks up Hastings Street from Chinatown. A bare-chested man with a flannel sleeping bag slung over his shoulders wandered around on the sidewalk in front of the bar murmuring to himself, lit up blue and red by a neon-tubed Molson Canadian sign in the window. Up and down the sidewalk, knots of men and women shuffled slowly back and forth, wandering out into the street or stopping to light cigarettes. The crowds thickened farther west, down the hill. Audrey parked and Wrists rolled down the window. A thick-armed bouncer in a black T-shirt, oblivious to the damp cold, sat on a folding chair reading a newspaper.

'Hey, where's the best place to park?' asked Wrists.

'That's the best place to park,' said the bouncer without looking up from his newspaper.

Inside there were twenty tables on a cigarette-burned carpet, a single man at each nursing a beer. Along the walls, a few women in checkered shirts with dark eyes under dark mascara plugged loonies into video lottery terminals, taking their time to press the buttons and watch the digital displays spin, not in any particular hurry for the outcome.

'I thought Vancouver was …'

'Was what?' Hector asked her.

'Exciting?'

'Wrists, what is it. Tuesday night?'

'Monday night,' said Wrists.

'Kid,' said Hector, 'nowhere is exciting on a Monday night.'

That night she noticed the mistakes.

Rodney kicked a skinny leg, grinned, then stepped on his instrument cable and slipped, yanking it out of the switch box. The guitar chopped out with a painful pop. He knelt and scrambled to plug himself back in.

Wrists and Hector rolled on, but Dick faltered, then picked it back up on the wrong count, a few bars out of time.

They started another song and the organ chords were an awkward half-tone wrong. 'D-minor!' Dick shouted. Hector looked up and stopped playing, hands frozen above the keys, confused. 'D-minor!' Wrists and Dick both shouted.

Wrists stick-counted a quick four and the Lever Men jumped into something fast and rock'n'roll, B flat minor, and Rodney dug into a big ringing tremolo arm chord and snapped three strings off his neck.

A man near Audrey turned to a woman sitting in front of a VLT. 'Is there a band on later?' he shouted at her.

'A what?' the woman shouted back.

'A band. On later.'

The woman shrugged and put another dollar into the VLT.

§

In the morning she found a gas station with a Tim Horton's off an exit halfway between Langley and Abbotsford. Wrists pulled the manilla envelope out of his jean jacket. Produced a thin pile of crumpled cash and gave each of the three other men twenty dollars, which they pocketed and stumbled toward the Tim's. Wrists filled the van with gas, and when he got the receipt he circled the date and total and stuffed it into the envelope. He shuffled through index cards with names and phone numbers and took one over to the pay phone on the side of the building. The other Lever Men came back with coffee and muffins and gave Wrists their receipts.

'Kelowna tonight?' she asked Wrists.

'Kelowna tonight.'

'I was thinking,' she said cautiously, 'I'd take us up the number 3 from Hope. Instead of all the way up the Coquihalla and then down from Kamloops. It's a little longer kilometres-wise, but if the weather is still bad up there around Merritt it could end up saving us a bit of time. Get a bit of a different drive. I mean, there might be snow up there too, but –'

'Sure, whatever you want,' said Wrists.

Audrey Cole beamed like a sunrise.

The van chugged up the winding Crowsnest Highway through the mountains and she kept to the right lane while station wagons and pickup trucks ground past her. Dick Move sat beside her, shuffling through a suitcase full of old dubbed cassette tapes. White-labelled tapes with hand-scrawled names, all of which featured hoarse-sounding men yelling over indistinct double-time punk rock, each new cassette somewhat indistinguishable from the last, all of them murky and tinny-sounding, like they'd been recorded inside a galvanized-steel garbage can. Every half-hour or so the music would slow and warp as the van stereo started to eat the tape, and Dick would jerk awake from a half snooze to stab at the eject button in a panic, then carefully spool out the copper-brown tape so that he could wind it back into the cassette, twisting the wheel with the end of a pencil.

She stopped every few hours so they could smoke. They each smoked a different brand of cigarettes and she got to know the smells. Wrists the thickest and sharpest, green and wet smoke. Dick, something grassy and spongy like damp earth just cut by a shovel blade. Hector's dry and hot, steam on coals in a cedar room.

In Princeton, Hector moved into the front seat. He had his own little case of white-labelled cassette tapes. Instead of music though, he played a hiss-heavy recording of an interview – a woman with a German accent interviewing a man with a British accent.

'But this wasn't the first Soviet expedition to the moon, according to your research,' said the German woman.

'Precisely,' said the British man. 'Since their original lunar visit in 1946, Soviet cosmonauts had established regular traffic back and forth from the moon, thanks to the V2 technology they had captured from the Nazis. But the cosmonauts only encountered the Lemurian civilization of the Mare Vaporum much later, in the 1970s.'

'And it was this Lemurian encounter and influence, you maintain, that contributed directly to the economic collapse of the Soviet Union.'

'We can only speculate. But we have seen, time and time again, the corrosive effect of exposure to Lemurian ontology – of Lemurian language even – on human culture. In Burgundy prior to the Frankish defeat, in sixteenth-century Livonia, in the Carpathians in the 1930s – these societies, upon encountering Lemurians and their alien ideas about non-sequential being, their whole concept of non-contingent identity ...'

'Not contingent on ...?'

'Not contingent, full stop. This is an epistemological framework built up from a language with forty-seven present-tense conjugations of the verb *to be*, and an as-of-yet uncounted catalogue of future-tense conjugations.'

'Those previous Lemurian encounters you mentioned had all been terrestrial diasporas.'

'Yes. Yes, exactly. Excellent observation. We can only imagine the alienness of the society the Soviets encountered on the moon. These Lemurian moon-colonists would be scores of centuries removed from their people's history, left to evolve on their own strange fork in the hostile moon environment. What did the cosmonauts hear and experience, and what did they bring back to the Soviet republics? We see the cognitive strain of this influx of terrifyingly different concepts manifest in convulsive failures throughout the collective industrial economies of the entire Warsaw Pact through the 1980s.'

'You don't claim to have invented this idea.'

'People have tried to warn us for decades of the dangers of the Lemurian moon society.'

'Which people?'

'People you'd expect. Charlie Chaplin. Wittgenstein. Marilyn Monroe. All deeply, deeply coded, of course ...'

'Heck,' said Dick from the back seat, 'you aren't making Audrey listen to your crazy moon tapes, are you?'

'So help me, Heck,' said Wrists, 'if Audrey walks out on us in Kelowna because of your crazy moon tapes, you are doing all the driving, all day, every day.'

[65]

Hector ejected the tape and put it carefully back into his case. Fiddled with the radio until he found a weather report. 'We can listen to the rest later,' he said in a hushed voice. Audrey did her best to nod in what she hoped was a non-encouraging fashion.

§

In Kelowna, Wrists had the bartender fill an empty detergent bucket with ice. In between songs he set his sticks on the snare, leaned forward, and plunged his hands into the ice up to the elbows. They played a stage with a stripper pole and mirrored walls to nobody. Occasionally orange-tanned men in muscle shirts came in and said loudly to the bartender, 'No peelers tonight, eh?' before turning around and heading back out the door.

Afterward, in her motel room, she opened her backpack and wrinkled her nose at the smell inside. Unable to tell if the smell of the band had already worked into her T-shirts and extra pair of jeans, or if it was her own body, her chemistry grown dense and musky like the men around her, the way a stick of celery changes colour in a glass full of purple juice.

§

She drove them up Highway 97 around the curves of the Okanagan Valley lakes, through little farm towns, past winter-closed fruit stands and old drive-in movie theatres. Rodney scratched a week's worth of scruff on his cheeks and chin. His self-buzzed hair had grown out in places long enough to show the spots he'd missed, giving his head corners and points. They stopped at a lakeside gas station bait-and-tackle shop with a sign advertising a four-dollar hot beef sandwich. Rodney dug in the back of his van for his tool box and produced an electric barber clipper. He bought a bag of disposable razors in the store, walked around the side of the building, and locked himself in the men's room. A line of drivers formed after ten minutes, shuffling from foot to foot. At fifteen minutes someone banged on the door with a fist. Rodney emerged with a raw, red cold-water-shaved face, smelling like green gel dispenser soap. His scalp freshly buzzed down to the #1 clipper guard and tiny dark hairs peppering his neck, shoulders, inside his ears. He took off his T-shirt and shook it; he was all ribs and grey tangled chest hair. He pulled a crumple of paper towel out of his back pocket and brushed hair off his shoulders. His movements were all slow and cautious, giving everything he did an exaggerated, slightly unreal quality.

'So we've narrowed it down somewhat,' he said later when they were back on the highway. She looked across at Rodney.

'Narrowed what down?'

'Well, you weren't going to Edmonton, or Nanaimo, or Vancouver or Kelowna.'

'None of those places,' Audrey agreed.

'You were coming down from Fort McMurray?'

'Up around there,' she said.

'There's a lot of jobs up around there,' said Rodney.

'Lot of jobs.'

'Not many you'd want to do for any length of time,' he said eventually. 'Especially not young, all-alone women, regardless of their ability to drive all night on two hours' sleep. Or even to keep men twice their size away at screwdriver point.'

She looked across at him and didn't say anything. She gave the van gas and passed a pickup truck full of bookshelves and chairs under a tarp.

'I got bored,' she said eventually.

'Bored?'

'It was boring. "Here's your map, follow it." I had …'

She stopped and stared out the window.

'You had …' he said.

'This truck, Rodney. You should have seen this truck. Big V8, lots of guts. Off the line or going up hills, nothing. Like …' And she pulled out into the other lane, to pass a silver Mazda hatchback with a dog staring out the back window. 'This amazing … and they give you a map. "Follow the map. Stay in your room."'

'So you left.'

She passed another car, revving the van's engine up into the red RPMS.

'It was going to be another few weeks before they rotated me out. But I just couldn't. I had to leave. Like, then. That minute.'

He watched her awhile, then said, 'Smart thinking, bringing that screwdriver.'

She looked at him. 'I'm not stupid, Rodney.'

He shifted in his seat and dug in the pocket of his jeans. Found a white pill bottle, cracked the cap, and shook out two white tablets.

'Headache?'

'They make me better.'

'Better than what?'

Rodney laughed and leaned against the window. 'You got it, Audrey. You got it.'

§

In Kamloops, they played to a room full of snowboarders who spent the set oblivious to the band, watching televisions above the bar playing videos of people driving snowmobiles off cliffs. The huge machines drove through white powder snow in slow motion, kicking up clouds against a blue sky, hung in space, giant machines, and the men and women driving wore ski helmets and bright jackets and kicked their legs out behind themselves, spread their legs, then brought them back in for landing. Young men and women in the bar drank beer and cheered each flying machine and landing. Someone stood on a chair and hollered when a snowmobile did an improbable leap off a craggy stone ledge and the driver lifted himself right up off the seat, spread his legs in wide splits. Afterward the bartender passed around a hat; a few people dropped loonies or quarters and a couple of five-dollar bills in. Wrists took the hat grimly and counted the money. Wrote the total on an index card and put it back into the envelope in his jacket.

§

She was somewhere on the swooping stretch of highway between the green pine-treed slopes around the Shuswap lakes, heading east toward the higher peaks of the Monashees. Wrists turned the radio tuner dial.

'Here's an old fave from the eighties to start another sixty-minute rock ride,' said the DJ.

A power-chord guitar riff started up: big ringing chords with echoey 1980s production values. It was something catchy that she recognized but couldn't recall the name of.

'Oh,' said Hector, sitting up suddenly, 'oh oh oh.'

'The money-maker!' hollered Dick. 'Turn it up, Wrists!'

Wrists turned up the volume and the three of them all sang along:

Spin that wheel, spin little girl,
Spin away that grain.
Cart that gold right out the door,
Dig that royal name.

Little Rattle, Little Rattle,
Little Rattle Stilt!
No-name, No-name
No-win game.
Little Rattle Stilt!

Pound that stilt, pound little man.
Pound that stilt and grab.
Grab a handful, yank it up,
Rip yourself in half!

And then a short guitar solo, which all three of them knew note for note and sang along with, vocalizing the lines with their own *ooh* and *whee* sounds, twisting in their seats to play their air guitars.

'I know this,' she said as it moved into the fade-out chorus coda. 'What is this?'

'This,' said Hector, 'is "Little Rattle Stilt" by the Fish Cans.'

'An immortal piece of CanCon rock history,' said Wrists.

'Edmonton, Alberta's greatest ever one-hit wonder,' said Dick.

'Whoa whoa,' said Hector. 'One hit? What about "Auto Motto Blotto"?'

'Not a hit,' said Wrists, 'not a real hit. "Auto Motto Blotto" was in minor late-night Canadian radio rotation when they were a regional fixture. "Little Rattle Stilt" was a bonafide Billboard Chart Topper in the U.S. American rock stations play it to this day.'

'Rodney,' asked Hector, 'are the royalty checks you get for "Auto Motto Blotto" comparable to the ones you get for "Little Rattle Stilt"?'

'Fuck off,' said Rodney.

'That's Rodney Leverman,' Dick said to Audrey, 'lead guitar player for Edmonton, Alberta's greatest ever one-hit wonder, the Fish Cans.'

'For six months,' said Rodney. 'I was in the group for six months.'

'During which time they wrote and recorded bonafide Billboard Chart Topper "Little Rattle Stilt,"' said Dick.

'How about we listen to something else,' grunted Rodney. 'Put on one of Heck's moon tapes. We can all hear about how space aliens were responsible for the FLQ crisis.'

'How come you guys never play that?' asked Audrey.

Wrists turned the dial and found a country-and-western station. Audrey was going to ask another question but Wrists gave her a look. She slowed down to let a family in a station wagon pass. In the back-seat window a little boy had his face pressed against the frosted glass. Audrey waved and the little boy sank down out of sight.

§

In Revelstoke, she walked out onto the street while they set up the gear. Walked into a linoleum laundromat and fished change out of her pocket. She bought a plastic sandwich bag full of powdered soap and put her pants and shirts, underwear and socks into the machine. An old woman in a raincoat watched a television bracketed into the wall above the counter. A man on an all-day news channel moved his mouth silently while small white text, too small to read, scrolled underneath.

She walked across the block to a thrift store. Bought socks and a new tank top and another pair of jeans. She found a red nylon sleeping bag, the interior fabric printed with red pheasants and grouses on a prairie-yellow background. Little travel bottles of shampoo and conditioner and toothpaste.

She went outside and walked up the street until she found a pay phone. Phoned the toll-free number on the back of her bank card and listened to a machine voice read her bank balance. She still had most of the Easy Money. She didn't expect there would be any more coming. Somewhere in the employment agreement there was probably a clause. Her parents had probably got a letter. 'Termination of employment agreement for Audrey Cole.' They'd be worked up and fretting, assuming they'd opened the letter.

She hadn't phoned home since the week before leaving Moose Leg.

She plugged a few more coins into the pay phone and listened to the bank balance recording at the bank again. There was still enough, enough to keep going.

'Dick,' said Wrists, after they'd finished their second set in Revelstoke. 'Hey hey, Dick.' He pointed with a drumstick.

Dick, bent over wrapping his guitar cable around his forearm, looked up in the direction of the stick. 'Whoa whoa whoa,' said Dick, dropping his cable.

Rodney was leaned over his speaker cabinet. He grabbed the handles on either side. Tried to pull it up from his elbows, bent over and extended wrong.

'Hey, boss, whoa whoa,' shouted Dick.

Rodney grunted and lifted the cabinet, then staggered and leaned backward, wincing. Dick ran over and moved in behind him, reaching around to grab the handles. He lifted the weight of the cabinet away from Rodney, who gritted his teeth with his eyes squeezed shut, caught in a wide bear hug between Dick and the cabinet.

'Heck, come here and give me a hand,' shouted Dick.

Hector took the cabinet and Rodney staggered away from them, eyes still squeezed shut, a hand on the small of his back.

'Boss, boss, what are you doing,' said Dick. 'Hey boss, how are you, huh? What are you doing?'

'I'm fine,' said Rodney, 'I just … just give me a minute.'

Audrey got up from the table she'd been sitting at and came to the stage to help him down. He reached down and took her hand. His hands shook. His fingers were long and thin and toughly callused, the knuckles swollen, beads on wires. She helped him down and could feel how slight and insubstantial he was. Helped him over to the table.

'I'm okay, just let me sit a bit,' said Rodney.

Wrists brought a bottle of beer over. Set it down in front of Levermann, glaring at Dick.

'What are you doing, boss?' said Dick. 'Come on. Here, have a drink.'

'Audrey,' said Rodney. 'Go get me my jacket.'

'Sure thing,' said Audrey.

He fished in the pocket of his jacket and found his pill bottle. Dick came back from the bar with a glass of whisky and he swallowed back a couple of white pills.

'What are you doing, boss? Come on. Take it easy.'

Rodney waved them away. 'Come on, go. We've got to tear down. We're all sick of this bar. Tear down and pack up so we can get out of here.'

They stood around evaluating him for a few moments and then Wrists nodded and jerked with his chin back toward the stage. The three of them walked back to the instruments they'd been in the middle of packing up.

'They think I'm an invalid, Audrey Cole,' Rodney said to her. 'Like I'm made of porcelain.'

'They'll get packed out and we can get out of here,' Audrey told him.

He had a mouthful of whisky. 'Don't you get tired of hanging out in empty bars, Audrey Cole?'

She shrugged. 'Tomorrow it's Nakusp. We'll take the ferry. I've never been on that ferry. And then we'll take the number 6 down through the Slocan Valley to get to Cranbrook. I've never driven that number 6. It should be a good drive.'

'A good drive,' agreed Rodney, finishing his whisky.

§

In Nakusp, they played a small stage rimmed in blue-and-peach terra-cotta tiles at the back of a Mexican restaurant. A few tourists sat at the other end of the room eating enchiladas. The busboy walked back and forth in front of the stage, carrying his bus bin full of sauce-covered plates through the kitchen door just behind Wrists' drums.

'I was going to get married,' Rodney said to the handful of people in the crowd. He twisted a tuning peg. 'There wasn't a date set or anything and we didn't have a ring and I hadn't actually asked her but it was more or less understood that we'd end up married. You know how it is, when it's more or less understood. This was a long time ago. Before I'd fallen in with these deadbeats here.'

Hector put two flat palms on the keys for a chromatic squawk.

'I wanted to learn this song. This one we're going to do next here. I mean, I kind of knew how to play it and a friend of mine was doing a set of shows in Winnipeg and wanted me to come out and play with him. Well, it wasn't just Winnipeg, come to think of it now, it was across the country out to Newfoundland and back for a solid month with a week in Toronto doing a residency at some kind of Toronto approximation of a honky-tonk off Queen West. We were to start in Winnipeg though.

'Anyway the song has this difficult bit in it. There's this kind of ... It's hard to explain. Mostly you're playing slide, so you're open-tuned with your brass slide on, but in the choruses you trade off the slide lines with this quick finger-plucked chord change, and that trading-off is just a bitch to get right. Uses different parts of your brain, see. But if you can pull it off ...' He ran his fingers quickly over the fretboard, something fast and complicated in a minor blues key. 'The point is, this song was in the set so I mostly wanted to go on this tour as a means to really nail it down.

'So it came down to me needing to take about six weeks off work – two weeks in Winnipeg to learn the set and then the month on the road and, hell, it would have taken me another week after a trip like that to dry out. Seven weeks. I had a hard enough time meeting my share of the rent with my going-to-be wife. We were saving for the down payment on a house. She liked to drive around on Saturdays and go to open houses. I said I need to go to Winnipeg for about seven weeks so I can learn to play a song. She told me not to come back and I didn't.'

§

In Golden, the day bartender propped open a back door with a four-gallon plastic pail of dishwasher sanitizer. 'You're early,' she said, wiping her hands on a black apron.

'We could get all loaded in early and be out of your hair before you open up,' said Wrists. 'Squeeze in a line check and be tip-top ready to go when folks show up.'

'Pete deals with the bands and Pete isn't here and there's people in the bar.'

'How about we just unload then, so we're not worried about the gear in the van driving around town then.'

'It's a fire exit. Don't block anything.'

The bar was a big old ski tavern attached to a two-storey main-street hotel, with timber-frame beams, neon signs for brands of interior B.C. beer Audrey had never heard of, and old signs from ski hills: *Widow's Peak Double Black Diamond, Runway to Paradise Quad Chair.* She sat at the bar and found an unfinished sudoku puzzle in the paper while the Lever Men brought in the gear. She'd gotten to the know the daytime smells of a bar over the last week, before enough people and their bodies and their new cigarettes came in and changed the chemistry of the air. Bleach and kitchen garbage, the previous night's cigarette smoke, deep-fryer oil, spilled beer. It was different from the hotel restaurant back in Canmore, stronger. The Lever Men finished piling the gear onto a short stage in the corner and Hector went across the street to get them all coffee in paper cups.

A girl with a blond ponytail and a puffy down-filled ski jacket came in and leaned on the bar. Waved at the busboy in the back of the room scooping ice out of the ice machine. Her mirrored ski sunglasses on her head reflected the bar lights' orange and gold. She turned to evaluate Audrey and the Lever Men.

'What are you guys, some kind of rock band?'

Rodney turned around slowly on his stool.

'We,' he said, 'are the Legendary Lever Men. One night only.'

'Lever men? Like, men with levers? Really?'

He swept an arm out to indicate something larger than the current room. 'Famous from the St. Albert Hotel in Winnipeg to the Red Lion Inn in Victoria.'

She pivoted on her heels and leaned an elbow on the bar. 'Are you one of those fun bands that play music people like to hear and everybody dances all night and it's great? Or one of those un-fun bands that play music no one knows and it's too loud so that you can't hear your friends and couldn't dance to it if you wanted to and people have to just wait it out?'

'We play all the funnest music beloved by the young people of today,' said Rodney.

'That's right,' said Dick, 'the funnest.'

She looked at Audrey. 'Are you the singer?'

'She's our manager,' said Rodney.

'Ah. I see.'

Around eight o'clock, the bar filled up with off-duty chairlift attendants, between-shift busboys, and just-finished day staff from the other bars and restaurants up and down the strip. They chattered in Australian and Québécois accents and drank pints of dark beer between sticky shots of cinnamon schnapps and Jameson's whisky. Everyone was wearing down-filled vests and toques despite the increasing heat. Audrey sat at a corner table, watching. Across the bar, Hector and Dick played pool with a group of young women, all of them laughing and drinking. The girl with the ponytail racked up the balls and bent over to break, staring across the table at Hector. He looked back at her with a cartoon fox look, a look she hadn't seen on any of the Lever Men before. His whole face transformed with the look he gave the girl in the ponytail while she broke, making him into some other, different man that Audrey had never seen before.

'Hector Highwater,' Rodney's voice said out of the PA speakers. 'Richard Move. Hector Highwater and Richard Move to the stage.'

When he climbed onstage, Hector whispered something in Rodney's ear. Levermann rolled his eyes. Dick Move held his hands together prayer-style. Rodney sighed and jerked his head toward Wrists.

The drummer just shrugged when Hector talked to him. Then he stick-counted a quick four and they all started up a country-and-western train beat, Rodney *chick-chick-chicking* a couple of palm-muted chords. The crowd looked up from what they were doing. Audrey watched. Usually they had about thirty seconds of attention before they lost a crowd.

Dick Move went to the microphone at the front of the stage, cleared his throat, and started singing 'Folsom Prison Blues.'

Someone in the crowd cheered.

He had a gut-deep easy baritone, and after Johnny Cash they did Willie Nelson, Townes Van Zandt, and Lee Hazlewood. They played these songs effortlessly, like they had been doing them every night for months. People clapped enthusiastically after each tune. In each song during the middle eight Rodney took exactly one step toward the crowd and whipped out a blazing-hot solo, which became more dexterous and complex as the night went on. People cheered when the Lever Men started into songs they knew and they moved some tables at the front so they could dance. The girls from the pool table danced right at the front, waving their arms above their heads.

They finished with 'Waiting Around to Die' and a woman at the bar with skull-tight grey skin and a small dog cradled in her buckskin jacket clapped and cried.

Later, Dick sat down heavily across from Audrey. His face was flushed, his breath lit up with whisky fumes. He coughed and leaned into the table toward her.

'Audrey, here's the thing,' he said, speaking slowly to assemble the words. 'We're going to stay late tonight.'

'We have to load out still,' she said.

'The thing – the thing about that. Heck and I, we talked to them. Talked to them.'

'Talked to … ?'

'The bar. Tender. Talked to him. He's also,' Dick paused to grin, pleased with what he was about to deliver, 'also the *day* bartender. See? Tomorrow. Day bartender tomorrow. So I've talked to him and we'll leave the gear here and load out in the morning.'

She watched him and didn't say anything.

'Okay, so we're staying late.'

'The thing,' he said, then paused to figure out how to assemble the next sentence. 'The thing, Audrey, is it's better if … they've got rooms for us, maybe, maybe you just go to bed early?'

'Maybe I'll stay,' she said.

Hector and Rodney sat down on either side of Dick, each of them with beer bottles. Dick took a beer and drank for a long time.

'Audrey,' said Rodney, putting an arm around Dick's shoulder, 'you've got a pretty good thing going right now, correct? Ongoing adventure, getting the van A to B, nothing doing beyond delivering us like mail wherever we're addressed for the day.'

'Sure.'

'So don't change the composition. Got me? We're going to stay late and maybe if you just go back to the room, then tomorrow we carry on and your good thing hasn't changed.'

'What might change?'

'Let her stay,' said Hector, looking at her over his bottle. He gave her the cartoon fox look from before over the top of his bottle and she inhaled and sat up straight.

'You guys are going to be so drunk in about half an hour you'll be passed out before I'm even done brushing my teeth,' she said.

Dick chortled and drank his beer. Wrists went back to the bar and leaned over to talk to the bartender, who nodded, then rooted around under the counter and gave him something.

Wrists came back and put a hotel room key down on the tabletop. A plastic pine tree with the room number embossed on it.

Dick got up and went back to the pool table, where the girls were doing shots of Jägermeister. Put his arm around the waist of the girl with the ponytail and started laughing at whatever they were laughing at.

'We'll see you in the morning, Audrey,' said Rodney.

'It's Lethbridge tomorrow,' she said slowly, chewing off the words, feeling her bright red cheeks and hating their bright-redness. 'Which is stupid because we were in Cranbrook last night and Cranbrook to Lethbridge is an easy drive, and Revelstoke to Golden to Cranbrook would have been an easy enough drive, but you did everything in the wrong order, so we've got to drive all the way back we already came. But whatever. We'll do it so you can get to Lethbridge in time to play for the dishwasher in the Lethbridge Shithole. We'll take the number 1 past Banff and then take Highway 22 down to Nanton. We'll miss Calgary and all the city traffic that way. Then over to Highway 2 and it'll be a good six-hour drive at least, so sleep in. Load your shit and I'll meet you later.'

She got up and then paused.

'If you can play music people actually like, why don't you?'

The other Lever Men all looked at Rodney, who thought about it for a while.

'It's not about people, Audrey. It's about us. We do things for us. You know how that is.'

She went up to her room and had a long hot shower. Then lay on the bed with her headphones on, listening to Link Wray as loudly as she could stand. Thinking about Hector's fox face.

§

They left Golden early and she wound the van along the twisting high-mountain ribbon of Highway 1 above the Kicking Horse River in the pre-dawn dark. The road was slick from overnight snow through the pass and she passed trucks in the ditch at Field.

At Canmore she took the first exit into town and pulled the van into the earliest gas station at the end of a long line of motels.

She stood filling the tank, looking at the mountains. The east face of Rundle Mountain, square and sheer, and the promontory that always reminded her of a chimney or a lighthouse, staring across at the north peak of Ha Ling. All the mountains surrounding the town looked slightly different, depending on where you were, the different angles or proximities showing you different characters and profiles of the rock faces.

She could get back in the van, she supposed, and just drive to her parents' house. Say, 'So long, Legendary Lever Men,' and get out with her backpack and head into the house. Sit at the table and drink hot tea and tell them all the stories over supper: Moose Leg and Valerie, and Wrists' van and how nothing exciting happens on a Monday night in Vancouver. She'd gloss over the truck driver and the screwdriver. Then she could fall asleep in her old bed, the bed she'd grown up in, and she wouldn't even need the headphones. No noise to block out. She thought about the surprise on their faces, opening the door and finding her there.

I could just go home, thought Audrey.

She paid for the gas and brought the receipt back to Wrists. They all stank, sweating out beer and whisky fumes. Dick and Hector were both curled up in the back, asleep, their balled-up jackets wedged between ears and shoulders for pillows.

'So it's Lethbridge and then Pincher Creek and then Calgary, and that's it?'

'Lethbridge, Pincher Creek, and then up to the Crash Palace at Two Reel Lake,' said Wrists.

'Two Reel Lake? Where's that?'

Wrists waved a hand. 'It's out, I don't know, northwest. It's a ways out from anywhere.'

'It's not really a place,' said Rodney. He opened his pill bottle and shook out a tablet.

'You guys draw much of a crowd in not-really-places a ways out from anywhere?' she asked.

Rodney swallowed a pill with what might have been a choke or half a laugh. 'You'll be amazed, Audrey Cole. You'll be amazed.'

3

'Troubled Member of Prominent Local Family Freezes to Death' was the headline, above a side column on the first page of the *Calgary Herald* City section. Audrey Cole read it sitting at her kitchen table, in the last beam of the just-about-to-set sun. Freezes to death, thought Audrey, ugh, and had a sip of her tea, then looked down at the picture and choked. She choked like she was on a soap opera receiving surprise news, and brown tea dribbled down her chin onto her chest.

The caption read 'Alex "Main" Aiver (pictured, centre), 42, had struggled with substance abuse.' And there he was. Black-and-white Alex Main, sitting at a bar table, in between two men, all of them holding beer bottles and staring, not smiling, into the camera.

They hadn't put his name in the headline. That was the first thing that popped into her head, once something eventually did. 'Member of Prominent Local Family' but not his name. That would burn him up. Just squeeze him up inside. Alex Main, relegated to the caption text, second billing to his family history, missing out on his last chance for real recognition.

She got up, angry, and made a quick jab with her foot like she was going to kick the chair. She didn't kick anything, just squeezed her fists and pushed them into her temples and took a deep breath. She sat back down and sighed.

'You fucked up a lot of things in your life, Alex, but staying alive should have been the least of it,' she said loudly. She heard a gasp behind her. She turned and Shelly was standing there with her mouth wide open.

'Sorry, sorry. Come here, baby,' said Audrey.

'Mommy mad,' said the little girl.

'Yes, Mommy mad. Come here.'

Shelly waddled over with her arms spread wide and Audrey knelt and wrapped her up in a hug, stood up with the toddler's face buried in her hair. She stood up with a grunt – Shelly wasn't as easy to pick up as she used to be. She buried her face in Shelly's hair and took deep breaths trying not to cry.

'What matter, Mommy?'

'Just sad, baby,' said Audrey Cole. 'Just sad is all.' And Shelly Cole hugged her back tightly and they stood like that for a while.

Police identified the body of a man found dead Tuesday morning in the alley of the 200 block of 7th Avenue SW as Alex Aiver. The grandson of Aiver Petroleum founder Dean Aiver, Alex was not involved in the family business but was well known locally as an event promoter and nightclub owner. Often known as Alex Main, he briefly gained notoriety after being fined for operating an unlicenced hotel and bar on a family property northwest of Rocky Mountain House.

Police would not release more details but said foul play was not suspected. They did note that he was known to them for his ongoing problems with illegal narcotics.

Aiver is survived by his mother, Susanne Aiver, and sister Catherine LeStrasse and her three children.

She squinted at the photograph. Alex between two men, in some bar, holding a beer. She knew both of them: Gurt Markstrom and the Skinny Cowboy. Gurt was a big man in a black leather vest with long black hair pulled into a tight ponytail. And the Skinny Cowboy, with his skull-thin face, his bolo tie, and sunken cheeks. The photograph was a tight crop so it was difficult to tell where they were. All three looked unsmiling into the camera lens, their pupils white from camera flash. Audrey pulled the paper close to her nose until the faces abstracted into individual grey printer dots and newsprint negative space. Not Alex and Gurt and the Skinny Cowboy in some unknown bar, up to god knows what. Just grey and black, newsprint and dots.

There was an address and time for a memorial service. She imagined sitting on a church pew. A photograph in a frame and a cherrywood box, and a vase of white flowers. A lot of people in black suits. She sat in the front row holding the little photocopied bulletin, and then Gurt and the Skinny Cowboy sat down on either side of her.

'How have you been keeping yourself?' the Skinny Cowboy asked her.

Audrey shook her head. Closed her eyes and pinched the bridge of her nose. Then she got up and stuck the newspaper clipping behind a refrigerator magnet.

She cooked a pot of spaghetti. Put a tongful of noodles and sauce into a bowl, then flipped it over onto a cutting board. Chopped it up into little half-inch spaghetti bites for Shelly.

'Use your fork,' she said to Shelly at the table. Shelly held her fork in a little toddler fist and ate fistfuls of chopped spaghetti with her free hand. Later in the bath she splashed with her tub toys while Audrey sat on the tub edge wiping half-inch spaghetti segments out from her hair, from under her chin, and off her chest.

Once Shelly was in bed, she sat at the kitchen table, holding the newspaper clipping.

'How have you been keeping yourself, Audrey?' she imagined the Skinny Cowboy asking.

The Skinny Cowboy is not coming to the funeral, Audrey, she told herself. Why would he come anyway? And who cares if he did? You're not afraid of him, Audrey. Who cares?

'Who's going to come anyway?' she asked herself out loud.

She picked up her cellphone and called her mother.

'Mom,' she said. 'Mom, are you still up?'

'Am I still up? Audrey, it's only nine o'clock. Hello, Audrey.'

'Mom what are you doing on ...' She looked at the article again. 'Mom, on Thursday?'

'Hello, Audrey. Good to hear from you.'

'I've had something come up Thursday. Can you come in and look after Shelly for the day?'

'How does Shelly like her new blocks? That building-block train set? Is she playing with them?'

'Mom, can you come down?'

'Thursday is the day after tomorrow, Audrey. I can come down tomorrow night, she's my granddaughter. I'm not doing much else. Wait, I'm volunteering stacking shelves at the library ... No, that's next week. No, I'm not doing much else.'

'Thank you, Mom.'

She walked around the house. Listening to the floorboards creak in the spots they creaked. Listened to the traffic grunt and rattle through the walls. Stood at the windows staring at the nighttime headlights through the windows. Her dirty windows, which she meant to clean every spring, in their peeling wooden sashes.

In the kitchen, the plaster on the walls bulged and wrinkled in a snaking curve behind the stove. Up to a discoloured spot in the ceiling where water had come through sometime in the past. Some old owner, who knows who. She opened the fridge and closed it, careful to give it a good shove to properly seal it.

She opened the door to the basement. Someone had cut a notch out of the wood at the bottom for a cat door, years earlier, and around the lumpy half oval the top coat of the paint was chipped to show previous colours of the door: taupe, mauve-grey, eggshell blue, milk white. She turned on the light and walked down the wooden steps, ducking her head as she went. Down to stand on the hard-packed dirt floor of the basement. The furnace rattled to life just as she got downstairs, and she stood on a patch of old carpet listening to it shake.

She needed to change the furnace filters. It was tough – they were an odd size and she'd only ever found them at a hardware store in the southeast, down Blackfoot Trail. She'd need to get them when she was on a grocery run for Joe Wahl, in his van.

She paid her landlord, Wade Clave, $950 a month for the house, plus her share of the utilities, which would get up to $300 monthly in the winter. Three hundred dollars and most of the heat would just evaporate right out of the badly insulated roof. It was a lot of money for her, but for a whole house downtown it was pretty cheap, all things considered.

She'd phoned Clave after about a year and asked him about the furnace filters. He never called her back. Eventually she changed them herself.

You should move out, her mother always said. *Why are you paying for all this space in this broken-down old dump anyway?*

It's a good deal for the size, Audrey would say. *Shelly gets her own room. You've got space. If Dad ever comes down, there's space for him. It's a good deal for the size.*

Her furnace, her steps, her carpet. Her shake, her bulge, her creak. She went back upstairs. Sat on the couch and turned on the TV news. She sat in the blue light of the television not really watching.

§

'Mum Mum, let's see magic,' said Shelly in the morning. 'Magic Glen magic.'

'Shelly, we need to have breakfast and take you to daycare,' Audrey said. 'Eat your toast.'

'Magic magic magic,' said Shelly, sitting in her plastic booster seat leaning her chin over a plate of peanut-buttered toast. She picked up a piece of toast and squeezed it in both fists, peanut butter oozing between her little fingers. 'Toast toast toast.' She squeezed and opened up both palms to show her mother the squished lumps of oily toast. Giggled and licked peanut butter from her fingers.

'Shelly,' sighed her mother. 'We have to go to Mirko's tonight to get a few things for Grandma's visit. We'll see Glen then. But now it's time for daycare.'

Her daughter threw back her head and wailed, a low to high full-throated tantrum cry that started in her diaphragm and peeled upward like a siren.

'Shelly, stop it or we won't go at all,' she said, knowing even as the words came out of her mouth that it was the worst possible thing to say.

Shelly snapped her head forward and back again and screeched, sliding out of the booster seat down into a puddle of crying toddler on the floor, sobbing and panting and keening. Audrey picked up the pieces of squashed toast and the plate and took them to the kitchen sink. Wet a dishcloth and wiped the table while her daughter cried on the floor.

She picked up the crying little girl and carried her to the bathroom. Sat her on her little stool and washed the crying girl's face and hands with a washcloth, then lifted her over a shoulder back downstairs. Pulled her arms and legs into her snowsuit. Pulled a wool toque onto her head. Shelly Cole sniffled and cried and her mom put mitts onto her hands, then led her out the door.

Reverend Joe Wahl stood on a chair in the corner of the long basement of the 12th Avenue United Church, stretching to fiddle with the volume of the small radio on top of a bookcase. The church was a few disconnected rooms in the basement of an old red-brick community centre. On the wall behind Joe, a table-sized poster listed the Twelve Steps in foot-high type. The long hall was split into little half-rooms by four-foot upholstered temporary walls, all tacked with crayon drawings, bright letters, cheerios, and macaroni glued on construction paper. Christmas tree cut-outs, sheep and angels and shepherd's crooks, chocolate brown, pine-tree green, vitamin orange. In each little room, red-cheeked babies and toddlers sat or played on the floor or held their plastic sippy cups with two hands at tiny wooden desks. A dozen children babbled and banged or squeaked in pairs and threes. A naked toddler ran across the room holding the diaper someone had been trying to put on him and was scooped up one-armed by a woman walking the other way, a stack of laminated time cards in her other hand.

'Miss Aphra, I have Stuart, where are his clothes?' she shouted.

'Miss Elba, I was changing him in the kitchen,' a voice hollered from behind a felt-covered half-wall, 'and set him down because Doreen threw her porridge at Keaton.'

'Okay, Miss Aphra,' Miss Elba shouted back, turning on her heel and heading toward a door in the back corner, the naked little boy dangling under her arm grinning at the room behind him.

The radio speakers crackled and 'The Wheels on the Bus' cut in mid-verse out of just one speaker. Babies looked up from their cups and blocks and clapped. Joe climbed down off the chair.

'Miss Anna,' he shouted over his shoulder. 'Shelly is here, Miss Anna.'

Miss Anna was a big-shouldered woman in neon-green yoga pants. She crouched down to touch Shelly's bright tantrum-red cheek.

'How's my big girl today?' she asked. Shelly threw her arms around Miss Anna's neck.

'Annannannaah,' said Shelly.

'She's a brat today,' said Audrey.

Miss Anna reached in a pocket for a tissue to wipe the little girl's nose. Then she picked Shelly up under the armpits.

'Okay, big girl, let's go have craft time.'

'Her grandma's going to bring her tomorrow and pick her up,' Audrey told Joe.

'Her grandma,' said Joe Wahl. 'You heading into the office early? Working late?'

'Funeral.' She took a note out of her pocket with an address and showed it to him.

'That's down Elbow Drive quite a ways,' he said. 'You can take the van.'

'I can take the bus.'

'Take the van,' said Joe. 'One less thing to worry about.'

Joe Wahl's van was a 1991 Ford Econoline, 240,000 kilometres, red, with a pair of barely-there-anymore soaked-through cardboard flaps on the floor that no one had pulled up since the last time it had been taken for an oil change. *Joe, you have to do maintenance on the van*, Audrey would say to him, picking up the key before a grocery run. *It's lurching. It's lurching and I'm worried about the alternator. Sure, sure, Audrey*, Joe would say, scribbling something in one of the coil-bound notebooks he kept in his aluminum desk.

The deal was you got a discount on monthly child care if you volunteered for the church. 'I have some moms who help with the meal prep,' Joe had told her over the phone when she first called him, 'and putting out the coffee for our weekly meal service on Thursday nights, and a dad who helps me run the Tuesday-night men's fellowship. There's a mom who helps me with the bookkeeping. I need help doing a deep clean twice a week – floors and windows and all the kitchen equipment. I need help getting the groceries once a week.'

'Getting groceries.'

'Yeah, you head down to the Wholesale Club off Blackfoot and 58th. I've got a list, doesn't take long. You just come down here and pick up the van and take the list. I give you our credit card.'

'Tell me about the van,' she said.

She went with him the first few times. Trailed behind him pushing the grocery cart while he slowly walked through the giant supermarket, stopping to squint at a paper list, then looking around the building for the right aisle, repeating this for each new item as if he'd never been in the place before and had no idea where anything might be. He took his time and shopped. He looked at price stickers and said, *This plastic wrap is forty cents off when you get three. Maybe we should pick up a few of these.* He put things into the cart in the wrong order: filled the bottom of the cart with lettuce and green onions, and then headed to an aisle for cans of tuna and cartons of beef stock. Audrey repacked while he shopped: pulled out the vegetables and laid down a floor of blocks and rectangles. Load-bearing cartons and cans at the corners, then an empty cardboard box on top for vegetables and other damagables. All the while memorizing and mapping the list and the store layout. Drawing up the new path for when she was on her own.

Now Joe left the key and the week's list pinned to the bulletin board in the low-ceilinged church kitchen for Audrey to go herself. How many cartons of milk, blocks of butter, cans of coffee. A second envelope had the church credit card tucked inside. Audrey came a few times a month, on Saturday afternoons when her mother was in town to look after Shelly for the weekend. The van struggled up and down Cemetery Hill and shuddered while it idled at the stoplights down McLeod Trail. She picked up groceries for Joe a few times a month and timed it for her own groceries, which she stacked in a separate end of the shopping cart from Joe's milk and butter and coffee.

'This funeral,' Joe said to her. 'Out of the blue? Unexpected?'

'Out of the blue but not unexpected,' she said. 'I'll take the whole day off work and get the groceries while I'm out.'

Joe shrugged. 'I'll make sure the credit card is in the envelope for you,' he said.

§

Downtown, she rode the elevator up through the silver-skinned glass building where she worked. In the elevator, an LCD television played a short reel of weekly news. Men in suits headed farther up toward law offices and engineering firms stood quietly with their necks craned up at the screens, reading the scrolling price ticker: natural gas per cubic metre, West Texas Intermediate per barrel, Brent Crude per barrel. The doors opened for her floor and she cleared her throat, then pushed between the men in suits when they didn't move out of the way.

She went straight to Harold's office without stopping to take off her jacket. Leaned in and knocked on the door frame. 'Harold, I can't come in tomorrow,' she said. 'I've got a funeral.'

Harold Goetz sat at his desk staring at the maps on his walls. The maps covered every part of the three walls surrounding him, held on long-ago papered-over whiteboards by magnets or pinned right into the drywall. High-detail maps of property lines, the intersections of farm sections and quarter sections, annotated with legal land descriptions and grid coordinates. A mesh of road and property lines, pinned up in no geographic order, snippets of Northern B.C. or North Dakota or Manitoba jumbled together – the only way you'd know one from the other would be to peer closely until you found a familiar town name, Billings, Weyburn, Minot, and then work outward.

It took a while for the words to reach the inside of his head.

'Audrey, for chrissake. I need you in here working, the place is falling apart. No one's here, Audrey, I need you. Have you heard anything from Kim?'

'Kim's still up above William's Lake,' said Audrey.

'Kim phoned this morning from the site in a lather and got four words into telling me she'd found something when her cell service cut out. Haven't been able to call her back – *cellular customer is not in service,* over and over.'

Audrey searched the maps and found the Central Cariboo Plateau, British Columbia. Kim's site north of Williams Lake was circled in red and surrounded by yellow and blue sticky notes with illegible scrawls in Harold's handwriting.

'She found something as in she found something? Like there's a find?'

'She literally said, "Harold, I found a –" and then the call dropped.'

They stood and looked at the map. Harold reached up from his chair to pull off a sticky note and move it up and to the left of a different sticky note.

'What kind of funeral takes a whole day anyway?'

'Harold.'

'Fine. Fine, Audrey. Go to your funeral, sure. Maybe we'll even still be in business when you come back. Wait,' he said, and shuffled through the paper on his desk. He found a pile of printouts and handed them to her. 'Get those to Thomas, he's heading into the field tomorrow. These are all the client boundaries. Tell him to keep his shit together.'

Harold Goetz knew the legal ownership boundaries of every acre of land between Yellowknife and Denver. Exploration firms phoned Goetz Environmental Consulting Ltd. and he would lean back in his chair with the receiver held under his chin.

Where are you looking? he'd say on the phone. *Right, north of the Cypress Hills there, east side of* CFB *Suffield. Encana has leases on either side of that. Probably sixteen years in that spot. That's north of the Enbridge pipeline? South. I know the spot. Sure, we can get down there and help you out.*

He made maps for the field archaeologists, for Kim and Thomas and Robert and whatever fieldwork hour-counting MA practicum students the university had lent them for the season. Road maps and property maps and terrain maps, satellite images from the computer giving a pixellated idea of the landscape. They went out into the field with the elevations, with the existing claims and leases marked. Well sites, pipelines, notations telling them who owned what, who got paid what royalty, how long they'd received it, and how long that arrangement would continue. The archaeologists took his maps and followed them out into the wilderness. They came back with envelopes and receipts. Motel room receipts with room charges for high-speed internet and adult movies. Dinner bills from chain restaurants: chicken wings, clubhouse sandwiches, beer schooners. All of which they brought to Audrey.

First she had to smooth all the crinkled slips and printouts, the carbon copies and sprocket-reeled printouts. When she had them sitting flatly, she started by sorting American from Canadian. Sometimes she had to lean into maps of Montana and Idaho pinned to her own wall, looking for a town name. She sorted by states and provinces and then cities and towns. Then she moved into taxonomy: Food, Lodging, Automotive, Equipment, Non-Work-Related, Other.

She sat between two computer monitors and entered numbers from receipts into a spreadsheet. She propped the receipts on a little stand. Each number on the printed page was marked with a streak of highlighter ink, different colours for different kinds of numbers, and her eyes scanned the page, reading first the pink numbers, then the yellow, then the blue and green numbers. Her fingers typed each number into a spreadsheet field while her eyes stayed on the paper. When she was done a page, she picked it up and checked the numbers on the screen, and when they were right, she set it face down in an open file folder and started the next one.

'Harold, is it okay if I use a highlighter to colour these numbers?' she had asked him a few weeks after first taking the job.

'All right,' he said, 'but make a copy first. Don't colour the originals.'

She made copies of the receipts and filed the originals. When she was finished with all the copies she fed them into the electric shredder.

Sometimes the archaeologists came to her cubicle with explanations.

'Those drugstore charges, Audrey,' Thomas would say, 'they're all above board. I was crazy sick. Some kind of northern muskeg super-virus. Something horsefly-borne.'

'Audrey, that dinner bill is cool,' Kim would say. 'Harold knew that we had to take the property owner out for some appreciation and he knows it's coming. You can't take these people to Denny's, you know? You can't take them to the Husky House.'

'Audrey, have you looked at the hotel bill yet?' Robert would say. 'I ordered the wrong movie. That's a mistake, that charge.'

She made photocopies of the receipts and then she highlighted the dates and amounts. Green for Routine. Orange for Unusual. Pink and red for Amounts in Excess of $500 and $1,000 respectively.

Between the movies and chicken wings, they inched over the earth described on Harold's maps. Digging and looking. Audrey had a limited idea in her head of the actual work. On television, archaeologists marked off squares of earth with stakes and string lines and dusted pottery clumps with little brushes. She imagined Kim and Robert bent down in clumps of prairie grass, blackflies and mosquitos buzzing above them, setting out their stakes and string lines. She didn't know if this was anything like how they actually worked.

They looked for signs of Indigenous habitation, for the stopover evidence of overland Hudson's Bay Company trappers, Catholic missionaries, Northwest Mounted Police camps. Pioneer settlements, red-river carts, or covered wagons. Any debris or refuse left behind, to show a route or datable journey. They looked for history in the marshes or meadow scrubland.

All clear, Harold would tell the client on the phone when they found nothing. *We'll get the paperwork to you and you're good to drill.*

At lunch, Audrey googled the funeral home address and plotted an online map to get there from the Wholesale Club. Printed it out and traced it with a red pen. She took the newspaper page out of her jacket. Unfolded it and laid it as flat as she could on the photocopier. She took the map and the grainy copy of the page back to her desk. Took a pair of scissors and cut away the copy columns to leave just the photograph of the three men.

§

Later she walked up 12th Avenue holding Shelly's mittened hand, the busy sidewalk lit by headlights, signal lights, brake lights. She walked slowly, as Shelly took careful steps along the cold sidewalk, her free arm held up for balance. They stopped at intersections and waited for the red hand to turn into the white pedestrian, and Shelly stretched out her little boot to step over grey lumps of the last snowfall still piled against the curb.

When they reached the ragged caragana hedge, brown and bare, that wrapped the fence around their little mustard-yellow house, Shelly tugged on her mother's hand and looked up seriously at her.

'Mom. Magic Glen magic,' Shelly said.

Audrey nodded. 'Yes. Let's go.'

Now Shelly walked a step ahead, pulling her mother along.

Her house was in the middle of the block, and down at the end was Mirko Lasko's Balkan Grocery, with its dusty awning and coloured neon window. In between was the long plywood wall around the hole.

There'd been houses there when she first moved into the mustard-coloured house a little more than three years ago. Narrow hundred-year-old two-storey houses, just like Audrey's. Then a couple of years ago they came and knocked them down. Knocked them down with heavy machines, then dug and dug, four storeys down below street level. Knocked down the houses and built the plywood wall around the hole.

The wall was covered in posters. Nightclub posters with the names of DJs and rock bands and theatre posters with the names of plays. Every day Marnie came by on her bicycle with a satchel full of new posters. Marnie was a razor-thin woman with a tattooed squid on her back, squid arms reaching down her own arms, tentacles wrapping around her shoulders, the squid body hidden under her T-shirt. She came by every day and propped her bicycle against the No Parking sign in the middle of the block. Pulled posters out of her satchel and hit them with a hammer-shaped staple gun, once in each corner. Marnie laid posters out in a grid, new ones up over the recently expired. Over months the paper grew thick and heavy, warping and crinkling in the wind and snow and sun, bulging around the staples. Then a City of Calgary truck would come and park with its hazard lights blinking and a man in overalls would use a claw hammer to peel the thick crust of poster off the wall. The paper came away in a scab strip, which he peeled away and threw in the back of his truck, leaving the plywood bare.

Every ten yards or so, the wall had a little window cut into the plywood, where you could stand on your tiptoes and look down to see the half-finished concrete and piles of old rubble that would have been an underground parkade.

They never built a parkade, though, and they never built a building. There was just the hole, and the wall around it.

At the end of the block, Glen Aarpy sat on his folding chair in front of Mirko Lasko's Balkan Grocery, under the awning out of the wind. His shabby oilcloth overcoat lit up by the signs in Mirko's window: neon-tube Open, Lotto 6/49, Orange Crush. On the other side of the big picture window, two white-haired men in aprons were slowly ringing up the groceries for the after-work rush. Morris Wirtz held up plastic tubs of olives and white cheese and Mirko Lasko looked over his black-rimmed glasses at the labels and punched the prices into the till. Morris put the tubs in a white plastic bag: green olives, green-and-black olives, different-sized blocks of cheese in milky brine. Handed the bag to a woman in a heavy felt coat.

She must be throwing a party, Audrey thought. Some kind of dinner party that you put out different olives in tiny bowls.

Glen was sitting on his folding chair looking up at two big men standing on either side of him. Paramedics: big men made bigger by their blue-and-yellow jackets. Coils of radio wire twisting out of bulky panels in the jackets. Shelly led Audrey up the sidewalk, then stopped a couple of yards from Glen and the paramedics. She pulled her hand out of Audrey's and stood waiting while the men talked, her hands clasped in front of her chest.

'Glen, if you see Shorty LeClaire, it's really important that you don't touch him,' said one of the paramedics.

'You can't touch him, not at all. His bare skin,' said the other.

'We're trying to get to everybody in the neighbourhood, but not everybody's around, so when you see people, tell them.'

Glen Aarpy looked back and forth between the big men.

'Tell people that they aren't to touch Shorty LeClaire's bare skin,' said Glen.

'That's right.'

'It's a fungal infection. It's in those big calluses on his hands. You know how big his hands are.'

'Don't shake his hand.'

'Don't shake his hand,' said Glen. 'And tell people this. Not to shake Shorty LeClaire's hand.'

'What about you, Glen? You keeping well?'

Glen Aarpy sighed and shrugged. 'I don't know about fungal infections. My own health issues are more microbial. Ill-intentioned spores in my gut biome. There's a malevolent microscopic kingdom down there squeezing out the more benevolent fermenters, which might otherwise bubble and burp the proper vapours out into my bloodstream. All of which leaves me ill-equipped to handle the various vagaries on any given day's agenda.'

One of the paramedics coughed into his fist.

'You want a cup of coffee?' asked the other. They pushed open the door and went into the fluorescent white grocery store.

Shelly stood patiently with her dinner-plate-wide eyes and hands clasped in front of her chest. Glen shifted on his plastic folding chair. Leaned down to root in the canvas bag he kept underneath, shuffling the papers inside. Shelly stood waiting while he puttered and rooted, and then he looked up.

'Oh, hello, Miss Cole. When did you get there?'

He had too few teeth and they were in the wrong places, all under a broom-bristle moustache, the whiskers of which looked to hurt the face they were so thickly rooted into.

'Shelly,' Audrey said, 'go ahead.'

On weekday mornings after rush hour, Glen Aarpy would get off the number 2 bus outside the St. Anne Apartments. He came into Mirko's grocery with his heavy backpack hitched up on two shoulders, and if Morris or Mirko had a customer, he waited, not talking to people inside the store by long-standing agreement. Once the shop was empty, he'd let himself into the back storage room where he kept his chair and his padded seat cushion. Outside he unfolded the chair, opened up his backpack, and pulled out a stack of bond-paper booklets with black-and-white Xeroxed covers: THE LUNAR PURVIEW: Calgary's Authentic Newspaper of Vigilance and True Voice.

'Every lie is a porthole into which the black waters of cold time lap and look and wait,' Glen Aarpy would declaim at passersby, while cars slowed and stopped for the red light a block ahead. 'And we can rivet that steel seal tightly as we might against the rime and bluster, but drip drop, drip drop, we can only float above our falsehoods for so long before the bottom goes out. Whereas the truth printed on a page will keep on your shelf high and dry, and your humble vendor's personal cost to produce is only sixty-five cents an issue.'

As long as Audrey had been coming to Mirko's – for a box of tea bags, for toothpaste or dental floss, a carton of milk, baby wipes, or after work or on a Saturday morning for a cup of the thick black coffee he kept slowly reducing on a burner behind the counter – Glen had always been sitting outside, yelling at people, shaking his handmade newsletters at them.

'Glen Glen Glarpy, I wanna magic,' Shelly said in a small, cautious voice.

He grinned to show her the black veins in his gums. Then he sighed dramatically. 'Baby Shelly Cole, I am delighted by your enthusiasm. If more people wanted magic, it would be a good deal easier to perform and produce. Unfortunately, magic is not only difficult for the practitioner but demanding on the audience, and the sort that I've made my practice requires of both participants the sort of keen, unclouded attention that is rigorously squeezed out of all of us like so much toothpaste by the circumstances of life.' He waved his hand around to encompass the building, the street, street lights, traffic. 'Their institutions do not absently grasp and pinch the tube willy-nilly. No, they roll from the bottom up from the first day of kindergarten so that years later every smear of cognitive gumption has been pressed out and left to stick to the bottom of the sink. Shelly Cole, because you are as of yet completely untouched by this grist pincher, you are the ideal magician's audience. An increasing rarity, however, and this difficulty in securing an appreciative audience has more or less drummed not only the desire but the ability itself from me of late.' Shelly's eyes were big and her mouth open in anticipation.

'In this atmosphere of pervasive, smothering skepticism, I find it more or less impossible to practise any sort of interesting magic. For instance,' he said, stretching and wiggling his fingers to show off the cracked nicotine-yellow nails and thick white knuckle hairs, 'I'm unable to produce the most basic misdirections and conjurations.' Then he snapped his fingers loudly and pointed at Shelly.

The little girl followed the line from the finger to the plastic zipper of her puffy jacket, which she unzipped a few inches and then gasped. A rolled-up tube of white printer paper protruded from inside her coat. She looked up at her mother and then at Aarpy, who motioned for her to give him the paper.

'For instance,' he said, 'I'm sure it would be altogether impossible these days for me to conjure up a little girl's favourite animal. I'd be unable to produce a ...'

Shelly waited a moment, making sense of this, then said, 'Kitty.'

'Right,' said Glen, 'a kitten. It would be out of the question for me to make a kitten with magic.' He patted the pockets of his pants and jacket. Then squinted at her coat again and pointed to her pocket. She reached in, then made a happy little squeal and produced a black Sharpie marker, which she gave to him.

'A kitten,' he said. 'Right. Just not possible.' He uncapped the marker and drew on the paper, flat against his thigh. A few quick lines and marks, then held it up: a crude cartoon of a dog with floppy ears and a bushy tail.

Shelly shook her head. 'No,' she said, 'kitty.'

'Right, a kitten. This is what I mean,' he said, drawing again. 'Proficiency in magic has more or less deserted me at this point.' He held up a drawing of a pig with two little slots in its snout nose and a single squiggle curly tail.

'Not piggy, kitty.'

There was one sheet of paper left and he scribbled furiously, then held up a duck with wide feet and an open bill, and a speech balloon, which said, 'Quack Quack.'

'No. No no, kitty,' said Shelly.

Glen Aarpy coughed and shrugged, then squinted his bushy eyebrows and pointed at Shelly's zipper again. She pulled it down further to produce another rolled-up tube of paper. She unfolded it and then squealed with delight. Turned to her mother and showed her: a black marker drawing of a kitten with little whiskers, licking an upraised paw, its long tail curling happily behind it.

'No, magic is altogether too thankless an occupation these days,' said Glen Aarpy.

Shelly giggled and clapped. 'Mommy, Mommy, itta a magic kitty.'

'It's a magic kitty,' said Audrey.

'Canna keep magic kitty, Mommy?'

'We'll put it on the fridge. What do you say?'

Shelly concentrated so that she could say as clearly as possible: 'Thank you, Glarpy, for magic kitty.'

'You're very, very welcome,' said Glen.

'Go in and show Mirko,' said Audrey. Shelly pushed into the hot bright store, and once she was inside, Audrey fished in her purse and found a $10 bill.

Glen inclined his head seriously and stuffed it in the inside pocket of his jacket. 'Here,' he said, handing her a copy of the *Lunar Purview*, 'take a paper.'

§

At the funeral home, a young man in a black suit led her into the chapel. A little pewter urn sat on a cherrywood podium at the front, beside white lilies in a white vase and a picture in a frame. Audrey thought about walking up to the front to have a closer look at the picture. See what they'd chosen. What they'd been able to find. Instead she sat down near the back.

A woman in an expensive jacket that she hadn't taken off sat in the back row, holding a designer handbag and staring straight ahead. Another woman sat a few rows ahead of her, holding a notepad and a pen.

There was a grey-haired man in a shabby leather jacket with his arm propped over the back of the pew. Wrists McLung was sitting next to him.

Wrists turned in the pew to look over his shoulder. He saw Audrey and didn't look as surprised as she would have liked. Puffed out his cheeks and looked up at the ceiling.

There was no one else. Audrey looked over her shoulder, watching the back door, but no one else came.

After a while the young man in the suit walked into the chapel, down the aisle to where Wrists was sitting. He whispered something to Wrists, who looked around the room, then nodded and coughed. Stood up and walked to the front of the room.

There was a little microphone on the podium, and Wrists spent a while adjusting this. He leaned onto the podium with his big hands on either sides. Coughed again and then he started talking.

'I guess I first met Alex Main after he bought the Alka Skelter from Sid Stein. Sid had hired me a while prior to that to be his doorman. "Wrists," Sid said to me, "we have a drug problem, a skinhead problem, and a people-having-sex-in-the-bar problem." He said my job was to do whatever I had to to fix these problems.'

The woman with the handbag in the back row exhaled loudly, stood up, and walked out of the chapel. Wrists waited for the door to shut.

'It was this real derelict bar, the Alka Skelter,' said Wrists. 'Right in the heart of old Victoria Park, on Olympic Way and 13th Avenue. This was before they bulldozed Vic Park to expand the Stampede grounds. Before the casino and all the condo towers. Proper sketchy, mostly vacant Vic Park. You went up a long, narrow flight of stairs. The building was old and there were places where the floor was thin and you could see down between the slats. You'd feel the floor bow when there was a room full of people. I mean, later, after Alex bought the place and people started coming, years later when the room was full, you'd still feel the floor bow.'

Wrists coughed into his fist.

'The drug problem was that everybody who came to the bar did drugs. It was a pretty quiet place before Sid sold it to Alex, and since it wasn't really busy, the only customers were friends of Sid's and they would come in and do drugs, and so it seemed like the kind of bar you could go and do drugs in. "Wrists, people think it's okay to do drugs in the bar and you've got to stop them," Sid told me. Sid did a lot of drugs and liked to do them with his friends in his bar. Most of Sid's friends liked downers and heroin and a few of them who considered themselves more exciting liked to snort cocaine. If they couldn't get their hands on powder cocaine, they'd go out onto the fire escape and smoke crack in the alley. Which was bad because it was a really sketchy alley that had a lot of its own crackheads occupying it already. Sid would send the bikers that sold him and his friends their drugs out into the alley to chase away these crackheads. The bikers would then come back later and sell the crackheads more drugs. All of which was just a really bad scene.

'Now, the bikers that sold Sid his drugs generally liked me. They liked me 'cause I'm a more or less together guy with my head on straight. I told them they couldn't sell drugs in the bar and they said, *Hey, no problem*. I found this surprising at first until Sid explained to me about his lawyer. Sid and the bikers shared a lawyer, the Skinny Cowboy. The Skinny Cowboy obviously isn't his name but it's what everyone called him. He was an old cowboy who lived outside of Turner Valley. He had long silver hair and weighed 120 pounds, maybe. Wore a silver cow-skull bolo tie and this proper old battered cowboy hat. He was some kind of crazy good lawyer, the kind that can keep bikers out of prison and city inspectors from shutting down empty, drug-infested, morally bankrupt bars. He'd come down and sit at the end of the bar and drink neat whisky. "Wrists," he'd say to me, "Wrists, you ever find yourself in any trouble and I'll make it go away. *Poof*." And he spread his fingers out like a magician. *Poof*.'

He coughed and looked around the room, doing his best not to look at Audrey.

'So mostly it was Sid and his friends, and Sid did his best to be involved in the running of the place. Sid really loved reggae music. He hired Bruce News, who owned more old roots-reggae forty-fives than any other DJ in town, to bring them in and play them in the bar.'

The man in the front raised both of his hands, fingers spread for victory Vs. Wrists coughed again.

'Hi, Bruce,' said Wrists.

'Hi, Wrists,' said the man in the front.

'Am I getting this more or less right? It's been a long time.'

'More or less,' said Bruce News. Wrists coughed again.

'Anyway, Sid loved reggae music, so he hired Bruce News, but he scheduled him on Tuesday nights because he was scared that if too many people came, Bruce would feel compelled to play different records to make people happy. "I don't want any kind of hippie dance party, Bruce," he'd say. So Bruce News played old reggae records to an empty bar on Tuesday nights. Which was why we had the skinhead problem.

'As you know, skinheads really love reggae music. Especially the real old crusty roots records that Bruce News played. Sid's bar was empty except for some strung-out junkies and punk rockers who went there to score drugs from bikers. So skinheads loved it because they had it to themselves.

'The Alka Skelter had everything that skinheads like except fighting. Fighting with junkies is a what-do-you-call-it, a non-starter. I think they thought at first that the bikers who sold Sid drugs would be good for fighting but these bikers didn't want any of it. They were on strict orders from the Skinny Cowboy. "No fighting anybody who doesn't owe you money, he told them. So they were stuck fighting with each other.

'You got about one good hour with them. They'd show up early, nine o'clock, right when Bruce started playing records. They drank a lot of beer, which was good for the bar. God knows junkies don't drink a lot of beer. They'd take turns walking up to Bruce and requesting songs. They were very polite to Bruce because he had all the records they liked and they were worried that if they antagonized him he'd start playing the kind of hippie dance music reggae that other people liked and the bar would get popular and they'd have to go someplace else on Tuesdays.

'About an hour in, though, they'd had enough beer and they needed to fight, and not having other options, that meant fighting with each other. One of them would sock the other in the face and they'd get a good brawl up. I'd get in the middle and then they'd run their mouths off to get a rise out of me, because as good as fighting with each other was, they all wanted a run at me and just needed the excuse. I was just barely smart enough to recognize this and not give them any. I'd just get in between, hold them apart, and tell the bartender to cut them off. They'd cuss me out with all kinds of skinhead bullshit to bait me into a proper fight, which I did not take. Eventually they'd leave.'

'Well, you took the bait once,' said Bruce.

Wrists sighed. 'Well, I took the bait once. I threw Curly Edwards down the stairs. It was a long staircase. I don't remember what Curly Edwards said except that it made me mad enough to throw him down the stairs. They said, "Next week we will come back and we will kill you."

'The next week I came to work on Tuesday. None of the skinheads came. I made it through the whole shift, waiting. I stood at the bar staring at the door. Bruce News played really great records and the whole place was empty all night.

'I shut the door at the end of the night. Nowadays there are a lot of condos and apartments around that block. There's the casino now. Back then they'd pretty much emptied out the neighbourhood to make room for the Stampede expansion, which hadn't happened yet. There was an empty lot across the street and boarded-up doors on either side of Sid's bar. I came out of the bar and there were six skinheads waiting for me. It was the middle of winter. They were all in their bomber jackets and those tight jeans they wear and a couple of them had those flat English-bloke kind of caps on. What's that pattern called?'

'Pattern?' asked Bruce.

'The pattern on that fabric they make those hats out of. It's not really a checkerboard, it's kind of …'

'Houndstooth,' said the woman with the notepad.

'Houndstooth.' Wrists snapped his fingers. 'Anyway, I remember thinking, these guys really don't dress for the weather.

'They beat the shit out of me. Beat me unconscious. I remember thinking before I blacked out, this isn't a run-of-the-mill beating, these guys aim to kill me. Apparently they dragged me back into the alley. It was minus thirty outside and they left me unconscious at 3:00 a.m. in this alley to die in the cold.

'Anyway, I ought to be dead. But I didn't die. I got frostbite and lost feeling in a few fingers. I lost toes too. I've only got six toes. Audrey, did you know I've only got six toes?'

Audrey shook her head. 'I did not know that, Wrists,' she said.

'Anyway, I didn't die. They had me in the hospital for a while, for the frostbite and the beating, and I had some broken ribs and a broken cheekbone and my eyes were pretty much swollen shut. As soon as I could stand and see, I split the hospital and went back to work. 'What the hell happened?' Sid asked me. He was pretty concerned. He gave me cash out of the till, I think whatever was in there, for the time I'd missed. Which, considering Sid didn't make any money from the bar, was pretty thoughtful.

'Now, when the skinheads nearly murdered me, the bikers were concerned. Sid was concerned. "I've had it," Sid said to the Skinny Cowboy. I'd showed up black-and-blue, missing toes, and Sid pointed at me and said, "I've had it," to the Skinny Cowboy. And the Skinny Cowboy turned on his stool to all the bikers and raised his hands with his palms out and said, "I release you." Which I did not understand the meaning of until the next Tuesday night, when the skinheads showed up. They were pretty surprised to see me alive, but not as surprised as they were when the bikers followed them up the stairs. I remember that the last biker up the stairs shut the door and locked it behind him.'

Wrists coughed. 'I remember the sound,' he said, 'that the door made locking.'

He leaned on the funeral-home podium staring at the back of the room for a while. The woman with the notepad sat staring with her pen hovering above the paper.

'The people-having-sex-in-the-bar problem was the easiest to solve, I guess. I'd just stand over people until they stopped. If people wouldn't stop just from me standing around, I'd spray them with the table cleaner. There was a cap of bleach per litre of water. You spray someone with that and they stop whatever they were doing.

'Listen, all of this sounds really interesting and cool when you tell it as a story, but it was mostly tiring and dull. Sid, for all his faults, was a sweet guy with a big heart but not much of a businessman, and it wasn't much after all that went down that whatever money he was running the place on dried up.

'And then one night the Skinny Cowboy showed up with this guy, Alex Main.

'"Sid," said the Skinny Cowboy, "Alex wants to buy your bar and I believe his offer is fair and equitable."

'That could have been my out. I could have left with Sid. "Thanks, Sid," I could have said, and headed out, and got a job in some other bar. Or, hell, a job in someplace that wasn't a bar. Bruce, you left.'

'I left,' said Bruce, 'got a job in some other bar.'

'But I didn't. I met Alex Main instead.'

Wrists stood at the front of the room leaning on the podium. He looked over at the pewter urn and the white flowers. He looked around not saying anything and eventually the young man in the suit from the funeral home walked halfway up the aisle and nodded, and Wrists walked off the stage.

Afterward, she signed the guest book and followed Wrists outside. He lit a cigarette and coughed. He smoked for a while without looking at her and she waited and he smoked.

Four years ago he'd seemed so old, she thought. When she'd met them on the highway outside Fort Saskatchewan. She was a skinny kid and they'd all seemed surprisingly old to her. She hadn't thought that men with grey-and-white hair and wrinkles around their eyes should have been driving around in a van full of beat-up old instruments playing rock'n'roll music to anyone who would at least partially listen. He didn't seem as old to her now, though, standing outside the funeral home smoking.

'I believe that's the most I've ever heard you talk, Wrists,' she said eventually.

'Yeah, I expect I won't speak for three days in order to recover.'

He smoked and didn't look at her and waited.

'You look like hell, Audrey,' he said eventually.

'Well, three years single-mothering will do that to a girl.'

'I guess so,' he said. 'I guess you were just a kid last time I saw you.'

'Last time you saw me,' she said, careful with the words, 'you were dropping me off at the Blue Goose Motel on 16th Avenue in the middle of the afternoon. That was,' she counted in her head, 'April 2006. No, not April, May. I remember there was one of those Calgary May snowstorms, and there was snow everywhere.'

'Right,' he said.

She waited awhile while he smoked. Part of her wanted to drive away in Joe Wahl's van, but part of her wanted to talk more.

'Were you planning on telling that story all along?' she asked. 'Or just when you saw me?'

He dropped his cigarette and then lit another. 'Maybe a bit of both. Maybe when I saw you. Some of the details.'

She took the cut-out photograph from her jacket pocket. 'Would you have told that story if the Skinny Cowboy had come?'

Wrists laughed, a short little snort that ended in a cough. 'He wasn't going to come. That woman with the notepad was probably a *Calgary Herald* reporter. "Disgraced Aiver Petroleum Heir Funeral Closes Book on Seedy Chapter of Local History." He'll have known that. He isn't going to show up someplace that will put him in the human-interest section.'

'Right,' she said.

'Right,' he said. Then after a pause, he said, 'Maybe not all the details. If he'd been here.'

She laughed with him this time.

'I had to talk to him, eventually,' she said. 'You must know that. When I found out. I didn't know what to do, and I was so scared, and I didn't know … I didn't even know where to start.

'I knew I needed to leave. And I knew … I wanted nothing to do with any of it. I wanted to leave altogether. So I realized I needed to talk to him. So I talked to him. You must have known that.'

'Yeah,' he said, 'I know that.'

'"I want to leave and never come back," I told him. "I don't care about anything else, I just never want to see Alex again." That's what I told him. And he said, "We can totally make that happen." *We can totally make that happen.* And then the next morning you were there. You showed up out of nowhere and told me to pack everything up and come and meet you down in the van. And you drove me to Calgary through a May snowstorm and dropped me off at the Blue Goose Motel.'

'Right,' he said.

She folded the photograph back up. Put it back inside her jacket pocket. They stood quietly outside the funeral home for a while.

'Do you still have the van?' she asked eventually.

He shook his head. 'Fuel pump fell apart outside of Wawa, Ontario. I was playing in one of Dick's punk rock bands and we were headed to Sudbury. No time to get it fixed. We traded it to a body shop for an older Econoline which was a bigger piece of junk but got us the rest of the way home before falling apart completely. I don't have that anymore either. The new act isn't on the road as much. When we do go out we mostly rent.'

'Right,' she said.

'I may have to go in there and see where Bruce disappeared to,' he said. He coughed into his fist. Then he looked up away from her.

'If you ever want to hang out …'

'I don't,' she said.

Wrists nodded. He stubbed out the cigarette he'd just lit. 'Well, good seeing you, Audrey. I guess I'll go see what's keeping Bruce.'

'Good seeing you, Wrists.'

PART TWO

THE ENGINEERS
FROM MUNICH

4

The snow started just past Red Deer on Highway 11. At first it melted on the black asphalt and shone wet under her headlights. The prairie rumpled with hills and thickened with trees and more and more snow as she drove west. By Rocky Mountain House, snow lay heavy on the road surface, cut into black ruts by some unseen up-ahead traffic. Everything in the Audi was in perfect shape though, and driving was easy. Brand-new winter tires that stuck to the road. The windshield wipers left no streaks, made no noise, and the headlights were bright and showed her the road through the snow. She turned up the heat and when the car got too warm she turned it down. She looked into the snow and sometimes headlights went past the other way.

She turned on the radio and turned it off. She listened to the tires on the road and drove with either hand, her arm propped up on the passenger seat or her elbow on the door against the window. Sometimes she opened the window and felt the cold wind and little taps of wet snow.

Audrey Cole was a small, skinny woman who had always had a hard time reaching and fitting the vans and trucks she'd driven throughout her life, vans and trucks sized for taller, fatter men. But tonight she hadn't even had to adjust the Audi's seat. Two hours out from Calgary and her lower back still felt good. The ball joint in her hip didn't hurt in the place it always did, where her leg swung ten to two between the gas and brake. She downshifted on hill grades and the clutch had a just-right sweet spot that only needed the smallest incline of her ankle. She held the steering wheel with one or two hands and propped one or the other arm on the window edge or elbow rest and could have driven two hours more, no problem. Like the Engineers from Munich had stood her on a stool and measured her, tailors with tape measures, pins in their mouths.

Headlights came close and receded, but the cars that made them and any people hidden in their glare were far away from Audrey.

The woman who owns this car takes it exactly on time to each scheduled appointment, thought Audrey. She phones the dealership the first day the Perform Maintenance light comes on. She nods when the mechanic suggests a differential check and a transmission flush on top of the regular oil and filter, and pays for it all without comment.

She opened the window for shrill, cold air and sucked it into her nose. It felt colder up here, out of the city. Her black leather boots were comfortable but not warm or particularly waterproof, and her cloth jacket had a collar but not a hood. Tail lights grew ahead of her and she passed a logging truck.

Audrey was alone in the car and alone on the road. Sometimes lights appeared on the horizon and came close, blinked past and disappeared behind, distant white then red, and she was alone then too. A person might be a few yards away for a moment, but she was alone even then.

'Car, you are perfect,' Audrey said.

She drove for a long time, and near Nordegg the hills moved tightly around the highway. Night and snow hid the shapes, but she knew the blunt peaks of the easternmost Rockies were low and close now. She drove past the trunk road that would take her north up to Hinton if she followed it. She saw a yellow Junction sign at the base of a hill, and she slowed down and turned onto a heavily snow-covered gravel road. A single pair of tire tracks led north and she drove slowly now into these hills.

The forest lasted and lasted and then parted into a cut around the village of Two Reel Lake. Dark except for a two-storey house with an old Pepsi sign hung in front and a Canada Post sticker in the window, lit up white by a single street light. One fuel pump and a white propane tank surrounded by unpainted concrete bollards. She'd stopped here with the Lever Men, the first time, years earlier. Wrists bought five packs of cigarettes. 'You never know how long you're going to end up being up there,' he'd explained. She remembered standing in the pale winter sun outside the van while Rodney filled the tank and Wrists bought cigarettes and inside Dick Move bought a scratch-and-win ticket and did not win.

'That'd be – when was that, Car? Three and a half years ago? Four years,' she said to the car. 'Haven't been back in four years.'

She drove through the village in the snow at two o'clock in the morning and saw no people. The light was on above the door of the aluminum-sided trailer with the RCMP sign in front, but the windows were dark. There were a few houses with long driveways closed in by tall pine trees. At the end of the last driveway was a car with a For Sale sign in the window.

She stopped the Audi, a hard brake that snapped her seat belt tight.

'It's my car,' she said out loud.

A cherry-red Honda Civic hatchback with black trim. An older model – late eighties, maybe 1990. '$600 OBO,' said the hand-lettered sign in the windshield.

That can't be your car, Audrey. Your car was totalled. An absolute writeoff. The RCMP officer who she talked to on the phone had said they'd towed it to a wrecking yard in Red Deer.

Your car was an '88. Squarer, boxier. This has a rounder front. This is a 1990, Audrey. Maybe a '91. But still, it was so close – the same cherry red, same hatchback.

'Car,' she said to the car she was sitting in, 'it's so much like my baby. But my baby is gone. A total writeoff. Towed off to Red Deer to get crushed into a cube.'

She realized she was stopped in a tiny village in the middle of the night. She gave the Audi some gas and drove out of the village, back into the dark forest.

'That car was my baby, Car,' she said, driving at a careful pace up the snow-covered road. 'I mean, it had problems. But it was the first car I'd spent any real amount of money on. It takes a while to scrape together $4,000 bagging groceries. Bagging groceries and bussing tables. That car was my baby.'

The road made gentle curves ahead of her and she drove into the snow streaks flying past her headlights.

She drove up the road between the trees, following the slow curves, and the Audi's headlights lit everything up white. Cast long shadows of the skinny pine trees. She made slow curves and the trees moved past her, their long skinny shadows turning around her as she drove.

She drove slowly up the road, leaning over the steering wheel. She was pretty sure that she'd remember where to turn. Just the one turnoff, as far as she could remember. Then she saw the sign. She stopped the car.

A big wooden billboard stood beside a side road leading north into the deeper woods.

Future Site of
CLEARWATER HAVEN
Luxury Wilderness Recreation Resort at
TWO REEL LAKE
Fishing – Skiing – Spa – Golf
COMING SOON!
A West-Majestic Development

There wasn't a picture – no artist rendering of the future resort, no evocative illustration of checker-coated sportsmen fishing luxuriously from expensive speedboats. No elegant blondes in bikinis sipping pink cosmopolitans on their cedar patios. Just the big words in an elaborate script, white on a brown sign.

There wasn't a fence. She'd worried there might have been some kind of temporary fence, chain-link with a padlock stretched across the road. But there wasn't a fence, just the big new sign at the turnoff.

Somewhere in the trees, the snow stopped. It was thick enough on the road though. She drove very slowly and the tires were good, didn't slide or stick. The road narrowed and the shoulders dropped off into deeper and deeper snow. It dwindled to a single car width and she slowed to a twenty kilometres an hour, second- and first-gear crawl, and felt her heart surge each time she cut through a low drift. She could miss a turn and slide straight into the snow, or worse, tumble right off a grade into space, falling through the treetops to crash on the rocks underneath.

The road wound downward and the forest opened up into a deep bowl valley. The sky split for a swollen seven-eighths moon bright enough to show her the long, frozen white surface of Two Reel Lake. Snow-covered granite boulders made a stony beach all along either shore. The lake and valley disappeared as the road curved back into the trees, and opened again when she switched back out, and she did her best to watch the road and not stare through the trees for glimpses of the white snow-covered ice. So when the woods finally opened up at the top of the lake, she wasn't ready, and stepped heavily on the brake, startled. She'd thought it was farther away yet.

'There it is, Car,' she said. 'The Crash Palace.'

The valley sides drew down around the dark mass of the building. A six-storey, red-brick building: window-gridded, sandstone-silled, flat-roofed, looming in the valley's vertex. Two arms opened east and west from a central block, and each of these had its own open-handed side, so that if you were to look down from a helicopter you would see a fat-bellied H, a steel I-beam that had swallowed something into its middle gut. Dozens and dozens of skinny windows set in the brick walls reflected Audrey's car headlights. The highest floor was smaller, a glass-and-steel later addition that had always reminded her of a little glass hat that the building wore. Hillsides and trees and lake surface magnified the building's scale, like an orange harvest moon just risen above the prairie, and made it taller and steeper than what she knew it was, but even if it were carted brick by slab away to the city and rebuilt on a dense Calgary street, it would still be tall and steep and heavy. Alone on the lakefront, the Crash Palace was huge and old and odd, not least for being so far away from plausible reasons for being built at all.

She shut off the car and the engine clicked, cooling. Snowflakes fell on the hood and melted.

She got out of the car and did her best walking across the yard not to step her insufficient shoes too deeply into any of the fresh drifts. Past the outbuildings down by the beach: the tool shed, the garage, and the little boathouse farthest out, where the trees reached the water. The wind was cold and then it cut off when she walked in between the building's arms.

The building reached around her, six tall storeys of lightless windows on either side around the narrow courtyard. She crunched through the thinner snowdrifts winding across the old concrete flagstones. There was a single step to climb to reach the eight-foot double door, the frost-dappled windows dark in the heavy brown wood.

She pulled the key out of her jacket pocket. It wasn't her house key and it wasn't her mail key, or the spare key for her mother's house in Canmore. It wasn't the heavy security key for the archaeologists' office. A thick steel key with a square of blackened masking tape stuck to the bow. Audrey Cole put this key into the brass lock and opened the door.

§

Inside, Audrey swam in night, standing in long, wide blackness. Her eyes buzzed in the dark. Windows that could let in the white moonlight were all too deep in the building. She felt at the wall beside the door for the light switch and of course it didn't work. No one had paid any bills here in years.

Her memory worked to create details in the blank space. Ahead and all around her would be the wide open foyer, reaching out on either side under the high, faraway ceiling. An open mezzanine looked down over a long rail from the second floor. If she walked straight ahead she should reach the brass-railed staircase, wrapped upward squarely around a copper-caged elevator shaft, the back spine of the building reaching up, away to the higher floors. The memories came back to her gradually in the dark.

The dark space stunk, rot and mildew, and damp despite the dry deadness of the air. She felt the cold floor through her boots. She listened for the sounds a building makes: hot water whistling in pipes, buzzing fluorescent lights, the thrum of forced air rushing through ductwork. The Crash Palace was quiet. No drips in sinks, no televisions on faraway floors, no laundry machines or pipes rattling in their brackets.

'Hello,' she said loudly in the dark. 'Hello, it's Audrey. Audrey Cole. I haven't been here for a long time.'

She took a few steps in the dark, shuffling her feet, careful of her toes, arms out ahead for obstacles.

'It's my key anyway,' she said, at normal volume, to no one. 'He left it for me and fuck him anyway and it's mine now.'

There was a parlour over to the left, she remembered. Bay windows and sofas, and a fireplace. She moved cautiously, anticipating furniture in the darkness, low chairs or tables lurking to trip her. She realized she was trying to be quiet, so she stamped her feet on the stone floor to hear the sound slap in the big space. Listened for responses, for scuttling animals, burrowed into the dry shelter of the walls and floors.

There could be black bears. Grizzly bears. Denned in the basement for their winter sleep. There are different kinds of bears and some of them you have to run away from at first sight, as fast as you can, and for some of them you need to just drop and play dead and hope for the best. Someone once explained to her these different bear responses that a person needs to know and she remembered cold horror in her stomach listening and imagining the fateful meeting someday in the future, face to face with a bear, and how she'd spend her last moments trying to remember which bear required which, making of course the wrong decision.

'Bears, be fair. Say which sort you are. Give us an honest shot.'

Something crunched underfoot. Tracked-in mud maybe. Dried bird shit. Upstairs there would be broken windows or vents. Chimney flues. Plenty of magpie and crow access for generations of brave bird explorers. The pine trees all around the lakeshore might sport nests lined with beak-stripped copper wire, kitchen silverware, shoelaces, fridge magnets.

In the cold parlour a wide bay window allowed enough light to make shapes. A sofa and heavy easy chairs. A coffee table. Piles of vague junk: bottles, boxes, books. And a brick fireplace, open, lined with black ash. She knelt and put her hand into the maw and felt a cold breeze from the flue. In an iron rack were logs and newspaper, and a box of matches.

Audrey crumpled newspaper into balls and made a little fire. Fed it with wood splinters and shavings until her fire was large enough to put a proper log onto, then stood and walked back to the couch. Rich orange light made the parlour an island of colour in the night. She watched the fire and felt the heat push into the room, chasing the chill that had worked up inside her from the wind, the concrete cold soaked up through her boot soles that had numbed her toes, her heels and calves. A fuzzy knitted afghan was folded in a corner of the couch and she pulled it around her shoulders, staring into the fire, feeling the heat fill the room, drawing dampness out of the wood and plaster, activating the air. The new light shrank the space around her, turned empty mystery into a room with couches and chairs and a view through the arch of a dark, empty lobby.

If there were residents, they stayed away. No small, clever locals drew in to the fire: weasels or porcupines burrowed in cupboards, nested in ducts. Badgers and blackbirds dragging straw, mud, burr bristles, pine-cone scales into the warm corners and dark crawl spaces. Leaving lucky stinkweed or thistle seeds around the building to grow out of any cracks they had the gumption to root down into.

She'd had a Christmas cactus, which sat on the radiator in her room upstairs. She'd had a few plants, she remembered now. She tried to remember the day she left, tried to remember if she'd thought of the plants while packing everything up in a rush. The day she left was a hectic sprawl of memories, but she was pretty certain she didn't think about the plants. There was a Christmas cactus, and a little ponytail palm, and a sprawly, scrawny thing with pale green heart-shaped leaves. She'd found them around the building in other rooms, and as people came and went she took to watering them and eventually moved them all upstairs to the bedroom.

They're dead, Audrey. They died long before the power went out and the heat was shut off. Died as soon as you weren't around to water them. You left with Wrists and that was it. Maybe if you go up to the bedroom you'll find some sticks of naked wood in a dried-out clay pot.

Outside, a coyote howled. Two notes and the swoop in between, the higher pitch a single solid tone. No vibrato, no waver. It echoed and stayed true, like two harmonics on either end of a just-intonated guitar neck. She shrugged out of the afghan onto her feet.

A second howl answered. Audrey ran into the mezzanine, away from her fire into the dark where she knew the stairs were, and she took the steps blindly. Leaned forward with her hands out, grabbing the upcoming step lips and pulling herself into the dark. She grabbed the bannister to round corners, brass cold in the ball of her palm, and ran up all six flights. At the top she wheezed, her legs and hips burning.

Upstairs the moonlight was sudden and full. An uncovered concrete floor spread uninterrupted to all four walls, the space broken only by a few skeletal steel wall studs at irregular intervals, too sparse to indicate their never-got-built floor plan. A few sheet-metal pillars, big strange polyhedral trunks stretching from the floor that had been the ceiling up into the new roof above them. All around, ten-foot-high windows showed the full panorama of the long valley outside, aluminum grey around the fat moon. In the distance a tiny blue flame wavered in the sky, the only flake of colour in sight – the flare of gas plant stack over on the far shore of the lake. Audrey stood at the window, looking, trying to catch a glimpse, watching for any motion. The grey cylinder of a theatre spotlight on a steel truss stood in the corner of the room.

Another howl went up into the night. Somewhere west, across the lake. But no motion. Then another call, this one farther out into the hill. A wait and then another. Then long quiet. She waited, but the coyotes were quiet and didn't show themselves.

She looked down at the beach, at the snow-covered outbuildings and the car, already powder white with snow.

You should build something into the landscape, Audrey. Go out there and install something on the lakeside. Something permanent, or at least as permanent as this heavy, empty building. A little 'Audrey Cole Was Here' marker. Before they send the bulldozers.

§

Outside, she picked her way carefully through the snowdrifts with the blanket wrapped around her shoulders, down to the lakeshore. The gravel was thick and cold under her boots. She stood at the ice lip of Two Reel Lake. Wind blew off the flat white lake expanse and sanded her with tiny stings of ice.

She took careful steps with her hands out wide on either side for balance, until the gravel gave way to snow-slick rocks, and she stopped, wrapped her arms around her chest, and stared out over the white lake.

There was no sign of morning in the thick dark sky. No sign, but soon. It had taken longer to get here than she'd planned. Longer through the narrow forest road out from the village.

It took you four hours to get here, Audrey. It will take you four hours to get back. You'll be on Highway 2 in the middle of morning traffic. You will be exhausted. You will fight to stay awake.

She gathered the flattest stones: load-bearing stones and platform stones, and feature stones, flecked and veined, fracture-sided or water-smooth. She stacked up stones into a small inuksuk until the cold pulled the mobility necessary for grasping and stacking from her fingers.

Audrey stood up to admire her marker, but then she was very, very tired. First with light-headed, risen-too-quickly vertigo, and then with deep, thick exhaustion throughout her body. You can't drive back, Audrey, she realized. You will fall asleep. You won't even make it back to the highway. You'll drift away and slip off the ledge of the road. Clatter through space. Crash and over.

'Car,' she said, 'we'll leave tomorrow. First thing tomorrow after we get some sleep. But we can't leave tonight because I'll fall asleep and crash you.'

Inside she stirred and fed the fire. Curled into the itchy blanket on the couch. Sleep for a few hours, Audrey, and then head back. She scrunched up as small as she could under the blanket. East at Highway 11 to get back to Calgary. Back home.

East. If you go west you end up in the mountains. You'd end up at the Athabasca River Crossing, halfway between Lake Louise and Jasper. There's a truck stop. You could stop for a bottle of water and a sandwich and a full tank of gas. You'll be able to go a long way on a full tank. The Engineers from Munich pride themselves on it.

Yes, Audrey, say the Engineers from Munich, *we pride ourselves on it.*

There's a lake on the way out there, Abraham Lake, she'd only ever seen it on maps, a long cut just inside the front range, and Highway 11 lips the edge for kilometres. She'd always wondered what colour the top of that lake would be on a winter morning driving west.

Did the Audi have a cassette deck? It used to be you parked at a truck stop and they had a swivelling wire rack of cassettes by the door. *Today's Top Country Hits, Countin' Down the Oldies, K-Tel Presents.* Swing through them. Odds are against Link Wray, but you never know.

Audrey, this is a modern luxury car, the Engineers from Munich tell her. *It has a* CD *player. It has bluetooth wireless connections.*

Right, says Audrey. *Bluetooth.*

Audrey, a full tank, you can drive all day, regardless of terrain, the Engineers from Munich tell her. *Regardless of terrain or inclement weather. You are a thoughtful, defensive driver, always aware of her changing situation on the road, no?*

I am, she tells them.

Then drive as long as you like. Snow, ice, high mountain roads, rapidly shifting conditions — we built this car for you to overcome any of these situations without material impact to your comfort or experience of the road.

Thank you, Audrey tells the Engineers from Munich.

They smile and clank their beer steins. *It is nothing, Audrey Cole. Enjoy your drive.*

5

She brought the van around the corner and stopped, staring over the steering wheel. The mid-afternoon sun, early-winter low in the sky, reflected white gold off the windows set into the six red-brick storeys. A huge, incomprehensible building, alone on the lakeside, nowhere near anything, like a turn-of-the-century Canadian Pacific hotel that had wandered off and gotten lost in the distant wilderness. A little cluster of outbuildings huddled near the lake, none of them square to each other, and a houseboat sat two-thirds of the way up on the beach, the bottom few feet of it wrapped in lake ice.

'I'll be damned,' Audrey said, leaning forward, as if being closer to the windshield would help her believe what was on the other side. 'This isn't even possible.'

'Well, it's possible enough to walk into and get a drink,' said Rodney. Rodney and Dick and Hector got out of the van and started heading toward the front door. Wrists was scribbling on an index card in the seat beside her.

She tried a few different questions in her head, and eventually she just asked, 'Why?'

Wrists shrugged. 'Alex will give a different answer depending on the time of day you ask him.'

The heavy wooden door opened into a cavernous mezzanine, floored in grey-veined marble, wrapped in dark-panelled wood, with a staircase wide enough for six people to climb abreast of each other, lined by a brass and wrought-iron bannister that swept up in a long curve to a second-floor balcony. It should have been stately, but the floor was patchworked by mismatched carpets and a green-wire tangle of Christmas lights wrapped around the bannister and railing. Extension cords ran around the room, duct-taped to the floor every few yards. The air smelled like cigarettes and roasting meat, sizzling over a charcoal fire in some hidden kitchen.

In the middle of the open room, two men stood behind a pair of folding tables. A linebacker-thick man with four days of rough black beard cut up a pineapple with a long-bladed chef's knife. He had a white apron tied around his bulky middle and held the knife in big hands furred in black hair. The knife blade rang on a bamboo cutting board buried in fruit: pineapples and melons, oranges and lemons, grapefruit and limes, whole or in stages of disassembly, slices, wedges, cubes. Extension cords ran to the table from the walls, and power bars sat on the table, out of which ran blenders and juicers. Bottles with steel speed spouts stuck in their necks: coloured liqueurs, tall clear vodka bottles, and stubby blue and green gin bottles. Lemon zesters and paring knives. Two-litre bottles of tonic and soda water. Champagne bottles, the foil peeled off their necks.

'You put it together like this,' said the other man. He took a pineapple round and cut it into two crescent halves. He slid one onto a long bamboo skewer, then an orange wedge, then a red maraschino cherry out of a jar.

'When you serve the rum punch, this sits on top of the glass,' he said. 'Just lay it right across there. Hey, Rodney,' he shouted without looking up from the table. 'You want a rum punch? Koop, make Rodney a rum punch.'

The big man picked up a bottle of rum in either hand, one white, one dark, and free-poured an up-and-down ounce and a half from each bottle into a tall ceramic tiki mask, a glazed face with ball eyes and an open O mouth. He poured red and orange and green juices out of plastic pitchers and scooped ice in with a steel scoop, splashing out a lot of the just-poured-in juice over the sides. He stirred it all with a steel spoon.

'Sure, but next time put the ice in first,' said the other man. 'Come here, Rodney, try this. Put the garnish on it, Koop.'

Rodney walked across the floor and took the tiki drink from Koop. He lifted the fruit skewer off the top and took a long drink.

'That is a hell of a good drink, Alex,' he said.

He was blue: vein-blue through tissue-paper-thin skin under the far-above-him lights. He had a young face changed by deep lines around his mouth and eyes. The blacks and pales, the whites and pinks in the wrong places, displaced by a long succession of sleepless nights. All made paler by a mop of peroxide-blond hair. He wore a white dress shirt over a black T-shirt, half-buttoned with sleeves rolled up, unkempt but not dishevelled, not wrinkled, as if he had put some care into the way he left it half-finished.

'Wrists, Rodney, tell me this is a long-lost daughter.'

'Alex Main, this is our driver, Audrey Cole.'

He shook her hand. 'Your driver. Fuck me. Welcome to Two Reel Lake, Audrey Cole. I'm Alex and this is Jerry Kopachek. What's ours is yours. And not just our rum punches. You guys, get your shit in here. They'll all start coming up in an hour or so, and I thought it would be cool if you guys were playing here in the foyer when everyone arrives. We'll prop the door and they'll hear music when they pull up. Some "Welcome to the Crash Palace" music.'

'It's going to sound pretty lousy down here, Alex.'

'Come on. Nice high ceiling, lots of space.'

'Hard reflective surfaces. Conflicting echo lengths.'

'You'll adjust.'

'I need a carpet,' said Wrists.

'Koop, find Wrists a carpet.'

'Just something that sits in front of a door to set my kit up on, so I'm not sliding around on this stupid floor every kick.'

'Extension cords,' said Dick.

'We'll find some. We need these ones to run the blenders. Audrey,' said Alex, looking up at her, 'go upstairs – go to the … fourth floor and find yourself a room. When you do, take the picture off the door and that way people will know it's taken.'

She pressed the round black elevator button and listened to the car rattle down the shaft toward her. The brass birdcage door slid open and she stood inside. Marked the thickness of the concrete floors as she passed upward from one to the next.

Audrey felt light-headed. It's just weird, is all, she told herself. It's weird and not what you expected. Driving through the landscape north of Nordegg past the village of Two Reel Lake, she'd gotten herself ready for some hidden-away ski resort, someplace that hunters and snowmobilers would spend a week over Christmas. Cedar and stonework in riverbank colours: rust reds and quartz whites. She expected two-handed lumberjack saws and crossed snowshoes mounted on the walls above rock hearths. Black iron wood-burning stoves and exposed timber beams. Painted saw blades: farmhouses in winter, orange light from the window highlighting blue snowdrifts, white snow-frosted pine trees, people on a sleigh ride with single-brush-daub faces. And a room half-full of not-really-interested elk hunters sitting around a fire after a long day out in the cold, not really paying attention to the music.

The elevator opened on the fourth floor with a ding. Vacuum cleaner brush-marks ran in alternating furrows down the long red carpet in the empty halls. On each door there was a photograph, stuck up with scotch tape or wire-hung in little wooden frames from nails. She walked between the doors looking at them all: flash-glare snapshots of groups, young people with bottles and plastic cups, arms around each other's shoulders, grainy in the dark. Or young girls and boys smiling against white portrait-studio backdrops. Little black-and-white square portraits clipped out of junior high school yearbooks, with braces and pimples. There were clippings from magazines, heavy metal singers with teased yellow hair, or skiers caught mid-air against brilliant blue skies.

The room at the far west end of the fourth floor had an old hockey card stuck in the brown wood by a red push-pin. Hakan Loob, said the hockey card. Right Wing, Calgary Flames. Number 12 in red and yellow, leaning forward over his stick, his mouth open in concentration, staring intently from behind a plastic visor. She opened the door. There was a sheetless mattress under the windowsill. A little Christmas cactus grew in a terracotta pot on top of the cast-iron radiator. One purple flower bloomed amidst the spiky green leaves. She put her bag and sleeping bag down on the mattress. She stood at the window, looking out at the pine-tree-green hills and the grey mountains behind them. Then she went to the door and pulled the red push-pin out of Hakan Loob.

They were bringing in the pig when she came back downstairs. Koop and Wrists carried either end of a long steel pole. Between them a burgundy pig hung tied around the steel, his feet chained together tightly in knots, upside down, mouth open where the pole split through him. A skinny man with black-framed glasses, black hair pomaded high above his head in a towering pompadour, came out of the back hallway.

'I've got the rotisserie set up on the back lawn behind the kitchen,' he said. 'Take him straight back out there so we can get the fire on him.'

Audrey followed them through a hallway in the back into a huge kitchen, white-tiled on the walls and floors, with restaurant-sized grill-tops, huge steel refrigerators, gigantic dishwashers fed multicoloured cleansers through long plastic hoses. Stock pots bubbled on grease-blackened gas burners, and the counters were covered in tubs of minced onions and celery, wholesale-sized cans of tomato, stacks of bagged bread and buns. They grunted and bumped, navigating the pig through this maze, and finally got it manoeuvred through a door in the back that led outside. The pompadoured man stood over a row of gerry-rigged gas grills, pulled together and lined up, the lids all removed, wavering heat blasting from blue propane flames.

'Looch, this thing is a monster,' said Koop.

'Bring it here, bring it here,' said Looch, waving them forward with two hands inside big quilted grey oven mitts. On either end of the gas-grill battery was a steel strut, and the men heaved the pig up and then dropped the pipe down into these struts. Looch fitted a crank into one end of the pipe and gave the pig a test shove. The whole spit turned above the gas flame and he grinned.

'I wanted to do it Hawaiian-style,' said Alex Main. 'You know, dig a hole and cover him up with coals and banana leaves like at a luau. But the ground is frozen. Anyway, Looch figured out this whole rigamarole and it ought to work pretty good. Should still get that long slow heat on him. We'll get that juice sizzling and smoking out there into people's noses in a good way all through the place.'

The Lever Men played while Alex welcomed people. They came in pairs or threes or fives. Audrey found a chair when they started arriving and sat in the corner so the band was between her and the crowd. She watched everything from between Wrists and Hector. Alex shook everyone's hands, clasped their elbow with his other hand and steered them in. Waved an arm to indicate the bar, the stairs, the musicians. He made this exact sequence of gestures for every person who walked through the door.

They brought suitcases, hiking packs, sleeping rolls, grocery bags full of potato chips, cheese twists, chocolate cookies. Some of them had guitars in hard cases or gig bags or just carried by the necks. Young people, twenty-year-olds in leather biker jackets and blue Canada Post jackets, poorly fitting thrift-store sport coats. Boys and girls in shapeless thick hoodies and down-filled vests brought suitcases and duffle bags. The tubes inside Rodney's open amplifier head glowed brighter orange as the afternoon went on. The Lever Men played surf licks or bossa nova chords, or two-chord country-and-western locomotive rhythms. Hector walked away from the organ and came back dragging a wooden chair. He sat down and played a few chords, then got up again and went to Koop's bar for a drink. Sat back down and picked up with the rest of them.

She caught glimpses through the window of the vehicles as they rolled to a stop on the long front yard. Pickup trucks, station wagons, Jeeps and SUVs. A yellow-and-black-painted school bus. She saw hockey sticks and skates tied together by the laces slung over shoulders. A van full of women in their forties with grey hair and crow's feet around their eyes carried milk crates full of records. People brought wardrobe bags for suits and dresses. Snowboards and snowshoes. Someone had a stack of jigsaw puzzles. A bald man with grey hair around his temples gave Alex a ukulele with a red bow tied around the neck.

A big man wearing a black leather vest and with long black hair pulled into a tight ponytail shook Alex's hand and pulled him into a tight hug. He hugged Alex and talked into his ear for a while. Alex listened and nodded and listened. Then he shook the big man's hand again seriously and gestured grandly into the room.

The big man in the vest looked around, and Audrey saw him make eye contact with Wrists. He waved and smiled a not-warm smile. Wrists did a little drum fill and waved back, not smiling at all.

Later, Wrists set down his sticks and went to the bar for a drink. Dick went with him. People in denim jackets with patches sewn onto the backs and shoulders came through the door and shook hands with Alex Main. Rodney walked out as far as the length of his guitar cable allowed and sat down on the staircase. He fingerpicked two chords, a drone pattern, no changes, flicked a treble note with his pinky occasionally, but otherwise sitting in the bottom strings. Grey-haired men in Hawaiian shirts, hockey jerseys, cowboy hats, leather ties. Two girls with matching black Bettie Page haircuts wore checkerboard-print dresses and had flames tattooed on the backs of their calves underneath black fishnet stockings. Leather vests and jean skirts. A group of teenagers in thick neon green and orange snowboard jackets, sunglasses up in their bleached hair, dragged an old TV set on a toboggan, hands wrapped in the yellow nylon rope.

Dick and Wrists came back and they played 'So What' and 'Take Five' and men with slicked-black pompadours danced with red-haired girls in starched skirts.

'Hey, Audrey,' said Wrists. 'Hey.' He snapped his fingers until Audrey looked at him. Rodney was back to the fingerpicking, the same two chords, same tempo, same static sheet.

'Go get a juice or something from Koop,' said Wrists. 'Go get him to pour you a soda water.'

'Wrists, I'm an adult.'

'You're an adult, Audrey, sure. Get a beer then. Get something to keep your hands full.'

'I think I might go upstairs,' she said.

'You're fine. Just stay sitting there. Nothing to be alarmed about.'

'My bag is –'

'Did you take the picture off the door?'

She took Hakan Loob out of her pocket and Wrists laughed.

'All right, good. There's rules here, Audrey, don't worry. There's rules and everybody knows to follow them.'

'Give us some "Stampede Breakfast," Wrists,' Rodney shouted.

'Your bag is fine in your room. Stay down here with us. Okay?'

'Okay, sure. What's the big deal?'

'Just stick close around.'

'Thanks, Dad,' she said.

Wrists started a quick two-beat country-and-western railroad shuffle. The crowd laughed and talked, and the racket they made filled the huge stone-and-concrete space with echoes. Beer cans and bottles opened and different smokes filled the air: cigarettes and clove, skunky marijuana, and from down the back hall roasting pork. The older crowd knew Dick and Hector and the even older crowd knew Wrists and Rodney and shook their hands at the bar. People went upstairs in twos and fours with their backpacks and sleeping bags and Audrey thought about her bag in the far room and wished she was upstairs to lock the door from the inside.

Looch started bringing food out of the kitchen: tubs of potato salad and coleslaw, trays of sliced white buns, all already buttered, and finally tray after tray of hot shredded roasted pork. People crowded around and loaded up paper plates. They ate roast pork sandwiches and the juice ran down their chins and they grinned and ate, and the smell of the hot roasted meat mixed with the dope and tobacco in the air, making it greasy and electric and alive.

Alex Main held a champagne flute out toward her. 'Here, have a mimosa. I know it isn't breakfast.'

'I'm okay,' said Audrey.

He shook his head. 'No, you have to have it. We use blood oranges. Koop squeezes them. Squeezed them today.' Bubbles ran up along the glass in the deep red-orange drink.

'I have this soda water,' she said.

'Of course you do,' said Alex.

He stood and waited for her to have a sip and it was fizzy and tart, not too sweet. He nodded approvingly and went back to shaking hands.

They got louder when the sun went down. Whether or not they turned up the amplifiers, she couldn't tell. Yellow bulb light replaced white and slowly greyer daylight, and maybe it was what and how they played and not the electric pickups and speaker cabinets reproducing the sounds. Harder and focused, chords and notes struck more tightly together, simpler rhythms, higher tempos. Not the men who'd dropped notes and ambled on and off the beat in Nanaimo and Vancouver. They got louder and the crowd broke apart, back toward Koop's bar, holding shoulders and shouting into each other's ears.

Eventually the Lever Men started playing Lever Men songs. They were same songs she'd been hearing the last two weeks, but they'd never sounded like this. The room and the crowd transformed them into something different. Rodney stood a bit in front of the band, on the floor level with the crowd, hands wrapped around the Telecaster neck and moving as little as possible, just his wrists and fingers and maybe a bit of his elbows. Staring somewhere just above and behind the crowd, and she understood. *The* Rodney Levermann.

The Lever Men played E minor and B minor, F and A minor, and the drunk crowd weaved together on the floor, dancing, a few close together with arms around shoulders and hips but mostly alone, their own set of hip and hand movements, nearer to or further from the rhythms in the music, kick drum snare drum, cocking hips, rocking up and down on heels, snare drum bass strings, wrists and necks, Hector's left hand, back-and-forth shoulders, wiggling and bouncing, bobbing or drifting. Some people covered distance in their dances, little orbits or slow approaches to girls or boys, and some of them stayed rooted, eyes closed, one heel correcting the travel of another. High droning up the neck notes sustained in the air, strings and keys, grinding in and out of phase as they played through the changes. Rodney played with his eyes closed and sweat dripped off his face onto the floor.

Audrey stood and didn't dance in the centre of the thick crowd, jostled side to side when shoulders or hips shuffled into her. Damp fabrics, slick arms, everyone's all-day built-up scents activated by the heat, all the liquor in their hands and guts sweet and tangy, and if the ceiling were nearer, all of their evaporations would recondense and rain salty and oily back to their faces and shoulders. She stood sweating with her head tilted back and her mouth open, close to the amplifiers, the speaker cones, soaking in the rumbles and high stings, letting the ranging waves rattle and shake her, hooks for the soft tissue between brittle ear and cheekbones. Hook and pull and space for all the buzzing, hot rays and pulses loose in the room. People near her kissed loudly, fingers pushed into each other's faces, eyes closed, tongue mouth lip noises smothered by larger sounds. Audrey rolled her neck back and listened to the landmarks. The Exshaw cement plant, Lac des Arcs, Morley Flats, Jumpingpound Creek.

§

She woke up hot in her sleeping bag, tied up in the fabric. She tried to straighten it around herself and couldn't. Found the zipper and fought it open. She sat up and put a hand on the warm radiator. Steam hissed on and off inside, pulses and gurgles, and a higher sustained tone keened from the copper pipe that fed the coils.

In the hallway, feet had scuffed and spoiled the long vacuum lines in the carpet pile. On either side of her, the pictures were down off all the doors, and someone had built a little pyramid of empty beer cans against the hallway wall. She heard low talking and giggles behind some doors. In the stairwell she heard someone singing badly on a higher floor.

Downstairs, she walked to the front door and pushed and it wouldn't open. She checked the lock. Pushed again and then turned ninety degrees, planted her leg, and pushed the door with her hip and shoulder. The door shoved open an inch and then another and no further. Snow blew in on a chilly wind. Outside, a foot and a half of snow had piled up against the door. She pushed it again, cutting into the drift, and got it wide enough to poke her head out. White snow and white light everywhere. Covering the cars and vans and erasing any footprints the crowd had left. There were drifts built up in the courtyard between the building wings, blown in as far as the door.

'They'll send the snowplow up the range road first,' Jerry Kopachek said behind her. 'That's west of here. Out to the gas plant on the other end of the lake. Then they'll do the east-west route off the junction. A couple of people live out there and there's the Long Twilight Sportsman's Retreat. But they won't even start that until tomorrow most likely. If it's going like this. They'll get to us in about two days.'

He smelled like coffee grinds and boot polish and old blue jeans. Maraschino cherries and white soap. A rolled-out-of-bed-and-into-shoes-and-socks smell.

'They'll call,' he said. 'I mean, they'll call to make sure we're all right, and we'll tell them that we'll be all right. You want a cup of coffee?'

He had already set up his tables. There were two big steel percolators, the kind you set up in a church basement when you need coffee for a hundred people. He peeled the foil top off a big can of yellow no-name grocery store coffee and filled the top filters of both perks. Then he started to unpack his bar. Pulled liquor bottles and juice cartons out of cardboard boxes. Bowls with cut-up fruit covered in plastic wrap. His knives and zesters, scoops and stirrers. Jars of olives and cherries.

He must pack it up at the end of the night, she thought. Take everything back to a fridge someplace deeper in the building to keep cool.

The percolators gurgled. Made steam and the smell of coffee in the cool lobby.

Alex Main came downstairs wearing a sportcoat over a black T-shirt and striped pyjama bottoms. He pushed the door and widened the opening in the snow farther than Audrey had managed, about thirty degrees. Koop poured him a cup of coffee and he sat on the steps.

'We're good for a few days, aren't we?'

'We can do a contingency menu with Looch.'

'What, disaster rations? Everybody gets a scoop of lentils and a cup and a half of water a day? It'll be a few days, not a few weeks. The menu as is is fine.'

'Shit, Alex, I need to get home,' Wrists said when he came downstairs. 'I need to get back to work. I need to see my daughter.'

'It'll be a few extra days, tops. Koop, they'll send the plow around tomorrow probably, right?'

'They'll send the plow around the day after tomorrow maybe,' said Koop.

'You're going to run out of material, Wrists?' said Alex. 'Come on, we'll pay you. You'll make new fans. A hundred bands in Calgary would pay me in blood to get locked up here with this crowd for two extra days.'

'We've all got to get back to work. We've got jobs, Alex. Lives and jobs.'

'Lives and jobs, sure thing, Wrists. I'll pay you plenty extra. The additional time at a higher rate.'

He explained it to people as they woke up and came downstairs, catching them on the stairs before they had a chance to see outside. Food for weeks, booze for months, all utilities intact, he explained. People had red eyes and yawned for the most part, asked if there was coffee and if there'd be enough to drink. They got the door pushed open the rest of the way and people went out into the snow. They scooped up handfuls of snow and threw it, or walked down to the lake and felt the wind and snowflakes. Mostly they stayed around Koop's bar, and when he declared the coffee ready, filled themselves a paper cup. Then Looch started bringing scrambled eggs and hot pancakes and white buns stuffed with leftover pork out of the kitchen by the trayful, and everyone ate and drank coffee.

The Lever Men sat around a table in front of the fireplace in the west parlour. Someone had started a fire but it had burned down to nothing. Audrey knelt on the cold floor, stirred and blew on the ashes, then put a log in to build it back up. Hector brought beers from the bar for all of them.

'I have to get back, Wrists,' said Dick. 'I have to get back to work. Tomorrow is the last day I have booked off.'

Wrists flipped through the receipts in his jacket envelope, squinting at the numbers and then writing on a blank index card. 'Yeah, I have to get back to work too,' he said.

'You have to get back to your daughter or Marla will murder you,' said Hector.

'I'm fully aware of Marla's nearness to murdering me at any given time, thank you very much,' said Wrists.

'We're starting a new job tomorrow,' said Dick. 'We're wiring a grocery store. The shop has this brand-new contract to wire the panels in all the new grocery stores in southeast Calgary. I can't miss Day One.'

'Well, unless Alex has a helicopter hidden somewhere in his goddamn lair here, we're not going anywhere until that plow comes,' said Wrists. 'When my ex-wife murders me, you can apply for my job.'

'Look,' said Hector, 'we're stuck. Okay? Take it easy, make the best of it. He says he'll pay us as long as we keep playing, so we'll keep playing. Unless you can find a pair of snowshoes and walk back.'

Dick grunted and stood up. He and Hector went to the bar, where the two women with Bettie Page haircuts were talking to Koop.

'I guess I never really thought about all you guys having, like, day jobs,' said Audrey eventually.

Wrists looked up from his index cards and squinted at her. 'You've seen how much we get paid any given night.'

'Sure,' she said, 'I just hadn't thought about it.'

'Dick is an electrician and Hector is a postie.'

'A what?'

'A letter carrier. I do some contract labour and I work the doors at a few bars in Calgary.'

'How old is your daughter?' asked Audrey.

Wrists put the receipts back into his jacket. He tapped his feet one two one two, alternating on the hard concrete floor.

'I'm not wiring up a grocery store, but I wouldn't mind getting out of here, Wrists,' said Rodney. His voice was slow and his eyes were unfixed on the back of the fireplace, somewhere past the slow orange flames.

'You're fine, Rodney,' said Wrists.

'I am altogether fine,' said Rodney. He raised his bottle and kept it near his mouth for two three four breaths before sipping. Staring ahead into the fire. Wrists took the envelope out of his jacket and put it back inside, watching Rodney drink. Then he looked at Audrey.

'She's six. She's seven in three weeks. I have to go and find the right princess for her. She's into princesses, see. Cartoons about princesses, and they make dolls of them and I have to find out which is the newest of these cartoons and which of the dolls she already has.'

'Can you ask Marla?'

Wrists snorted. His eyes followed Dick and Hector to Koop's bar, where they leaned on the table laughing. The women with the Bettie Page haircuts had new dresses, the same starchy cut but different patterns, with matching bandanas in their black hair. They laughed and Dick talked with his hands, opening his fingers and framing shapes. The women laughed and Koop put tiki cups with long red straws in front of them. Wrists watched them and pushed back out of his chair.

'It's going to be fine, Rodney,' he said. He picked up his beer and weaved through the crowd toward the bar.

'What about you,' Audrey asked Rodney. 'Are you an electrician?'

Rodney watched Wrists disappear into the crowd, then reached into his jacket pocket. Produced an unlabelled orange pill bottle. He winked at Audrey and held a finger to his lips. Shook out four white pills. 'How old are you, Audrey?'

'I'm twenty, Rodney. I keep telling you that.'

'Right. Right, Audrey.'

He tipped back and dry-swallowed the pills with a wince and cough. '"Little Rattle Stilt" gets played at a remarkably dependable rate by radio stations that do a certain format, for which I get a royalty cheque worth around 3,000, maybe 3,200 bucks every three months. Sometimes a bigger one-time chunk if it gets used in a car ad. There's an old CBC made-for-TV movie about Doug Flutie that it's in, and there's a nice cheque any time that gets rerun.'

Audrey did the math in her head and didn't ask him any of the other questions she had. Rodney kept shaking the pill bottle in the same four-four backbeat, staring off across the room at wherever Wrists had vanished away to.

'Did I ever tell you about the time I met the Devil, Audrey?' Rodney asked.

'Who?'

'The Devil. Satan. I met him at a bus stop.'

'You never told me the story about the time you met the Devil, Rodney, no.'

'It's a pretty good story,' he said. 'You'd remember it.'

'Are those your usuals?'

He looked at the bottle, scrutinizing it like he was seeing it for the first time. 'These? These are – I have it on good authority they're a good substitute.'

'Good authority?'

'My … interim … pharmacist.' He coughed and slapped his chest.

'As long as they make you better,' said Audrey. 'Right?'

'Well,' said Rodney, 'there's different sorts of better.'

§

Audrey walked aimlessly around the building, up the stairs or the elevator, and everything felt a little smaller in the daytime, the hallways narrower, the brick and concrete thicker and heavier. Upstairs, she stood at the window watching a group take push brooms outside onto the lake top. They shuffled on the ice, pushing snow out of the way in strips. Cleared a long space and slid-stepped back to the shore for their hockey sticks and a tennis ball. Eight of them in ski jackets and toques, no skates, sliding on their shoe soles, passing and batting the ball around. Mostly they chased the ball out into the snow when someone shot it wide and away.

Down the shore from their game, a houseboat sat half-beached, dragged up onto the gravel, dipping frontward into the ice. A full-sized houseboat with a plastic slide curling down the back, one you'd drive past sunning on a lake in the British Columbia interior some summer afternoon, drifting across the Shuswap or Mara Lake, shirtless drunk men lazily steering or diving from the rooftop into the cold lake water. The Two Reel Lake houseboat was rimmed all around in icicles. A tennis ball missed a pass farther up the frozen lake top and slapped hard against the fibreglass wall.

She wandered around getting more and more bored – itchy, agitated bored. She started picking up the empty cups on the floor. Stacked the red plastic cups into a long sleeve. Wrapped her fingers around as many beer-bottle necks as she could. Brought them all to the main floor and stacked them behind Koop's folding table bar while he poured liquor and juice.

In the kitchen Audrey found an empty coffee can and walked through the lobby emptying ashtrays.

'Hey,' said Alex Main, crossing the floor toward her. 'Hey, what are you doing? You're a guest. Go take it easy. Have a seat, get a drink.'

'Well, I've taken it pretty easy all day,' she said. 'I'd rather keep busy.'

'Koop and Looch can do all that stuff,' he said. 'Get a drink, take a nap.'

'I just get a little nuts if I don't have something to do,' she said.

He furrowed his brow as if this caused him some kind of deep confusion, then sighed and shook his head. 'Well,' he said, 'maybe Koop can show you how to make some drinks. Koop, show Audrey how to make some drinks.'

Koop shrugged. 'Make some drinks. Sure.'

He showed her how to make a Caesar: how to salt-and-pepper-rim a glass. This much vodka and then shakes of hot sauce and Worchestershire sauce. He took the cap off a big bottle of Clamato juice and she sniffed the tomato-and-sea-creature tang. He took the lid off a jar of pickled asparagus and put a vinegary spear in each red drink. People woke up late and trudged downstairs and asked about aspirin, and Audrey made them Caesars, which they stirred groggily with the asparagus.

Koop showed her how to free-pour liquor, the right up-and-down motion to get an ounce out of the speed spout. He lined up beer bottles for her to practise pulling the caps off. When people walked by, they hollered at them to come take these freshly opened test beers. He showed her how to twist the cork out of a champagne bottle. Peeled off the foil and untwisted the wire cage. He wrapped his big fist around the cork and twisted the bottle until it popped off undramatically in his closed hand.

The big man in the black leather vest walked through the crowd, chatting and shaking hands. He'd pull people aside and whisper in their ears, and they'd nod. They'd think to themselves, concentrating, like they were counting something in their head, then nod and shake his hand. He had a little notepad in the pocket of his vest. He'd grin and make a few marks on the notepad with a stubby pencil and move on.

'Who's that guy?'

Koop followed her gaze around the room. 'That guy … Oh. No one in particular. Don't worry about him. Here, I'll show you how to make a Manhattan.'

When the sun went down, the Lever Men plugged in and fired up again, and the crowd came back in from outside, stomped snow off their boots and shoes. They came down in groups from their rooms upstairs, bleary-eyed, men in pyjamas and girls in sweatpants and hooded sweatshirts. A few of the older rockabillies had new suits, and their boot heels clipped on the concrete when they danced. Everyone crowded around Koop's bar. Koop plunged two hands into the cooler and brought up six bottles of beer at a time, lining them up and snapping off the caps with his opener, pop-pop-pop, the caps flying behind him and clattering somewhere on the floor. Koop scooped ice into plastic cups and stirred rum punches, twisted the half-pulled-already corks out of wine bottles. People took two drinks at a time and milled around while the Lever Men rattled through their songs. Joints were lit and passed around and the air got thick with skunky smoke.

Audrey helped Koop open beers and rotated new bottles out of boxes into the ice to chill. She cut up limes and lemons for him on a little cutting board, stacked glasses. As the night went on, there was less to do and he was just fine doing it himself. She sat in a chair behind the bar and watched people drink and dance and kiss and drink. Everyone was sloppy and groggy, from drinking all day after drinking all night, and they danced out of time with the music and not for very long. Fewer people danced, and more sat in chairs or on the floor, passing around cigarettes and joints. A group of kids, they seemed like kids, in lumpy sweaters with scraggly hair, sat around on the floor near her and passed a square of tinfoil back and forth. One person held the tinfoil and another held a lighter flame underneath it and they took turns inhaling the smoke from whatever substance sizzled on the hot metal.

She got in the elevator and pressed the button for six.

On the top floor, the building was empty, no interior walls other than the middle spine of the elevator shaft, just wide open space, with pipes sticking out of the unfinished concrete floor in places, future plumbing for future rooms. Electrical conduit, the ends capped with plastic plugs, and wires tied off with black electrical tape twisted out of hollow steel posts, like scrubby cacti in a cold desert.

She wandered into the west wing. Alex and Looch stood in the corner. Everything was white from moonlight. A heavy theatre spotlight stood nose down in the corner, like a cannon, plugged into the wall. A pair of hunting rifles leaned against the window glass.

Alex opened up a window and the night rolled in heavily. He picked up a rifle and held it up to his cheek, sighting down the barrel into the darkness.

She followed the barrel line out into the night, and on the white lake coyotes milled in a circle, grey shapes under what must have been a full or nearly full moon.

'They got into the garbage last night,' said Looch. 'Even with all the noise in here. Right up to the back door and tore apart the garbage bags in the cans.'

'You've got to thin out a scavenger population as a demonstration to the whole what-do-you-call-it,' said Alex. 'Biome. Go find your leftovers elsewhere.'

He fit the stock tightly into his shoulder and pulled the bolt. Behind him Looch hoisted the spotlight up in its strut. It sat on a wheeled base that he rolled back and forth, balancing the light to match the rifle-barrel vector. 'Hit me with the light.'

Looch pulled the lever back with a heavy clank and the spotlight turned on, a long beam of white light. He was dead on them: a circle of light on the ring of coyotes, their eyes bright green glass, and they froze for a moment in the sudden unexpected daylight. Alex pulled the trigger and the rifle report cracked hard and loud in their ears, slapped back off the glass at them. The coyotes jumped and scattered and one leapt awkwardly, twisting in the air, then hit the ground and staggered, ran to catch up with the rest. They ran out of the light and Alex fired again. Audrey slapped her hands over her ears too late and the shot banged deep inside her head. Outside, the coyotes howled and their racket echoed with the rifle crack off the hills.

'You missed him,' said Looch.

'I might have hit him in the tail,' said Alex. 'Well, yeah, I missed him. That's a shock for him though.'

He handed the rifle to Looch, who pulled the bolt and the empty shell spat and rang on the concrete floor. He pulled more bullets out of his jeans pocket.

'Audrey Cole,' said Alex Main, 'come here.'

The rifle was heavier than she expected. She took it from him and the weight pulled her arms down. She hoisted the barrel and brought the stock against her shoulder, holding it across her body like she'd seen in Westerns and police dramas.

'This is a bolt-action rifle,' said Alex. 'It's going to fire one round at a time. You can have three rounds in the magazine inside there. Like this.' And he showed her how to slip the bullets into the metal top of the wooden rifle body. 'Each time you fire, you'll need to pull the bolt, and that will load the next round from the magazine into the chamber. Pull it.'

She pulled the bolt and heard the sound the mechanism made, shunt and clank, preparing the bullet and rifle, with a hard backward pull. She put her cheek down against the cold wood and pulled it tighter up into her shoulder. It was already heavy and her arms wobbled under the weight.

'Closer and tighter,' said Alex, and he reached around her. He reached, and his hand closed around her small fingers and pulled her grip further up the barrel. He enclosed her in a reach to move her arms and she felt the heat moving off him and his chest and diaphragm against her back. He leaned forward to pull the stock back into her shoulder and she felt his breath on her neck.

'Always treat it like it's going to go off,' he said. 'Don't point it at anything that doesn't deserve it.'

She squeezed an eye shut and stared down the grey barrel length out the window into the night. She breathed from her stomach muscles to stiffen her body and hold the weight steady, and her lungs filled and emptied quicker than his behind her. She felt the difference in their size in the length and pace of their breathing. She felt his body all around her own.

'Now it's going to kick back like a bastard. So you're only going to squeeze your finger when you've got a full breath in you. So steady yourself, feet up to shoulders.'

She inhaled deeply and squeezed her one eye tightly. Pulled the trigger and the noise and force shook her backward. A tremendous crack, split, and echo, and he squeezed his hands around her fist and shoulder and soaked her up into his own body when the explosion shoved her backward.

'Yes,' he said beside an ear ringing with gunshot.

6

Audrey woke up cold and thirsty on the couch in enough grey light to know it was morning. She couldn't remember falling asleep. The fire was burned down to coals and the room had a blue woodsmoke tinge. Her eyes stung and her sinuses were full. She dug in her jacket pocket for her phone. The phone said 7:45, and three-quarters battery, and No Service. She sat up, pulled on her socks and pants. Stiff and bent from a poorly curled sleep on the lumpy couch. She knelt in front of the fire and blew the embers larger and larger until the flame caught the new kindling.

She walked into the mezzanine, morning showing her how the space was and wasn't what she'd remembered in the dark. The car of the birdcage elevator sat behind its sliding brass door. The red carpet on the stairs was mud-tracked and worn out, faded in trails like a schoolyard lawn. Plastic poly sheets lay spread over the floor across the room under the arch of the east wing. A sheet of plywood sat on a pair of sawhorses. A circular saw, extension cords, and a toolbox on the floor. A caged construction lamp hung from a wire hooked over the strut of a stepladder. Everything furred in grey dust.

How long ago had they all cleared out? Did they think they were coming back? She hadn't found a specific date in her online searches.

She went to the bay window and pressed her forehead against the cold glass. Outside, the weather had stirred up, woken in the night, and a quick wind blew ribbons of new snow out of the sky. A skin of snow covered the car. She could hear the wind through the glass, whipping off the lake.

She hugged the afghan around her shoulders. Away from the fire it was cold, cold, cold. If she'd come in July, the floor would be cold, colder than the air. In December, the air and every surface underneath shivered with bone-deep cold, and even if she could stand it for the moment, she could feel the hard blood-thickening limit lurking not so far away.

She stood near the fire, staring out the window at the white-topped lake. The houseboat was gone, she realized. She hadn't noticed in the night. The stretch of beach where it had sat before was empty. How big a flatbed truck do you need to take a houseboat away? What kind of crane to hoist it off the gravel? You would have to drive so slow through the switchbacks, up and down those slopes, lowest possible gear, the weight above and below. Pilot trucks with blinking yellow lights and Wide Load signs ahead and behind.

Maybe they sank it. Scuttled it. Blew it up. Chopped it up with axes. Burned it piece by piece in the fireplace and wood stove. What's a houseboat made of? You can't chop up fibreglass and steel with an axe. Can't burn prefab plastic in a firepit. Maybe they sailed it to the middle of the lake and cut a hole in the floor. Watched it sink from the beach. Maybe it was out there under the ice, cold-water algae and winter lake weeds growing inside, a meltwater reef. She turned from the door. She needed to pee.

The light in the windowless washroom didn't work because none of the lights anywhere worked because there was no electricity. She propped the door open with a cylindrical metal garbage can for a sliver of light. The mirror was cracked and balls of old paper towel littered the floor. She twisted the faucet but no water came. The pipes must have frozen and burst during the first winter without heat. Down in the basement there would be slabs of ice. Slick stagnant puddles run down from broken plumbing. How many winters had had their way with the place, without heat and electricity to protect it? Not more than three. Maybe just one. How much time did a winter need to wreck a naked, unheated building? She lifted the top off the toilet tank and there was no water for a flush. She peed anyway.

She opened her phone and it said 8:01. Shelly was awake now. Audrey's mother had been awake for a few hours already. Read the newspaper and boiled water for a plunge pot of coffee. She would put cereal and milk in a bowl and sit across from Shelly while she ate. Madeline Cole would make Shelly eat more cereal than the toddler wanted. They would sit together on the couch and Shelly would watch cartoons.

She won't panic, Audrey told herself. She'll be worried and try to call me but she won't panic. There's a voice-mail message waiting on the phone, as soon as you're back in service. *Audrey, where are you?* it will ask you. There will be a few of them. She'll fret but she won't panic.

She went floor to floor, walking down the hallways, past closed or opened doors. Rows of evenly spaced doors down the either-wing hallway, staring at each other across the scuff-faded doors. With numbers they'd be hotel room doors, but they weren't numbered. Some of them still showed a square of back-folded masking tape, a thumbtack or a plastic push-pin that used to hold up a paper picture.

Bare mattresses lay on the floor or leaned against the wall. Half-made beds, the sheets knotted or pulled half off to the floor from the last person rolling out before leaving. She opened closet doors and found black T-shirts hanging on wire hangers, beer boxes, a crate of records, or nothing but an empty room. Soap slivers and mostly curled-empty tubes of toothpaste. Bottles everywhere: beer bottles and whisky bottles, two-litre pop bottles and mostly beer bottles, all of them empty, probably. A plastic card table with a game of Monopoly, all the cards and piles of money still sitting where they'd been left, about two-thirds into the game, all the property cards sitting out, some green houses on a few blocks, the mid-grade orange and red stretches, everybody still with enough cash to get by, the green and yellow properties split up among a few different players. A game with hours left in it that no one was close to winning.

Some of the rooms were empty, no beds, no furniture, no detritus or leave-behinds, nothing to indicate anything had ever happened there at all.

On a third-floor wall someone had written in black lipstick IT'S NOT YOURS.

On the fifth floor, the door to Alex Main's old office was open. If it had been closed, she might have weighed going in. Debated, lingered in the hallway. She might have wanted the right circumstances or a carefully prepared frame of mind. The right cold, cutting quip to say out loud in the empty room. But the door was open, so she went in and didn't think too much about it.

His desk was buried in loose paper and surrounded on the floor by beer boxes. A fax machine sat on a folding chair, the unplugged cord dangling off the side. There were empty bottles and old coffee cups and cereal bowls full of white ash and cigarette butts. Paper stacked up in piles on the desk and floor, crumpled loose paper, printer-sprocket-reeled invoices, torn-open envelopes, newspapers back-folded to half-finished crossword puzzles. Black-and-white photocopied posters covered the walls: scratchy photographs of rock bands, big black block-letter dates and names: *The Salt Licks with the Ugly Fuckers. Cheryl Rae and Her Raenettes. The Mants with the Von Zippers. Bruce News and the No Clues.* All with the same footer: *The Crash Palace, Two Reel Lake, Alberta.*

'Alex, I'm going through your stuff,' she said.

She opened the desk drawer and shuffled through stubby pencils and packets of dried-up cigarettes. She found a flashlight. She flicked the switch and the still-alive battery gave her white LED light.

At the back of the office a wall-sized oak cabinet lined the room wall to wall, full of rows and rows of guns: hunting rifles and shotguns, all of them oil-clean and shiny behind locked, streak-free glass doors.

She went back to the fifth-floor hallway and looked down the other way to the big door at the opposite end of the hall. Up here there were just two doors: the office and the bedroom.

You should go over there, Audrey. At least to see what happened to the plants.

She looked at her phone but the higher elevation hadn't changed its No Service message. Then she went back downstairs.

On the main floor, she walked down the back hallway to a steel door with a wire-mesh window. She shone the flashlight into the windowless kitchen. White tile and stainless steel, grill tops and blackened iron burners. Cold black grease stank in the deep fryer. Dirty dishes filled the sink: a cookie sheet with blackened dried cheese and a coffee mug full of grey fuzz. She turned a burner dial and the stove didn't light. She lifted the lid and the pilot light was out.

If there was gas, you'd have blown up already, Audrey.

There was a stack of five-gallon plastic water cooler jugs in the corner, the kind a uniformed man rolls into offices by the dollyful once a week. Full and still sealed. She found a clean pitcher on a shelf, upside down, the inside free of dust. She pulled a heavy cooler jug from the stack and carefully peeled off the plastic top. Splashed water into the pitcher, swished out her mouth and spat in the sink. Then wet her face and took off her shirt to wipe her chest and under her arms. Patted herself dry with paper towel.

Last of all she went to the ballroom. She opened the double doors on the second floor and stood looking into the large darkness, feeling the space and the stale air. She turned on her flashlight and went inside.

The hardwood floor ran off a long way in any direction, scuffed and dirty, the muddy prints and scrapes and bits of gravel and cigarette butts casting outsized shadows behind her flashlight beam. Straight ahead of her, a long counter ran most of the wall, stools stacked on top, the shelves behind lined with glasses and bottles. The room stretched out left and right, some high tables on one side, more stools, some of them knocked over on the floor, and the other way the floor reached maybe sixty feet until it stopped at a high stage, with a red curtain pulled tightly across. Along the wall sharing the double doors were banquette seats around lower tables. On the far wall her flashlight beam picked out framed posters. In the middle of the floor the light dazzled back at her from a mess of broken glass, not just glass but mirrors, radiated outward around the stem of a mirrored sphere like a fallen Christmas ornament. She shone up at the ceiling and could see the wire where the mirror ball had hung, the base still up there, the glass fallen, or pulled down. Pulled down, thought Audrey.

She walked back to the bar and shone the flashlight along the counter. Behind a stack of dust-skinned rocks glasses stood a little plastic hula girl with a plastic red hibiscus in her hair. She played a little plastic ukulele. Audrey reached out and touched her with a fingertip and she bobbed back and forth, wobbling on the spring mounting her bare feet to her green plastic base.

They'd go through this mess, eventually. West Majestic Developments, whoever they are. This mess was a long way from being Clearwater Haven. There would be men in tailored suits wearing hard hats. They'd have the drawings with them: the blueprints and elevations and plans that they'd turn into estate villas surrounding eighteen holes of golf. Guided bow-hunting excursions. Heli-skiing. Only these piles of trash standing in their way. They'd assess the wreckage while tapping on their smart phones. They'd bring trucks. Temporary fencing. They'd set up an aluminium-sided trailer on cinder blocks and a pair of plastic port-o-potties. They'd bring diesel generators and construction lights to shine on early winter mornings when the crew starts before sunrise. Before all that though, they'll need to get rid of all of this. Men in gloves and overalls would haul out all the garbage: the mattresses and furniture, the stage lights and tall stools, all the empty bottles. Her empty Christmas cactus pot. They'd pull apart the banquette seats and Koop's bar with crowbars. Fill their trucks with everything and haul it away, to Rocky Mountain House, where in the landfill it would just be more garbage, and get slowly covered by other construction debris, supermarket cast-offs, tied plastic grocery bags filled with dirty diapers and Kleenexes and potato peelings from a thousand other households, and it won't mean anything. She picked up the hula girl and took her out of the ballroom.

Shelly knew how to work the two remotes, one to turn on the television and one to turn on the cable box. She knew the numbers for the different kids' stations. Four channels that played her favourite shows at different times, and she knew the schedules well enough to flip from one to another. Her grandmother had probably made herself a pot of coffee and then got distracted by the toddler, making sure she ate her breakfast. Once Shelly had her attention filled up by the cartoons, Madeline would microwave her mug for half a minute, then sit beside the little girl on the couch. Fill in sudoku puzzles, or maybe knit, while the toddler changed channels.

Audrey turned on her phone and waited while it hunted for a signal before telling her there was none, and then shut it off and put it back in her pocket. She wouldn't have to go far to get back inside the network range. The highway past the village. She could stop before the junction and make a call.

'Mom, I'll be there soon, I'm fine, don't worry,' she would say. 'I'll be home soon and I'll tell you all about it. I'll tell you the whole story.'

You can tell your mother the whole story, all of it, when you get home, Audrey.

In the meantime, she's leaving a voice-mail message every twenty minutes, Audrey thought. She put the hula girl in the pocket of her jacket. Zipped it to her chin and went outside. She stopped to lock the door on the way out.

§

The car started easily, and she sat with the defrost on full blast, waiting while the air warmed and ate into the skin of ice on the windshield. Still half a tank of gas. Not bad for all that driving last night. She tried the radio but couldn't find a signal and shut it off. When the air was warm and the window was wet enough for the wipers to clear, she put the car in gear. It turned easily enough in the snow, but the drifts were deeper than last night. She drove away from the Crash Palace.

She drove slowly up and down the hills through the forest. She was five minutes up the road when it happened. Not quite back to the fork at the billboard. The road rounded the crest of a hill and sloped down through a curve. Audrey turned the wheel, and the tires slid on ice hidden underneath a drift. She downshifted and turned into the skid, but the car slid ditchward. Audrey braked harder than she meant and the wheels locked. The car slid back end out, in a wrong-way spin, and the rear tire dropped over the ditch lip. She lurched forward, caught hard by the locked seat belt. Her stomach contracted. She pushed in the clutch and stepped heavily on the gas – the tires spun. She put it into reverse and gave it gas, turning the wheel toward the middle of the road, but the car didn't move. The tires spun, whining loudly, and then the car dropped, snow and gravel giving out under the other tire, and she jerked against the seat belt again, head and neck a short shock, only a half-foot of movement down and back but sudden and unexpected.

Audrey Cole sat in the car staring into tree trunks, hot air blowing into her face from the dashboard vents. She put her foot into the gas and heard the tires spin in free space behind her.

She was panting. She caught herself panting and grabbed the elbow rest tightly. She made herself take a deep breath and hold it inside her chest, then release it slowly.

She undid the seat belt and turned to look behind. The back of the car stuck out, downward off the road, in a high drift.

'Car,' she said, 'come on, Car. You can do it.'

She pushed the gas and heard the tires whir in the empty space they'd already cut in the snow. Then the engine stalled.

She sat in the car for a while, she couldn't have said how long.

Audrey, your car is stuck and you are a long way from anywhere. The village is up ahead through the snow. Walk to the village and get help.

No, the wind is too cold. Wait here a little while. Sheltered from the wind where it's warm.

Audrey, you can sit here and the snow will fall and cover the car. White snow will cover the glass and it will get dark. Sunlight will have to work harder and harder to get through the thickening snow covering the car. You will turn the car off and wait ten minutes to conserve the half-tank of gasoline before turning it on again. You will keep the darkening car just warm enough this way until finally it doesn't turn on again. You will try to open the door but the snow will be too thick. It will be dark and you will go to sleep.

The Engineers from Munich nodded seriously, sipping their steins. *Yes*, they said, *that is correct. We're sorry, but yes, that is what will happen.*

Audrey turned off the ignition and put the key into her pocket. She zipped her jacket up to her chin, then got out of the car.

Her feet sunk into snow up to mid-shin. She took a step for a look at the rear of the Audi, hung up on the ditch edge, a snowdrift furrowed out in two dirty trenches by the rear tires. She stepped out of the ditch onto the road. The snow covered only her feet. The wind cut through her jacket fabric and stung her eyes. The wind made her ears ache.

How long a drive is it between the village and the lake? Between the lake and the turnoff with the billboard? Between the billboard and the village? There's the winding hilly stretch of road along the lakeside. Up and down and curving. Then the road from the village into the valley. She tried to remember intersections. Aren't there driveways or junctions? Forestry service roads? She tried to picture the drive, start to finish. How long, Audrey? How long a drive? Twenty minutes? Half an hour? Twenty kilometres an hour she'd been driving. Longer than half an hour. The wind gusted hard and her eardrums ached. How far is twenty kilometres walking uphill in the snow?

Water soaked through her boots and socks. The tire tracks she'd left last night were already full of snow and each step was ankle deep. She tried to step over deeper drifts. The wind blew through her jacket and drew tears out of her eyes.

She stopped fifty yards down the hill and looked back up at her stuck car leaning on the lip of the road.

Maybe someone would be on the road. Maybe they'll plow it out.

She walked down the hill with her arms wrapped around her chest and sometimes wide for balance when she staggered in the wind. She looked back up the hill at the car, stuck on the lip of the ditch.

What happens is you'll get tired and slow down. You'll want to sit down eventually, for a rest. She could see the white lake top through the trees. You'll get tired and sit down.

We're so sorry, said the Engineers from Munich.

She shook her head and slapped her cheeks. Come on, Audrey. You're no good to anyone dead in a blizzard. Go back and wait it out. You're not so far, and that will be a whole lot easier. Go back and make a fire in the parlour fireplace. Dry out.

She turned and walked back the way she'd came up the hill, back toward the Crash Palace.

PART THREE

THE SKINNY COWBOY

7

'**A** man was here,' her mother said. 'He left you a letter.'
'A man? What man?'

'Some funny old man dressed up like a cowboy.'

Audrey stood on the threshold of the kitchen with her jacket still on, staring at her mother. Madeline Cole was chopping up an onion and had a tiny onion tear in the corner of each eye. Shelly sat on the floor, legs spread out, leaning over a pile of multicoloured construction paper. She drew on the pages with a thick washable marker and her hands were smeared with marker ink.

'Some funny old man dressed up like a cowboy,' said Audrey in as measured and calm a fashion as she could manage. 'Did he come inside?'

'No, he just stood at the door and asked if Audrey Cole was here. He said he had a delivery and gave me an envelope. That's it stuck to the refrigerator door there.'

And there it was, held to the door by a magnet, next to Glen Aarpy's magic kitten. A white envelope with the name *Audrey Cole* printed in small type across the front.

She hung her jacket on the back of a chair and sat down on the floor across from Shelly. The little girl stared up at Glen Aarpy's kitten and did her best to replicate the drawing. Drew wobbly oval faces with triangle ears and poky whiskers. She held the marker in a closed fist and struggled to drag it around on the paper according to the template up on the fridge door. Held her drawing up to squint at it in relation to the original, then grunted and started over on a fresh sheet.

Madeline looked curiously at the envelope, then at Audrey, then back to the envelope, repeating this several times in increasingly exaggerated fashion to try and elicit a reaction from her daughter. Audrey responded by getting more and more absorbed in her daughter's drawing.

Eventually they ate dinner.

Later, when everyone else was asleep, Audrey stood in the kitchen alone, looking at the envelope.

You could just throw it out, she thought. You could drop the unopened envelope into the garbage and then take the bag out to the alley and throw it in the dumpster. The truck would come in the morning and hoist it up along with all her old tea bags, orange peels, used paper towels. Crush and squash it all together and drive it to the landfill.

You could take the unopened envelope to Goetz Environmental Consulting and drop it in the shredder. Let the steel teeth cross-shred it into illegible confetti, impossible to ever reassemble.

You could drop it in the sink and set a match to it. Turn it into black ash and then wash the ash down the drain.

She took the magnet off the envelope, opened it up, and unfolded the letter inside.

Audrey Cole,

I'm contacting you as the executor of Alex Aiver's estate. By now you know about the fact and manner of his death, and as an interested party I'm sure you have questions.

As you well know, Mr. Aiver had been long estranged from his family. You will not be surprised to learn that a battalion of lawyers with immense resources at their disposal endeavoured long and hard to ensure that, prior to his death, he and any of his beneficiaries (in the case that any were to be discovered) were completely cut off from any and all proceeds or entitlements of the family's collective industries. Similarly, they invested time quietly acquiring and disposing of his numerous debts in order to quarantine them-selves from unforeseen risk or unintended consequences. Whatever remained in his own name he'd long ago managed to squander in a manner with which I'm sure you are more familiar than anyone.

All of this is to say, in as concise a manner as I can manage, that the execution of the Alex Main estate has largely been a formality, in that there is nothing to execute. Alex died with whatever was in the pockets of his pants. (Had he been wearing a jacket, he might have lived a little longer, I suppose.) There is nothing else.

Over the years, Alex gave a few things to me. For safekeeping. I came across one of these trinkets recently and thought of you.

I need to stress that what is enclosed is not the property of Alex Aiver, and in a strict sense, I should return it to his sister or some other family member. However, I believe the point to be moot as the Aiver family has discharged themselves of this recently as well. I understand that the developer who acquired the property has plans to turn it into a boutique resort. (All those walleye, you know, just waiting to be caught.) I would imagine they've changed the locks already. I consider it, therefore, as I said, a trinket. A memento. A harmless and inconsequential one, and nothing more, and supply it as such.

I hope you aren't overburdened with any of this, and wish you and your daughter the best.

Sincerely,

The signature was just a scrawl.

She turned the envelope and a single key fell into her hand. A thick steel key with a square of blackened masking tape stuck to the bow. She stood quietly in the kitchen holding it, staring ahead, not looking at anything.

'I want to leave and never come back,' she'd told him. 'I want to never see Alex again.'

'We can totally make that happen,' he'd replied.

She found a clean mason jar and dropped the key inside. It pinged as it hit the glass. She set the jar on top of the fridge. Thought about crumpling or shredding or burning the letter, but instead put it back in the envelope. Later she put it in the drawer of her night table.

Awake in bed, she thought about him finding the house. The Skinny Cowboy walking up 12th Avenue, looking through the gap in the caragana hedge and thinking, *This is it, Audrey Cole's home. Audrey Cole and her daughter.* This raced around her mind like a plastic train on a well-constructed toy train track. Each little boxcar packed with a set of carefully chosen lawyer words that didn't seem so lawyerly considered on their own.

She stared at the ceiling, wide awake, while the train ran around the curves and through the junctions, over and over.

§

The next day was Sunday, and in the afternoon Madeline Cole packed her clothes and toiletries back into her black suitcase. She peeled the linen off the hide-a-bed and folded it carefully. Then she heaved the creaking mattress back inside the couch. Put the square sofa cushions back in place. She picked up the linen with every intention of walking it to the back of the house to the rattly old single-piece washer-dryer Audrey had found in the *Bargain Finder*. Audrey cut her off and took the linen from her.

'I'll take care of it, Mom.'

Madeline shrugged.

Shelly sat down on the floor in front of her grandmother. Folded her arms and stuck out her bottom lip. 'Gramamama,' she said. 'Gramamama, don't go. Stay night.'

'I have to go home, sweetie bear,' said Madeline, leaning over to hug the toddler. 'I have to go back home to see Grandpa, but I'll be back so soon. And you'll call me on the phone. And I'll be back so soon.'

'Tomorrow?' asked Shelly.

'I won't be back tomorrow, no, baby. But soon.'

Shelly waddled away to the other side of the room. She pulled her toy blocks out of the Rubbermaid tub and moaned quietly to herself. Picked up blocks and dropped them on the floor, over and over, moaning melodramatically.

Madeline rolled her suitcase to the door. Pulled on her jacket and her toque. Audrey stood hugging the linen against her chest.

'Audrey, you know I have a busy month coming up. Helen at the library is on a six-week cruise to Alaska so I'll be in twice as often. And then we have the annual general meeting for the historical society. I have a haircut and I have to take the car in.'

'Don't take it to the dealership,' Audrey said. 'They're ripping you off. Every time you take it in for an oil change they find some phantom problem that needs fixing and you just go along with it.'

'I have to take the car in and I'm getting my hair cut and coloured. What I'm saying is I can't be down on a moment's notice. But obviously if anything happens you give me a call and I'll make arrangements. I'll figure something out if there's an emergency.'

'Mom, we are perfectly capable of handling anything that happens,' said Audrey.

§

In the morning, Audrey stopped at the doorway to Joe Wahl's office.

'Joe,' she said.

Joe Wahl looked up from the aluminium desk in his closet-sized office at the front of the church. He always kept the door open, and Audrey would see him in the morning when she brought Shelly down the stairs. Scribbling on a yellow notepad, or squinting at the screen of his laptop. He wore wire-rimmed glasses that he'd pull half-off any time he needed to look at something, leaving them hanging off an ear by one arm, the lenses under his chin.

Across the hall, the toddlers clamoured around a little wooden table while the Misses did their best to sort them out for breakfast. Audrey could see the back of Shelly's head, sitting in a little wooden chair. Shelly Cole sat in her chair holding her favourite green plastic cup, watching the Misses, waiting for her morning milk.

'Audrey. Hi, Audrey.'

'Hi, Joe,' she said.

He waited.

She was going to say *never mind* and head up the stairs, but he waited and didn't say anything, and just watched her. She felt held in place.

Audrey, she said to herself, you wanted to talk to him, remember.

'Joe,' she said eventually, 'you're a minister.'

'I've got paperwork,' he said. 'Something from the United Church of Canada. Signed by the moderator. I've got something from St. Andrew's College in Saskatoon. I can provide you copies if you need.'

'And you do – I mean, it's more than just the sermons. You do weddings. You're involved in the ...'

'Are you getting married, Audrey? You need an officiant?'

'You're involved in the – I mean, there's a legal side.'

'Sure. I've got duties as stipulated by the province. It's more than just the sermons, sure.'

'You do funerals.'

He nodded slowly.

'When people die ... how much do you know about ... I mean, how much involvement do you have with the ... with the estate?'

Joe pulled his glasses half-off, one arm hung off one ear, and squinted at her. 'You have estate obligations from that funeral the other week?'

She stood in the doorway, framing the answer that was also a question in her mind. 'No. I mean, I guess not. They didn't say anything about obligations.'

'They didn't say – You're talking to a lawyer?'

'No. I mean, I heard from a lawyer. Sort of. We didn't talk directly.'

'The funeral. Is this a family member?'

She felt the pained expression on her face and knew she couldn't help it being there. She didn't say anything, but she realized what she was saying was loud and clear anyway and flushed.

'When this lawyer described the situation regarding the estate and the instructions around its distribution, were you surprised? Disappointed?'

'No,' she said. 'No, it's not that. It's just ... it's just that they found me, Joe.'

Joe nodded and leaned back in his chair. When he nodded, the lenses of his glasses knocked against his Adam's apple. 'Audrey,' he said, 'you're a pretty private person.'

She nodded quickly.

'I've known you what, a year now? Year and a half?'

'Shelly started daycare two years ago,' she said. 'A little longer than two years.'

'Two years. You bring in your daughter, you go to work. I don't know much about you. You get the groceries for us a few times a month to save on child-care costs because you're a single mother. Your own mother comes and stays with you once or twice a month so you can get a little break. But I don't think you take breaks, Audrey. And so you're worn out and tired and in a haze, just like all the other single mothers who bring their kids to our place because with the subsidy we're the best rate in the inner city. I see that tired haze a lot and so I don't ask questions, and anyway,' he said, leaning back over his desk, 'you're a pretty private person.'

'Pretty private, Joe,' said Audrey Cole.

He sat and didn't say anything, just watched her, tapping the end of his nose with his fingers. He sat watching her and the silence made her itchy.

'It was all going to be temporary,' she said eventually, just to say something to fill the silence.

'Temporary?'

'You know,' she said, casting around, 'all of it. Working at Goetz. Needing a daycare subsidy. It was a step to get started. Something in between until ...'

'Until ...'

She wanted to stop talking and run away. Stop talking and turn around and walk out.

You could tell him more, Audrey. You could tell him the whole story. Joe Wahl was a lumpy, absent-minded man who ran a daycare out of his church. Who ran his church out of a community centre basement. He held a men's fellowship on Tuesday nights, and a lot of recovering alcoholics sat around in the basement drinking coffee and chatting or they played euchre sometimes. He used the kitchen to serve free meals to street people on weekends. Audrey, you could sit in his office and tell him the whole sad story of your circumstances. He hears sad-circumstance stories all the time. If ever there was someone to talk to, it's lumpy old Joe Wahl.

'Pretty private,' she said instead.

'Well, Audrey, I mean, I don't know. Generally if a lawyer needs someone to do something as part of the estate execution, they're pretty clear. They'll tell you. So if there aren't any obligations, then there aren't any obligations. So from that perspective – the legal perspective – you're probably done with it all.

'And sure, they found you. It's what they do. They've got to do their due diligence and wrap up the loose ends. They're not trying to invade your privacy. Well, I guess they are, in a manner of speaking. But it's just what they do. They track people down, even people who don't want to be tracked down. They do it all the time and they're good at it.'

Audrey just nodded.

'As for anything else? As for grief and healing and closure? Now, that's definitely the part that I have some knowledge about, if you ever need someone to listen.'

She nodded again, the smallest nod she could manage.

'I don't know if that's helpful, Audrey,' said Joe. He pulled his glasses back up properly in front of his eyes.

'That's helpful enough,' said Audrey. 'Thanks.'

§

'It was all going to be temporary, kiddo,' she said later to Shelly while the little girl splashed in the tub.

Shelly sat in the bath, surrounded by floating toys. Plastic ducks and whales and frogs, all bright yellows and blues and reds, and a little submarine with a monkey inside. Shelly pulled a string on the back of the submarine and a little propeller spun, churning the submarine through the sudsy bathwater.

Audrey sat beside her on a little plastic stool, the latest copy of the *Bargain Finder* in her lap. Audrey liked to read the *Bargain Finder* while Shelly was in the tub. She liked to hunt for appliances, to see if she could upgrade the old washer-dryer that didn't really dry their clothes. She kept an eye out for refrigerators. She had a feeling that their fridge was on its last legs and she wanted to get ahead of the breakdown if she could. Instead of waiting around for Wade Clave to do something about it. Find something more reliable and send him the receipt.

Tonight the *Bargain Finder* stayed folded in her lap. She leaned against the wall, not really looking at anything, and talked, not really to her daughter.

"'This house is too big, Audrey.' That's what your grandma always says. This house is too big and we pay too much for it. She's right. But I found it and it was cheap for the size, all things considered, because I got a good deal on it. A goddamn good deal, Shelly.

'I thought we'd be glad to have the space. And we are. You like having your own room, your Big Girl room. Your playroom. You like having space to keep your train set up. We've got space when Grandma comes to visit.'

Shelly dropped the whale and the frog over the side of the tub. Leaned over the tub side to pick them up back up, slopping water onto the tiled floor. Usually when Shelly did this, Audrey would mop the water up and scold the little girl. 'These tiles,' she'd usually say, 'they're barely grouted. This water will be dripping on our heads downstairs.' But tonight she just stayed leaning on the wall, not really looking at anything.

'I was probably overcompensating a little bit. I was living in a little studio apartment in Renfrew that I could practically touch every corner of. It wasn't big enough to lie down on the floor. You were just a growing little peanut inside Mommy still.'

Shelly looked up at her mother and grinned. 'Peanut! Peanut!'

'That was hard but not the hardest. I mean, before that I lived in the Blue Goose Motel on 16th Avenue for two whole weeks. That was hard, kiddo.'

Shelly pulled the cord and the monkey submarine zipped through the water, kicking up a soapy wake. Shelly giggled and slapped her hands on the water top, splashing.

'I was washing dishes at a fish-and-chips restaurant, living in a 400-square-foot studio, getting more and more pregnant. I was applying for other jobs. I think I'd applied with Harold already. And then I found this place. And I thought, You know, when we're a family, we'll want the space.

'I couldn't afford it. I can barely afford it now, and Harold pays me more than I was making washing dishes. But it was all going to be temporary. I was going to figure …'

She stopped and watched her daughter splash for a while.

'I was going to figure out something else, eventually.'

Shelly slopped more water over the side of the tub. Looked up at Audrey. 'When Gramamama come back?'

'She'll come back in a few weeks, baby. It's just us for a little while.'

Shelly bunched up her face in a frown. 'I miss Gramamama, Mommy.'

'I know, baby, you love your grandma.'

When Shelly was in bed, she went downstairs and poured herself a glass of water. She sat at the kitchen table, facing the refrigerator. It was an old off-white fridge with a bad condenser that hummed and rattled loudly on and off in the night. Glen Aarpy's black-marker kitten smiled at her from its creased paper home. Above the freezer sat the glass jar. She stared at the glass jar, drinking her water. After a while, she stood up and pulled it down and, yes, the key was still inside. She set it back on top of the fridge. Poured herself another glass of water. Sat down again, listening to the fridge.

8

S he sat, wet and shivering, on the couch. Her fire had gone out while she'd been away, and any warmth it had brought into the building had vanished. All the woodsmoke humidity was already soaked up into dry concrete, with just a burnt smell left behind in the hard cold. The wind outside whipped against the glass, tearing and spilling winds blowing thick white snow down into the valley. Truckloads of snow. Boxcars of snow. Sea cans of snow.

She'd walked, arms wrapped around her shoulders, and head pointed forward, up and down the hill in the louder and louder wind to get back.

Her phone said 1:45, and No Service, and a third of a battery. They drain faster, she knew, this far from their towers. Run down while searching the air for grippable frequencies.

She pulled the blanket around her shoulders on the couch and squeezed her arms around a pillow. The cold leached upward from the concrete into her damp jeans and jacket.

She hugged the pillow, hands in front, prayer-clasped around her cellphone. The plastic box made no sound. Didn't move or vibrate. She leaned her face toward it in case the rings were too quiet to catch. She opened it and it didn't make any sounds or tones and didn't hold the small searching voice of Madeline Cole back in Calgary. *Audrey, where are you?* it didn't ask. *Audrey, Shelly is fine, she isn't worried, take your time, be home safe when you can,* it didn't say. Her phone said 1:47 and No Service and a third of a battery.

When she was in junior high, they had gym class first session a few days a week. In the late fall and early spring, the girls changed into their terry-cloth shorts and loose T-shirts and went outside to run. They ran across the grass playground, then single file out the chain-link fence and onto a gravel side street, and ran a long loop around the south end of town, down the length of Policeman's Creek and back. They ran single file on cold mornings when their breath puffed and clouded, and the cold always made her ears hurt. Like she'd jumped off a wood pier into a cold lake and the lake water plunged into her ears all the way into the middle of her skull.

She sat on the couch shivering, pain in her numb wet feet, and her ears hurt deep inside her head, like running along Policeman's Creek on an early October morning.

Audrey Cole heard a sound then, something soft and inquisitive, and turned her head. A tiny orange kitten sat on the floor under the archway. Little triangle ears twitched and it opened its mouth to mew.

Audrey stared at the kitten without moving for a long time. It leaned away from her stare, squashing backward into its shoulders. They looked at each other, only moving to blink.

'It's okay,' said Audrey. The kitten hopped up and turned, padded quickly away across the mezzanine, then disappeared behind the renovation clutter at the far end. Audrey watched the floor where the kitten had sat.

'That happened,' she said out loud, to hear her voice in the room. 'I saw that.'

'Yes, I believe you,' Audrey said back to herself. 'There's a kitten in here. That happened.'

She stood up then. Shook her legs to try and get feeling back in her feet. Her wet clothes clung tightly all over. She walked to the fireplace to see about her dead fire. Last night's ashes were cold in the iron rack. She crouched on her heels and crumpled up newspaper. There was a thick pile beside the firewood, drugstore flyers and a three-year-old *Calgary Herald*, and she didn't ration but clumped up several pages. She picked up the matches and then put them back down.

You have enough time, Audrey, she told herself. Time to do things right. In the seventh grade you learned to start a fire with a single match. You did it last night.

She opened up her pocketknife and peeled kindling slivers off a fire log. Her hands shook. She had to start and stop with the knife, shaving the wood until the amplitude of her shake grew too wide, and she set everything down to hold her knees, breathe deeply for an interval, then started again. She made herself think about the steps during these pauses. Only think about the steps and nothing else. Cut the kindling and then pile it in a teepee around the crumpled newspaper. Then the matches. Then wood around the fire and wait. Once all that was accomplished there would be a new set of steps to decide and execute.

She struck one two three four matches that her shaking put out and the fifth little flame she held steady long enough for the newsprint to catch. The fire grew and she put her smallest quarter log in when the kindling had all taken. Waited sitting on the floor until the little flames moved and sank roots into the wood.

Just a little bit of warmth, but make use of it, Audrey.

There was a card table in the corner, with a pair of wooden dining room chairs. She pulled them over to the fire front. Then she took off her boots and socks. Curled her bare arches away from the cold concrete. She hung her socks off the back of a chair, then tugged off her wet pants and hung these over the other. She lay her jacket flat on the seat of a chair. She set the pillow down on the floor and sat in front of the flames with the blanket around her shoulders.

If there were a farm around, it might be a barn kitten. She didn't know the roaming range of a barn kitten. How far it could manage to get lost. There weren't any farms or barns nearby that she knew of though, none that you could see from the top-floor window. None that anyone had ever pointed out to her across the lake. She hadn't seen new lights the night before across on the other shore.

She sneezed and her nose ran. Her lip was damp and her stomach hurt. She'd stopped for pizza, the night before. Earlier in the evening, before seeing the Skinny Cowboy. She'd stopped at a pizza-by-the-slice place on 1st Street, the size of a coat-check alcove, slices rotating under a hot lamp in a glass box, the man behind the counter blue and red, lit by the Open sign in his window and the reach-in Coca-Cola cooler behind him. Eaten a cardboardy slice of Hawaiian pizza on a paper plate before everything else, at maybe six o'clock. That was the last time she'd eaten, and once she ascertained this duration her stomach came alive and hurt.

She couldn't count to herself the logs she'd burned the night before. Hadn't made a tally as she'd fed the fire. She stared at the stack of cut firewood, wondering about how long they'd last, smallest to thickest burning, and didn't have an idea. She might have wood for six hours or she might not have wood for ten.

She thought about an hour spin cycle in a tumble dryer: it lasted an hour and was quicker than a hanging rack in front of a wood fire.

There are steps to execute in order and this one right here is the hard one, Audrey.

§

Later her pants and socks weren't dry but she pulled them on anyway. Her stomach hurt. There was a cardboard box under the card table, full of worn paperback science-fiction novels and Dungeons & Dragons manuals. Make the trip once, Audrey, she said to herself. She emptied the box. Then she dug in her jacket pocket and found the flashlight from Alex's office.

In the kitchen, she shone the flashlight beam around the steel-and-tile room and walked carefully into the path it showed her. Past the refrigerators, which she did not open, not wanting to find whatever mould and moss had grown into the last allowance of air sealed inside. At the back of the room, the wire-rack pantry shelves were still stocked. Cardboard cereal boxes had been chewed and shredded, inward and outward, all the grains and Os taken away. Flour bags split open, the white innards spotted with black mouse droppings.

It's been at least one winter and one summer, she guessed. A winter's worth of cold and a summer's worth of hungry critters with easy access to the place.

There were plenty of cans and jars, all of them rodent-proof. She hunted for anything salt-packed, pressure-cooked, unexpirable. Filled her box with chickpeas, green beans, tuna, and tomatoes. She took a carton of table salt and a zip-lock bag of ground black pepper. She moved slowly, held up by the range of her flashlight and the need to set it down for free hands. She tracked down a can opener and a spoon. She put the pitcher she'd found earlier into the box, propped the box into the crook of one arm, then picked up the water jug she'd opened in the morning. Her hands and knees shook, in the cold air, in the cold fabric of her damp clothes.

She sat in front of her fire and opened up a can of chickpeas, a can of diced tomatoes, and a tin of tuna. Shook some salt out of the carton onto the top of each can and started to eat, a spoonful from each. She picked up a can at a time for a spoonful, chickpeas, tomatoes, tuna. Told herself to eat slowly and go easy on her stomach, and didn't. Her hands shook picking up the cans. Tomato juice ran down her chin.

She was about halfway into the chickpeas and then stopped. She looked down at the can in her hands and the other two cans on the cold floor and the splatters of tomato juice and chickpea brine that had splashed down onto the concrete.

'Audrey,' she said, 'there's bowls in the kitchen. You could have brought a bowl.'

She set down the chickpeas and hung her head into her chest and laughed, crying a bit at the same time.

'Kitten,' she said loudly. 'Kitten, you should have reminded me about bowls. I'm pretty ridiculous here, Kitten. Help me out.'

She opened a second can of tuna and set it out in the middle of the floor.

'In case you feel like company,' she said to the back of the room.

§

She sat in front of the fire until her hips got sore. She wished she had something hot to eat. Something baked or with a crust. She had seen flour and sugar sealed in plastic jugs on the pantry shelves. With some of the water and her fire maybe she could make a pancake. Maybe she could wrap bannock dough around a stick above the coals.

She stared out the window at the falling snow, which was falling maybe a little more thickly than it had been earlier.

She thought about not checking her phone for the time, to save the battery, then checked it anyway, and it was 3:14.

'Kitten, it's barely been an hour,' she said to the room.

It's barely been an hour, she thought, but you don't have many hours now, and you're still damp. The sun will go down, she thought. It will be dusk in another hour and black middle-of-the-Alberta-winter night in two hours. You have to leave now if you have any chance of making it to the town. Your clothes are still damp but you need to go.

Or you could stay. Build up the fire. Spend the night. Leave first thing in the morning, dry and properly prepared. There are clothes around the building. She'd seen balled-up sweaters in messy rooms, and she was sure she remembered a pair of socks.

It will get dark fast. No street lights. Last night the moon had been big and white, but the road curved between high trees and she still didn't know how far it was. She thought about the coyotes, yowling in the night, and the long steep sides of curving road snaking along hillside.

'Audrey, if you get trapped in the dark in damp clothes in that cold, you will die,' she said.

§

Audrey turned away from the window, and her first step back toward the couch she kicked an empty beer bottle by mistake. The bottle rolled across the floor with a harsh glass ring and clanked loudly against the far wall. She bent down to pick it up and the bottom was full of shrunk cigarette butts, whatever heel of beer they'd been dropped into for extinguishing evaporated long ago, leaving just a paste of ash and paper behind in the brown glass. Audrey stuck out her tongue and made a face.

'Fined for operating an unlicensed establishment,' the newspaper article had said. There must have been a big bust. RCMP up from Nordegg. She imagined the confusion. People running around when they spotted the flashing lights coming up the road. People running around, flushing things down toilets, hiding, looking for any evidence in plain sight.

'Were you around for that, Kitten? All the action? All those scared kids emptying plastic baggies into the toilets? Must've been something.'

She put the bottle into her cardboard box.

She walked around the parlour, looking under the couch, in the corners, and found more beer bottles. Brought them all back to the front of the fire and stacked them in the box. She filled the box with brown and green and clear beer bottles and pushed it against the wall.

'How did it go down, Kitten, when they showed up? What did he say to all those big RCMP officers in their big jackets? How did Alex explain it all?'

She went back into the parlour and put a new log into the fire. Stirred and blew the flames higher. Tried to sit awhile longer on the pillow, close enough to the fire that she could feel the heat on her face and on the skin under her clothes. When it got too hot, she scooched backward. She pushed forward and backward every few minutes, hunting for comfort in the fuzzy boundary between the hot fire front and the cold chill radiating from the hard floor.

§

In the summer a kitten could eat a cricket, she supposed. It could track down a Cheerio missed by mice and magpies. The stony lakeshore must grow marshy in places, rocks giving to reeds, and a kitten could learn to pounce on a young frog. Birds would elude it, but would a kitten eat an egg? Mice, of course. The walls and ducts must run rampant with mice. Clean water for lapping up would drip from split pipes in the basement. There were worse places for a clever kitten to get stuck.

§

She wandered around the building carrying her cardboard box, picking up bottles. They turned up in twos and fours in the empty rooms upstairs, in clusters around old mattresses or sitting alone on radiators. She slid open the brass elevator cage door and found a Scotch bottle with a finger of brown liquor still in the bottom, the cork stopper still in the neck.

Wandered around picking up bottles, and when she got too cold she headed back downstairs to the fire. She'd found a few more boxes and she sorted the bottles: brown and clear domestic bottles, green import bottles. Sorted them by colour and then sat on the pillow to warm up until the fire felt too hot.

The bottles rang and clanked in the box while she walked around.

The glass clanked and the wind howled. Louder and shriller on some floors. The pitch of it changed in some rooms. Sometimes she opened the door to a room and the glass was cracked or a pane broken, and she found snow blown inside, swirled in little drifts around the window, in the corners. A broken window on the fourth floor was furred all over in thick white frost. The walls and floors showed old water stain rings where previous snows had blown in and melted.

She took her bottles downstairs, then went back to the kitchen with her flashlight. Hunted in the dark until she found a box of green plastic garbage bags.

Up in Alex's office she found a roll of strapping tape.

She walked from room to room, and when she found a broken window she pulled out a green bag. Tore it from the serrated border. She bit off a few inches of strapping tape and covered the window with plastic. Sealed it up with tape against the cold and snow. The wind howled or

[170]

whistled or moaned, depending on the size or shape of the break or crack, and she muffled these sounds with plastic bags and tape.

Some rooms had broken windows and others did not. Some rooms had empty bottles on windowsills or sitting in corners and she made an inside-her-head map for the next things to do.

§

There were worse places for a clever kitten to get stuck, but this kitten was pretty little. And if at least one winter and summer had had their way with the place empty, it must have come after the evacuation.

Probably they'd come up recently in a van or truck, someone who'd known someone who'd been up here before, back when it was the Crash Palace and not just an empty building in the middle of nowhere.

I know this place, someone told someone else, this crazy place. We'll have it all to ourselves.

Knowing the conditions, you'd pack accordingly, like you were camping: sleeping bags and a butane stove, flashlights and lanterns, hot dogs and buns, potato chips and beer. Everything but a tent. They came up and camped out in the empty building and someone told stories about the crazy things they'd got up to here.

And someone with a kitten in their jacket. It would have wandered off while attention was in a bottle or a kiss. They'd have conducted a search the next morning. Calling and looking behind doors, under couches. But there was too much crawl-into-able darkness for a spooked thing so tiny. Audrey imagined a teenage girl crying as they got back into their van and drove away.

§

The light got grey and murky and there was less of it. In the valley-shadowed east side of the building, the darkness piled up in the hallways and in the corners of the rooms. She kept to the west side, pulling curtains open wherever she could to let the sparser and sparser light inside.

At home, this time of year, she could go days without seeing the sun. Wake up before sunrise and head out the door, Shelly's mittened hand held in her own, everything black and dark like the sun was nowhere near rising. Just the street lights and the headlights of the snarled-up, sliding-around-in-the-overnight-snow traffic. She'd drop Shelly off at 12th Avenue United Church for daycare and walk downtown, and she could be inside the elevator on the way up to Goetz Environmental Consulting before the sun came up. Her little desk was on the inside of the building, nowhere near a window. If she stayed at her desk for lunch, she might not see the low-in-the-sky noontime sun. And then when she got out of the elevator and back out onto the street, that small, pale sun would be long gone. Just headlights and street lights as she headed back through the cold night to get her daughter.

Audrey sealed up a last few windows, and though the wind wasn't quite as loud, the building wasn't any warmer, and she headed back to her fire to rewarm. Sat on the pillow rubbing her legs to keep the blood flowing. Blowing on her fingers.

She looked over and the tuna was gone out of the tin.

§

When she was warm enough, she found a broom in the kitchen and went up to the ballroom.

She set the flashlight down on the floor to aim the beam as best she could across the room. The white light showed her a wedge of the huge, empty space. Threw enormous shadows off the debris littering the floor and dazzled off the broken glass. The rest of the room large and blackly invisible around her. She swept the floor. Pushed the cigarette butts and bird shit and broken glass and splinters of mirror together. Swept and then went back to the flashlight to turn it forty-five degrees. She swept the room a wedge at a time, doing her best to stay inside the cone of light. Swept everything together into the middle of the room around the smashed stem of the fallen mirror ball.

'They're going to tear all this apart, Kitten,' she said. Her voice was big in the empty room and she looked around in the dark. 'I googled it. I went to the website. "Clearwater Haven at Two Reel Lake." They're going to gut it and rebuild it into a whole new thing. I saw pictures on their website. Not pictures, "artist's renderings." A big modern ski-lodge-looking thing and a bunch of little cabins all along the lakefront.'

Her breath clouded while she spoke. She was hoarse from the dry air, but talking made her feel better.

Audrey pointed the flashlight beam toward the bar. The bar top was completely covered in empty bottles, broken glass, crumpled napkins, and paper towels. Fast-food wrappers and squashed pop cans. She moved the bottles one at a time down onto the floor. Swept all the trash around to her pile in the centre of the room.

She shone her flashlight around the bar: the mirrors were broken and it looked like the lightbulbs had been broken in their sconces. Some of the liquor bottles had speed spouts in the necks, the openings clogged with hardened sugar. A few had cork stoppers. She found a two-thirds-full bottle of bourbon and a bottle of red Cinzano. There were cocktail shakers under the bar, and a few of them sat open-end up, the insides fleecy with dust. There was one with the cap on and when she popped it open the inside was clean. Then she shone the flashlight upward.

In a corner behind the bar there was a black iron ladder, bolted into the wall, leading up to a square panel in the ceiling. She'd never noticed it before. She pushed a stack of boxed glassware out of the way and lifted herself up a few rungs, then a few more, right up to the ceiling. Reached up and pushed the panel, which lifted easily aside and provided entry to black space, wide enough for someone larger than herself to hoist themselves up and through.

Audrey climbed two more rungs, took a deep breath, and moved her head and flashlight beam up into the hole.

Ahead, a short tight passage led along the steel ribs of the ballroom ceiling. She moved the flashlight and saw a wider space beyond, a room, above one floor and below another. Inside a bulkhead, she thought, in some uneven slice of this overhigh second floor. She set the flashlight down and took a deep breath. Then pulled up, careful of her head in the small space, and hoisted herself by her elbows all the way into the crawl space. She found the flashlight and pointed the light up to see her clearance. Enough to stand crouching on the ceiling steel.

The crawl space opened into a wider room, split in the middle by ductwork and electrical conduit. An old mattress lay across the ceiling beams, a tangled sleeping bag on top. A two-by-eight plank sat across a pair of cinder blocks holding a little lamp and some books. Balled-up tissue paper, an overflowed ashtray. Crumpled white paper. She picked up one of the paper lumps and unfolded it: a pharmacy bag. Dozens of pharmacy bags with addresses from Edmonton, Vancouver, Red Deer. Tylenol 3s and codeine, Percocet, lorazepam.

A metal panel with a speaker grill hung on the wall: an apartment lobby door buzzer, pulled out and brought up here, bolted crookedly into a beam. Wires ran into it from an opened conduit. A row of white buttons, each with a black dial-punched label:

MEZZ
KITCHEN
KOOP
LOOCH
OFFICE
BALLROOM
BEDROOM

She pressed 'Mezz' and held the button, listening to the nothing that came over the speaker. She pressed 'Office.' But there was no electricity to bridge her across the wires down to the space underneath. No crackle or static, no linked-up distance.

'So this is where you were, all those nights we couldn't find you.'

She shone the flashlight under the plank shelf and saw a set of keys and a plastic zip-lock bag. It was full of cash: wrinkled $20 bills, almost an inch thick. She took the keys and the money and crawled around to orient herself back toward the ladder.

'Well,' she said, and she couldn't finish the sentence. She sat there holding the keys and money and her breath caught and she choked a bit.

'Well, I'm in your nest here,' she said, 'and I want to say exactly the perfect thing that will, I don't know, I don't know what.

'I don't know, if you walked through the door, if I'd have anything to say.'

Then it was dark: complete black dark all around her. The flashlight was in her hand and she flicked the button up and down but no light came back. She shook it. A blue afterimage of the room's shape in the white flashlight beam hung in her eyes for a moment like soap film on a window and then slid slowly away. Her breath was loud in the small space. She breathed loudly in the thick blackness and listened carefully around the sides of her breathing to make sure it was the only sound.

Her breath caught and she thought she'd panic but instead she laughed. She laughed and it surprised her because it should have been frightening but fuck him anyway, right?

'Fuck you anyway,' she said in the dark.

She sat there in the dark, and that's how he felt after all, alone up here. Sure, he had his lamp and the electricity worked, but when he nodded off up here it was like this: perfect thick smothering darkness. Nodding off listening to the other people in the building out of his tiny mesh speaker. This was what it was like to be him at his bottom-barrel worst, and she was glad she'd driven all the way up here and glad the Audi slid off the road and glad she was stuck for the night, glad for all of it, to feel like him at his worst.

She thought about a time she'd been looking for him. She'd been living there for four months and the lake finally thawed out. Early April? She stood out on the lakeshore and saw a fish jump out of the water. A walleye. She assumed it was a walleye. Someone had told her that the lake was so full of walleye that they'd called it 'Two Reel Lake.' Something about fishermen needing to bring an extra reel, for all the fish they'd be catching. Alex had probably told her.

She got excited. Because she'd always assumed it was just another load of bullshit. 'Bring your extra fishing reel, sucker.' That's what she'd always assumed, those first four months while the lake was still frozen.

It was a really beautiful night – near sunset and the lake was quiet, and the fish jumped out and glittered in the sun like it was a postcard.

She ran inside to find him. She wanted to tell him about seeing that fish. To share her excitement with him.

'But I couldn't find you,' she said out loud. 'I mean, of course I couldn't. When could anybody ever find you, if they needed to? And I guess this is where you were.'

She sat in the dark holding the flashlight.

'It probably wasn't this cold though,' said Audrey.

She put the bag of cash into the pocket of her jeans. She put the dead flashlight in her other pocket. Crouched over these full pockets pressed into the tops of her thighs.

Walk on your hands and feet, Audrey. Feel for those ceiling beams with your hands. Take them one at a time and only go ahead when you've found the next one. Each time you reach forward you're going to feel for the top of that ladder. It will probably be on the fifth or sixth beam.

She breathed carefully in the dark, then reached forward with an open palm for the first ceiling beam.

9

On the third morning at the Crash Palace, she lay under the pheasant-pattern sleeping bag and watched the plaster ceiling turn grey and then white in the slow morning. Stayed in the sleeping bag as long as she could stand the growing wet heat before finally standing up.

Outside, the world was still brilliant white with snow, the road still undisturbed by any snowplow. Footprints ran all around the snow outside, from the front door down to the beach, criss-crossing, running around, doubling back, to the outbuildings, right out onto the lake top. The snow dug up and rolled around in, snow-angeled, trenched and piled, balled-up into intermittent snow figures, some of them wearing black leather jackets or checkered flannel lumberjack coats. Audrey stared out at the snow and the white glare of the just-risen sun hurt her eyes. She pulled on her pants and carried her bag down the hall to the bathroom, to brush her teeth and take a shower.

She opened the door and found a young man with a shaved head, mismatched earrings in off-centre parts of his ear cartilage, sitting on the tiled floor with his arms wrapped around his knees, crying. He sat and cried wetly, his nose running, breathing in fits and starts, and didn't look up when she came into the room.

Audrey stood there for a minute, thinking about whether she should stay or go, and then he looked up and saw her. His breathing caught and his eyes were panicked and he choked trying to catch his breath.

She put down her bag and knelt down across from him. 'Hey. Hey, it's okay,' she said. 'It's okay.'

'I ... I ... I can't ... I can't ...' he wheezed and sniffled. He probably wasn't more than nineteen, thought Audrey. His eyes were red and crusted around the edges and his nose looked raw and painful.

'Take it easy. Take some deep breaths.'

The door opened and a girl in a snowboard hoodie and sweatpants poked her head in. 'Nick! Oh my god, I looked all over for you. Nick, come on, come back to bed.'

Audrey grabbed her bag and stood up.

'Nick, come on, get yourself together. You just need a little sleep. Just a little sleep and you'll be okay.'

'I can't ... I can't ...'

Audrey squeezed back out the door. She went downstairs to the third floor and showered in the empty bathroom there.

She thought she'd slept in, but downstairs the mezzanine was still empty except for Koop unpacking his bar. She took one of the coffee percolators to the kitchen and filled the tank with cold water out of the sink. Carried the heavy pot back slowly, careful not to let any water slosh out the top.

In the kitchen, she flipped up the icemaker lid and reached in with a steel scoop. Filled an empty bucket with fresh-made ice cubes. The scoop was moist from the thick air in the lobby and grew white with crystals in the cold confines of the icemaker bottom. She dug it through the ice and cubes stuck to the damp steel like children's tongues.

'How come no one pays for anything?' she asked Koop.

Koop had cartons of salt and ground black pepper and shook them out with either hand onto a dinner plate. He jostled the plate back and forth to blend the salt and pepper together.

'Huh?' he asked eventually.

'No one pays for any drinks.'

He ran a lime around the lip of a glass and twisted it in the salt and pepper to rim the edge. 'It's like a ... a what-do-you-call-it. An all-inclusive.'

'An all-inclusive,' she said.

People came slowly down the stairs and she shook Tabasco and Worcestershire sauces into the salt-and-peppered glasses. Koop lift-lower poured vodka and Clamato juice.

They drank all the coffee and she made more.

§

'Audrey Audrey Audrey,' said Alex Main, walking up to the bar while she poured ice into a cooler tub. 'Audrey, you're killing me. They're playing cards upstairs. Go play cards. They've got one of the TVs hooked up on, I think, the third floor, they're playing video games. Go outside and play in the snow, when was the last time you played in the snow, Audrey Cole?'

'I haven't played in the snow since I was a kid, Alex,' said Audrey.

'See, that's the whole point. Get a drink, go play in the snow. You're up here to get away. You're on a retreat. A vacation. You and everybody else, you've left everything behind. There's nothing to worry about, all the booze you can drink, so just relax. Just relax, Audrey.'

She looked past him, out the window. A group had built snow forts, walls of packed snow several feet high, facing each other forty yards apart on the wide slope down toward the lake. They knelt behind the snow, packing snowballs together.

'Why is any of this even here?' she asked.

He cocked an eyebrow at her. Turned around to look at the window with her. People were throwing snowballs at each other behind packed walls of snow. In the middle of the stretch between the two forts, someone was lying on their back, staring up at the sky, smoking while snowballs whizzed by overhead.

'You ought to come out when we have a real party, Audrey Cole. I mean, nothing against Wrists and the band. Rodney Levermann is a goddamn legend and we are happy to put him on, and obviously there's a crowd for it. But you ought to come when we have a real party in the summer. We have a DJ up in the ballroom and another downstairs on the main floor and I like to set up a PA out on the beach for a party out there. We'll have four hundred people up here. The tents wrap the whole beach. And we will go four days straight, everyone dancing twenty-four hours a day, non-stop. You ought to see that, Audrey Cole.'

She looked over at him. He was watching the snowballs fly overtop the smoker lying in the snow. He was older than she'd first thought.

Maybe. It was hard to tell. He might have been Dick's age and he might have been Wrists' age. But he wasn't as young as she'd thought at first.

She watched him and he stayed looking out the window.

'I guess there's two answers, Audrey Cole.'

'Two answers.'

'The first answer is, my great-great-grandfather saw a map on a wall in Toronto. A long time ago. Alberta isn't a place yet. He sees a map on a wall that purports to show where the Canadian Pacific Railroad is going to run through.'

'The Canadian Pacific Railroad.'

'A long time ago, I said. He sees this map and has visions of the opportunities such a thing would bring about, for a man with the means to capitalize on the knowledge. And being a man of means, he heads out west to acquire just the right piece of land to start to build the amenities that all of those soon-to-be-arriving railroad passengers would surely desire.'

'But the railroad runs ...'

'In the family folklore, it is still a matter of debate whether the ultimate route changed in the intervening time or whether the old man just didn't know how to read a map.'

A snowball landed a foot from the smoker's head. They did not flinch.

'What's the other answer?'

Wrists walked up to the bar. He looked at the two of them. Then turned around to have a look at whatever they were both staring at through the window. Audrey pulled the cap off a beer for him.

'Well, Alex,' he asked, 'how about we take everything upstairs to the ballroom? Play on the stage tonight?'

Alex Main thought about this for a while, then turned to Koop. 'Koop, what do you figure? Want to set up upstairs tonight?'

'Well, it sure is a lot of trouble moving all this shit up and down the stairs twice a day when there's a fully functioning bar up there.'

'We do have the new PA all wired up there,' said Alex, scratching his chin. 'It'll be good to hear it in action.'

Koop stood behind the bar in the ballroom and turned on the lights. The black cylindrical theatre lights pointing at the stage came up gradually, the bulbs taking time to heat up. Halogens hanging above the bar dropped circular spotlights onto the counter. There were lights set into the glass shelves behind the bar that lit the bottles from below, casting shadows in the colours of the liquors inside: honey brown, melon green, cherry red, smoky orange. Lights diffused behind etched glass shades hung over the tables and sat in wall sconces. They shone on the black leather banquettes and stool cushions, on the long black wood bar counter, on the black-lacquered stage floorboards. A spotlight up in the rafters pointing at the big mirror ball made spots of light turn in a slow season around the room's hemisphere. Koop lit little tea-light candles and set them in rocks glasses on the bar top. He set a couple of them on either side of a little plastic hula girl who bobbled on her spring stand when he picked up and set down bottles.

The Lever Men moved their gear gradually up the stairs, a drum and amplifier at a time, and Koop and Audrey relocated the bar in cardboard boxes.

'Rodney,' said Wrists from the stage, 'get up here, let's get you set up and checked.'

Rodney sat at the bar with a glass of whisky at the end of his arm, staring at the stage. The skin in his face was white and damp and his eyes stared through a film into nothing in particular.

'Wrists is looking for you,' she said.

'Rodney, get up here and give us some guitar volume,' said Wrists.

Rodney set the glass down on the bar, a few fingers of whisky still inside, and slid off the counter. Took a few steps toward the stage, then turned around to pick up the glass again.

Later in the day, when the sun went down and the crowd moved up into the ballroom, they couldn't find him. The crowd filled the space with noise and heat, made the trapped air in the big space humid and full of chatter. They smoked the air blue and peppery.

'Audrey, have you seen Rodney?' asked Wrists. She shook her head.

Koop scooped ice out of his well into steel shakers. Poured and shook, strained and poured. He slid orange wedges and cherries onto toothpicks and laid them over glass tops.

'Audrey,' said Hector.

'I haven't seen him, Hector.'

She walked through the crowd looking at pairs and crowds and couldn't find him in a conversation. People sunk in the banquette seats over their drinks and he wasn't around any tables. In the back corner, men cut white powder on a tabletop with the edge of a credit card and he wasn't one of them.

She poked her head in the men's room. The big man with the black leather vest stood at the sink beside a skinny kid in a rock-band T-shirt. The kid's eyes were glassy and his nose was bright red and running. The man in the black leather vest glared at Audrey and she shut the door again quickly.

Audrey was walking through the ballroom looking at each table for Rodney when the lights went out.

The lights went out and the room plunged into dark. For a second everything was quiet, as a hundred people stopped talking all at once in the sudden darkness, then the black room erupted. Everyone talking, gasping, a few people shouting. The ballroom was pitch-black, cut off from the moonlight by thick walls, the deep black heart of the building, and Audrey stood frozen like a bag had been dropped over her head.

A few seconds passed and then lights appeared. People lit their cigarette lighters and held them over their heads. On the bar at the far end of the room, Koop's little tea lights flickered, then moved and floated upward, as people at the bar picked them up, raised them to try and extend the range of their glow.

From the stage Wrists shouted as loudly as he could, 'Hey, quiet, everyone. Quiet for a second.'

The crowd rumbled and muttered and tittered.

'Koop, I think you blew a breaker,' shouted Dick Move.

'I'm on it,' yelled Koop, his voice moving across the ballroom. 'Everybody stay put and don't hurt yourselves.'

Audrey walked carefully through the crowd, between the dark lumps of people without enough light for faces. People walked slowly, following the red cherries on their cigarettes like the phosphorescent lumps at the end of antennae on the kind of deep-deep-sea fish that sunlight never reaches.

'We're on it, everyone,' yelled Koop. 'No need to panic.'

'Everybody stay put and we'll have the lights back on in no time,' shouted Dick.

She walked carefully through the crowd, feeling for chairs, high tables, people. She found the ballroom doors and stepped through them. Outside on the second-floor balcony, white moonlight streamed through the windows, bright after the darkness inside, bright enough to see. She stepped over a couple sitting on the floor of the open elevator, their shirts open, arms wrapped around necks kissing, and neither of them was Rodney.

A tall, skinny man leaned on the brass bannister at the top of the stairs, looking down into the open moon-silver mezzanine. He looked over at her when she came near, and nodded, recognizing her in the moonlight.

'You're this Audrey Cole who's been looking after them the last few weeks,' he said.

He was a rail-thin man with an old, gaunt face, wearing a wide black cowboy hat. Long silver hair that was tied into a ponytail under the hat brim. The white full moon lit him up on the balcony and she could see roses stitched in silver thread into the shoulders of the old leather jacket he wore in spite of the heat.

'Audrey Cole and the Legendary Lever Men,' she said.

He didn't laugh at this but nodded seriously in agreement.

'This is your first Alex Main party?' he asked, staring down and through the window out at the lake.

'I guess so,' she said.

'I appreciate that he does these rock'n'roll nights still. His bottom line on the electronic music is obviously much better. He can get a medium-name DJ up here for a few nights to do dance music and really pack people in. The summer dance parties you'll see every room filled and then the whole lakeshore stacked with camping. Tents, RVs, the whole deal. So I appreciate that he sets aside some winter weekends for rock 'n' roll, which is close to my own heart, for whatever that's worth.'

'Have you seen Rodney Levermann?' she asked, after he didn't continue. 'They're looking for him in there.'

Outside, coyotes were howling their pleading, whining howls. He waited a little while, listening to them.

'When I first met Rodney, he was the guitar player for Sue Father. This was 1980 probably. Sue Father was my favourite singer and her band was my favourite group. They played two hours a night every night for three years before falling apart. They played naked. Before every set they stood out in the alley and took off all their clothes and spray-painted themselves with matte black carpenter's paint. Each of them put on a pair of safety goggles and spray-painted each other's faces. They were loved in Calgary by maybe thirty half-psychotic paranoid twenty-year-olds, and hated everywhere else on the entire continent, and they played every night: Golden Nakusp Abbotsford Victoria Bellingham Eugene Eureka Santa Rosa Petaluma San Jose Santa Barbara San Diego. They pulled down water pipes and flooded venues and hung from lighting rigs until they crashed and they stepped though stage monitors, they kicked glasses off bars and threw up on promoters and jerked off on paying customers and after they got kicked out they'd set up in the parking lot and play, Marshall Stacks turned up to ten, until the police came. For this they had all their teeth and limbs broken, and then being on crutches slowed them down significantly so they were easy chasing down for all those thrown-up-on and jerked-off-on hostiles from their previous trip to town, who'd rebreak and run over and generally cripple them, leave them naked, spray-painted black, in ditches from Missoula, Montana, to Charlottetown, PEI. They were banned from every club and bar in every state and province and detained at the border and thrown in holding cells. All of this made them particularly well suited to playing rock 'n' roll and they were the best band I ever saw.'

He leaned over the mezzanine railing, looking down, watching through the big windows into the courtyard.

'I saw Sue Father for the last time at a Vietnamese restaurant on Jasper Avenue in Edmonton, a few years back. She'd picked a fight recently and been hit in the face and mouth, and because her gums were weakened by acrylic poisoning from all that spray paint years earlier, her teeth had all fallen out. She had them in a little cloth bag.'

He reached inside his shirt and pulled out a little cloth bag on a shoelace. Tilted it up and a dozen brown lumps, like little melted sugar cubes, fell into his open palm.

'She said to me,' and he said a name here that Audrey didn't quite catch, '"The only good these ever did was to keep me from swallowing my own fist up to the elbow. Maybe they'll be better as a good-luck charm." I never heard from her again.'

He poured the little lumps back into the bag and tucked it back inside his shirt.

Outside, coyotes howled. She looked to where he was watching, and between the building walls past the courtyard she could see there were men outside, running on the lake top. They'd taken off their jackets and shirts despite the cold and were running bare-chested on the snow-covered ice, yowling and whooping along with the whiny shouts of the coyotes. They ran and slid and fell over in the snow, staggered back to their feet, slid and crashed into each other, laughing and shaking and howling in the night.

The big man in the black leather vest poked his head out the ballroom doors. The thin man in the cowboy hat waved him over.

'Gurt, why are we all standing around in the dark?'

'Breaker went,' said the big man. 'I was going to find Alex.'

'Don't worry about finding Alex,' said the thin man. 'I'm sure Wrists and Koop are already figuring it out. Let Alex keep at whatever he's up to. Just go back in there and make sure nobody freaks out in the dark until Wrists and Koop fix it.'

'Sure thing, boss,' said Gurt.

'Well, it's been good talking to you, Audrey Cole,' said the thin man. He drank the last of his whisky and walked past her with Gurt to the ballroom doors.

She went downstairs and then outside. The howling men had come back to the shore, their wet, cold skin glistening in the moonlight. They ran past her back to the building, shivering and shouting. Audrey stood alone on the lakeshore. She hugged her jacket against the wind, looking around for the nobody that was there. She looked down the snowy beach and saw yellow lights in the houseboat.

Inside, Rodney sat on an upholstered bench, tilted at the angle of the boat, his brown leather jacket in a heap on the dirty floor. He had rolled up his shirt sleeves and was tracing the faded green lines of his tattoos for a pair of teenage girls. They wore men's plaid shirts and jeans and passed a crumpled joint back and forth.

Audrey held her hands up like she was approaching a barn kitten with a sack, palms out. 'Rodney.'

'That's a hand drill,' Rodney said to the girls, pointing at his forearm. The veins high enough to cast shadows under his clenched fist. 'And that's our Saviour, prostrate in his grave, before the Assumption.'

'Hey, Rodney, it's me. It's Audrey. Hey.'

'What's the Assumption?'

'Well, every day you and I and your neighbour and the mayor of Regina wake up and start regretting. Regretting all the infinitesimal hurts and harms we inflict in all directions like so much grapeshot.'

'What?'

'But there isn't a blunderbussload of screws and nails that the Lord won't step in front of for our sakes.'

'Rodney. Hey, it's me.'

Rodney blinked his eyes and smacked his lips to get moisture moving in his face. 'This here is Audrey Cole. She's here to make me do things I'm not up to doing.'

'Ha ha. Yep, that's me.'

'What about that star on your elbow?'

'In Russia, before the …' He smacked his lips together. There was a whitish crust around the corners of his mouth and his eyes were heavy and mostly closed. 'Before the revolution, they'd tattoo stars on each other's knees, in prison. It means "Never again on my knees."'

'You doing all right, Rodney? Feeling okay?'

'But it's on your elbow.'

'Well, I'm still on my knees,' he said. He looked up at Audrey. 'Right? Things I'm not up to doing?'

'You sure don't make yourself easy to find.'

'A little too easy, I guess.'

One of the girls took a deep pull on the joint and the paper crackled. She coughed and exhaled a huge cloud of smoke that filled the tight space. The houseboat had a plasticky damp interior and Audrey felt like she was in a campground shower.

'Hey, kid,' Audrey said, 'do me a favour, don't give him any of that.'

'What I want is a file,' Rodney said to Audrey.

'He hasn't really been having any of this,' said one of the girls.

'What has he been having?'

'A coarse-rasped carpenter's file. And a teaspoon and a steak knife and a box of strike-anywhere matches. I'll cut off each match head and put it in a bowl and then eat them, a spoonful at a time. Eat a box of match heads and swallow the file. Bang.'

The girl shrugged. 'I didn't ask.'

Rodney pitched forward, caught himself, straightened back up.

'A set tonight and then they'll plow us out tomorrow,' said Audrey. 'Tomorrow or the day after. Hey, you could play that song with the slide part. The one you played in Revelstoke. I want to hear that one again. The one you learned in Winnipeg.'

He looked up at her and squinted an eye. He chuckled and shook a finger at her. 'You're all right, Audrey. You're all right. If I weren't broken down and old enough to be your father, I'd court you. I'd woo you.'

'Come on, we need to go in there. Wrists is tearing the place apart.'

'How would a man go about doing that? Wooing Cole? You'd need to be some kind of timed rally-race titleholder. The fastest time on the Crowsnest Highway the second week of January in a three-speed Hyundai

Pony. No heat. Pissing in a cup to keep from stopping. Your picture in the paper next to the timekeeper pointing dumbfoundedly at his stop-watch with the proof. You know anything about these rally races, Audrey?'

She wanted to open up her wallet and unfold the Mitsubishi Lancer. Explain to him about the tires and the safety cage. She wanted to tell him about Tommi Mäkinen and his consecutive World Rally Championships. And the Elbow Falls Rally Race, and the Athabasca Crossing stage rally. The Sentinel Peak Rally Cross, and the kind of car she needed to enter all of them. And how all those races were just on the other side of the normal world everyone else knew about, and all you needed was to know the right gravel escape hatch to drive your Mitsubishi Lancer down, and you could slip out into a world you made yourself.

'They need you on the stage,' she said instead.

One of the girls pulled down the last of the joint and carefully crushed out the cherry against the cold lip of the laminate table. She opened up a mint tin full of ashes and roach ends and put it inside.

'They need you on the stage. Then tomorrow they'll plow us out, and I'll take you all back home to Calgary.'

'Home,' he said, and sighed.

'Come on,' said Audrey. She kissed him on the cheek, and the rough bristles on his face left salt and an old beer film on her lips. His face was rough and raspy and he smelled like whisky. He focused his eyes on her and took time to work enough moisture into his thick mouth to speak.

'Okay, Audrey, let's go.'

When she brought him inside, the lights were back on. She led Rodney into the ballroom, through the crowd to the stage. He put a foot up on the stage and didn't move for a while. Dick Move reached down and helped him up. They pulled Rodney up onto the stage and he slowly, gingerly, started to sort through his gear, turning on his amplifier, opening up his toolbox. He pulled out his rifle-range ear protectors and spent some time trying to figure out how to get them properly onto his head.

She looked around for the skinny man in the cowboy hat she'd talked to by the stairs but didn't see him anywhere.

Onstage, Wrists started to tap out a shuffle while Rodney slowly put on his guitar. He turned off the amplifier standby switch and stood at the microphone with his eyes half-closed. The other Lever Men joined Wrists' simple shuffle, a walking bass line padded with short organ chords.

'I'm waiting for the bus,' Rodney said into the microphone. 'Over there in Ramsay, in Calgary, across the street from the Shamrock Hotel. Waiting for the number 24 to Ogden.

'That's when he sat down next to me on the bus bench. The Devil.'

The volume was up on the Telecaster and it began to feed back as Rodney talked.

'He leaned into my field of vision and said, "I'm going to do some magic." He held out his hands palms open at this point as people do when they're doing magic tricks.'

Wrists shuffled and splashed the floor tom, the ride cymbal. The Telecaster was feeding back and Hector had picked up a drone note on the organ to match the tone. Rodney talked with his eyes closed.

'He said, "I'm going to permanently change one, and only one, thing about your life." And then he snapped his fingers. The number 24 rolled up and the Devil stood up and got on the bus. The door shut and I just sat there, stupefied. Had to wait half an hour for the next bus.'

Rodney's eyes were open now and he stared into the crowd.

'What did he change?' someone finally shouted from the crowd.

'That's how I know he was the Devil,' said Rodney. 'The real Devil.'

10

Downstairs, she wrapped herself in the blanket and went outside. The sun had gone and there was no twilight, only night. But the night was full of light, deep dark greys, brushed-blackboard slate greys, and old highway-top greys that diffused the cloudy sky from the swollen moon somewhere above the sky's floor. In the bottom-floor windows of the Crash Palace, orange light from her fire flickered and pulsed. Snow fell and cold wind blew on her face, not as harshly as the morning but cold enough, and she squeezed her eyes tightly until tears pressed out of them, tears that sat, wet and warm, then chilly, on her cheeks.

Audrey walked down to the beach, picking her way between hard snowdrifts, on a swooped path cut down to the bare gravel by wind skipping off the lake. The drifts carried on across the ice, grey crests that snaked into a maze of white lines on a black plane. She put a foot out and swept an arc of powder snow off the black ice. Put weight forward and the ice swelled downward, flexing in a circle and then *crack*, giving in the centre, like a windshield chip.

It's thicker farther out, Audrey.

She took a breath and then jogged forward, running on the ice, and slid, arms wide for balance, tottering but gliding all the same, and she screamed without meaning to and the sound echoed out and back in the valley bowl. She coasted to a stop, windmilled her arms for balance and stayed upright, then put her hands forward on her knees and laughed, choking for breath while she did. Behind her, two thick black lines of exposed ice tracked back several yards to her last bootprints. Audrey straightened and stood on the hard frozen top of Two Reel Lake.

She came out to the lake a lot, the six months that she lived here. When the place was crowded for a party, to get away from the press of people. Even in between the parties, there were always people around – someone staying a few nights in one of the rooms, some friend of Alex or Gurt or Looch, passing through, crashing for a night or a week.

Most of them stayed inside though. So she always had the lakeshore to herself.

One night in May she saw a little blue plus sign on a stick and she really, really needed to be alone. She stood by herself on the lakeshore, terrified. There may have been a party going on behind her in the building. It was hard to remember. She just remembered feeling so all alone and scared. Scared and anxious, and eventually to open up her lungs and start her heart back up she'd leaned back her head and yowled like a coyote.

'I was so scared,' she said out loud in the night.

The steps to execute tomorrow are: the snow will have stopped and the wind will have died and in this new situation you will get home. You will dress for the weather. Making do with what you can scrounge in the building. You will go back to the car better suited for the walk than you were. You will probably not get the car unstuck but you will try. If you can't get it unstuck, you will find anything useful in the car and then walk to the village. It's a long, long walk but you'll prepare and it won't be snowing. Tomorrow, when the snow stops, all of this will be manageable: steps to execute.

She leaned back and yowled in the night.

Coyotes ran out of the trees on the far bank, right through the line of her gaze. Two, four, seven of them. Blue and black in the dark. They slipped out of the dark out onto the ice, far away. She stood and watched them run along the lip of the lake, far on the opposite shore.

The coyotes stopped across the lake and she wasn't sure how far away they were.

She'd never been good at gauging distances. On familiar highway stretches she sometimes passed signs giving distances, odometer test section markers posted by the Canadian Automobile Association, and these quantified the internal landmark map she'd made herself: the coulee bridges and ranch brands on number 2 south of High River, or the sequence of tourist traps through the Purcells; the Enchanted Forest, Crazy Creek Falls Suspension Bridge, Miniature Land. Watch your dashboard here and do the math as you pass each ordered sign and you'll know how far a kilometre is in terms of lived experience. She always meant to count or record, but she'd fall behind slower traffic and make a pass in a straightaway when the double line turned dotted, and once she'd regained her speed she'd forgotten to count. She meant to count because she never properly knew how far a kilometre was.

The coyotes milled around, in and out of the trees. They didn't yelp or whine, just ran quietly. They felt far. Far enough that she couldn't tell if their faces were turned toward her. How far can you safely be from a pack of coyotes alone in the dark? Too far to see the white moonlight reflected back in their glassy eyes. She took a step back without turning and put her foot ankle-deep into a snowdrift. Then she turned and took quick walking steps back along her black path. At the shore she turned and the coyotes were running along their original vector, far away, opposite across the lake toward some other point farther up the far shore.

The ground was solid and she howled in their direction and this time they howled back.

§

Inside, she drank whisky out of the bottle and watched her fire, curled up on the couch. She'd pulled off her pants again and hung them to dry on the chair. The whisky hurt her stomach and pulled acid high into her chest but she sipped it anyway. Small amounts into her mouth that warmed her tongue and throat.

She heard a sound: lapping. Turned to see the kitten licking the tuna tin. She watched the little cat and it stopped licking and looked up at her.

'Kitten,' said Audrey. The little cat contracted backward but stayed put. It watched her for a while, then lowered its face back into the bowl. Contracted backward again, like it had in the afternoon, but stayed at the bowl.

'I get it, Kitten, don't worry. Not everyone wants company.'

Audrey stood out of the blanket and built up the fire. There were fewer logs and she didn't think they'd burn through the whole night for her. She stood in front of the fire and the floor wasn't cold on her bare feet now and the heat on her bare legs felt good.

'Come on over here, Kitten, this will warm you up. Come on, get closer. Come on.' The kitten lapped at the bowl and looked up at her. It sat still, watching her.

'Well, Kitten, we'll burn up all this stuff tonight and stay warm. And then tomorrow the snow will stop and I'll find warm clothes and we'll be able to get the car started again,' she said. She stirred the fire and enjoyed the sparks and crackles. An ember spit out and burned the top of her foot. She winced and swore but she stirred the fire more and the heat felt good up the front of her body.

'You know what though, Kitten? Even if the car doesn't start, whatever. We'll just walk back to town. I mean, it's a long way. But it's not like it's the worst thing that ever happened to anybody. Walking through the snow a few kilometres. There are more clothes around the place and we'll bundle up good. If the car doesn't start, we'll just walk back to town and get help there.'

The kitten stretched and then walked carefully across the room. It sat down on the warm concrete in front of the fire and purred. Audrey started to reach out for a pet but stopped herself.

'You know what that miserable son of a bitch had stashed away up there, Kitten? He had $1,600 in a zip-lock bag. Sixteen hundred dollars in twenties and fifties. We'll walk back to town and buy a cup of coffee from the gas station and we'll buy that old Honda Civic. What'd they say, $600 or best offer? We'll buy it with cash. A hot cup of coffee and we'll drive that Honda Civic out of town.'

The kitten purred and she reached out to touch it behind its ears and stopped herself again.

'I got excited last night, Kitten, because I thought this car for sale in the village was my old car. My baby. But we've established that it can't be because it's not as boxy as the '88 model, and besides which my old car was in fact totalled and crushed into a cube just over three years ago. So there's that.'

Audrey took a sip of whisky out of the bottle and made a face. She had a drink and sighed.

'Shelly is going to love you, Kitten.'

She reached for it and it scampered away, under the couch. She saw its little green eyes, reflecting the firelight back out of the darkness.

Audrey had a sip of whisky and made a face. She put whisky and red vermouth into the cocktail shaker. No ice to shake it with. Just a little bit of the Cinzano, Koop had told her. You just want to kiss it. Some places use a spritzer bottle. A spritz kiss of Cinzano mist.

'Hold tight, Kitten, be right back.'

She went outside barefoot and bare-legged. Shook the shaker and stuck it into a snowbank to chill. She hopped from foot to foot. The wind blew on her bare legs and she hugged her arms. She wanted to take off the rest of her clothes and run out to the lake again. Slide on that stinging ice, supported above the black bottom by a skin of cold. She wanted to run, feeling the ice melt under her feet with each step.

If the coyotes came back, she'd just run with them, barefoot on the black ice. Run amongst the hot fur, ropy muscles. Howling in the night. Run and break a sweat and get hotter and hotter.

She gulped breath and her lungs felt overly large and underused.

Inside, she sat on the pillow sipping her Manhattan straight from the steel tin. She stretched her neck up as best she could, sitting straight, and sharp clenches held the muscles, hip bones to skull bottom tight and sore. Another night on this sofa won't help, she thought. The whisky was sweet and the sharp steel lip of the shaker added an electric metal taste.

Another night on that sofa and you won't be able to walk tomorrow, Audrey. Maybe it folds out.

She pulled the cushions off and, yes, there was a metal handle. She pulled and the interior creak-clanked open and out, a mattress accordioned into thirds, spring-spranged out with her pull, unfolding brown steel legs. She pulled the mattress out flat and in the flickering firelight couldn't get a good idea of the colour or condition, which she decided was for the best.

'Kitten, it's a goddamn Christmas miracle.'

She lay flat on the mattress, and the springs creaked underneath her. Spread her arms and legs open and wide and tilted her head back. The padding was thin and she felt the springs. It smelled mildewy and old. It was heaven. All she needed was a kitten to tickle behind its little ears.

'C'mere, Kitten. We've got a bed. I bought a bed like this for Mom to sleep in when we moved Shelly into her own room. Found it in the *Bargain Finder* and the guy – this kid named Rusty – brought it in the back of his Ford F150. He had a nice new one, Kitten, one of those extended cab deals.' She giggled. 'Just between you and me, Kitten, this Rusty – maybe I ought to buy more furniture out of the *Bargain Finder*.'

She giggled and rolled over, legs crossed backward at the ankles behind, and reached out for the Manhattan.

I probably made this too sweet. Should've found a spritzer.

She remembered the umbrellas. Stood up and walked over to the table. Unfolded an umbrella and set it on the lip of the shaker. If it's too sweet you could put a little more whisky in it, Audrey. The fire was hot and she shrugged out of her shirt and laid it across the chair. She felt her pants, and the fabric was dry and hot. She pushed the chairs away from the fire. Felt inside her boots and they were dry.

'The shitty thing is, Kitten, and we won't dwell on it, is that almost-but-not-quite-identical to my beloved Honda Civic will basically be a one-way trip back. Can't drive it, see. Not regularly. You see, Kitten,' she said seriously, 'I've got no automobile insurance. And let me tell you, our little household is close enough to the wire, financially, that a $400 driving-without-proper-insurance ticket is the last thing we need.'

She had a drink.

'I mean, it's one thing to drive around Joe Wahl's van under the care of the 12th Avenue United Church's automobile insurance. But I'm still looking at – what did they quote me last time? – $2,400 annually. Two hundred bucks a month, twelve months a year, to insure a vehicle. Harold Goetz does not pay this single mother that much, Kitten. No sir.

'How's that for a boring, stupid problem?'

She had a long drink and pointed a finger at the kitten.

'That's his fault.' She stabbed a finger into the mattress. 'His. Fault. His crash. Didn't just wreck my car, he blew up my insurability for a decade.' She spread her fingers wide. 'Kablam.

'I'd brought it up here, from Calgary. Up from the airport. Brought it up here and then he took it out and crashed it. A total writeoff.

'You know what the worst part was, Kitten? He comes in the door … ' Audrey looked around to get her bearings and then pointed at the front door. 'That door. And he just hands me a phone and says, "You've got to talk to this cop. You need to explain to him,"' and she chewed off the words: '"You need to explain to him that it's your car and it was fine that I was driving it."

'That's what he said, Kitten. After he killed my baby.'

She rolled over onto her back. Lifted up her feet and flexed her toes.

'I mean, I did. I let him drive it, Kitten. My baby. I let him take my baby out for a drive and he crashed it. I gave him permission. Sure, I said. And he crashed it.

'Kitten, I'd like to tell you about all the good reasons that surely I had, but the truth is mostly I was just coasting downhill in neutral, and it was easy. It was easy and exciting, and then it got dull and repetitive. And then I started to get a little smarter and it got … worrisome. I was a little slow on the uptake, Kitten. Maybe wilfully so. I mean, I lived out here for, what?' She counted fingers. 'Five months? Wrists drove me back to Calgary in May. Six months. So maybe a little wilfully slow figuring out why all these kids were coming out to stay here for three nights at a time and why the only money changing hands was going to large men in black leather vests.

'But he crashed it. My baby. A total writeoff. I was so mad, Kitten. Just livid.

'I'd like to tell you that was the moment of clarity, but of course it wasn't. It took a little blue plus sign on a stick a month or so later. And then everything went from worrisome to scary and then I understood a lot of things awfully clearly.'

She drained the last of the whisky and squeezed her eyes shut.

'Kitten, the hardest thing I ever did was to get the courage to ask the man in charge permission to leave. You had to ask him, see. Nothing happened without him saying so. I spent a few weeks worried, not knowing what to do, and then one night I went out and stood at the lakefront and yowled like a coyote. And I realized I just had to go ask the man in charge to leave. And he said, "Sure thing, Audrey Cole, we can totally make that happen." And I never heard from him again. Until I did.'

She thought about making another drink, but the bottle seemed far away. The bottle seemed far away and as hot as the fire had been, there still wasn't much warmth in the room. The cold was out there, squeezing the building. She pulled the blanket around herself more tightly and the bedsprings creaked.

'We've got a windfall now though, Kitten,' she whispered. 'We'll buy that Honda with cash and still have a thousand dollars left over. A thousand dollars of Alex's hidden-away-in-his-secret-painkiller-nest money. That'll solve a few single-mother problems.'

She thought about all the voice-mail messages that were piling up inside her phone. *Audrey, where are you, we're worried*, her mother must have said, every hour and then every half-hour. And then at a certain point the mailbox would have filled up. *The cellular mailbox is full*, a digital voice will have told Madeline Cole hours and hours ago.

I'll be home soon and I'll tell you everything, Mom. I'll tell you and Shelly everything. Moose Leg and the Legendary Lever Men and the six months I lived at this crazy building in the middle of nowhere. And Shelly's dad and the funeral and why I wanted to come back up here to see it all one last time before they knocked it down.

'I mean, Kitten, we can't complain,' Audrey whispered, lying on her back. 'We love Shelly and you'll love her when you meet her tomorrow. I mean, who knows, Kitten. Who knows?'

PART FOUR

HAVE YOU LOOKED ON THE MOON?

11

A few days after the funeral, she thought she saw the Skinny Cowboy. She stepped out of the silver office building, feeling the early evening, colder than the morning wind, cut through her jacket, and was thinking about maybe catching the number 3 bus the seven blocks south to 12th Avenue United to pick up Shelly. Audrey, it's pretty cold, she thought, spend the few bucks and take the bus.

So she walked to the corner, and she saw him. She saw the Skinny Cowboy on the opposite corner of 5th Avenue. A skinny old man in a brown leather jacket underneath a wide black hat. Her stomach dropped.

The light turned to Walk and a crush of people started crossing. Has to be him, she thought. The Skinny Cowboy stopped in the middle of the street and, without looking to either side, squatted down and kicked both his legs back, arms out in a prone push-up, right on the asphalt. The crowd parted, people looked down, surprised, and bumped into each other, trying not to step on the man lying in the middle of the road. He put his ear down against the black iron City of Calgary manhole, listening. The light blinked Don't Walk red and the crowd made it to the other side, and Audrey hadn't even moved, still staring. The Skinny Cowboy jumped up, pushed his fists into his pockets, and finished crossing the street, stepping onto the curve a few seconds after the red hand finished blinking. He walked right past Audrey and she got a good look at him: his long hair wasn't silver but a cheap drug-store-bottle red dye job, and his long black duster jacket wasn't the soft brown leather with the roses stitched into the shoulders, and he coughed into spindly fingers with black-painted nails. He walked by Audrey close enough that she could smell dispenser hand soap and mouthwash, and he was a young man maybe in his late twenties and he wasn't the Skinny Cowboy at all.

§

She got a phone call from the daycare a little after lunch. 'Shelly threw up,' Miss Aphra told her, speaking loudly over the shouting toddlers in the background, 'and she has a fever. You need to come and pick her up.'

'You're killing me, Cole,' said Harold when she stood in his doorway.

'They need me to take her out, right now. They get strict when they think the kids are contagious. Zero tolerance.'

'I ought to have a zero tolerance for the kids I hire booking out halfway through the day any time they feel like it,' Harold grumbled. 'It's not a goddamn petting zoo we're running.'

'Harold ...'

'Sure, sure. I need all the expenses for Christina Lake filed tomorrow.'

'I can't ...'

'I need all of that to the bookkeeper in time for quarter end and the latest I can go to see her is Thursday so that means tomorrow.'

She turned around and walked away before he could say anything else. Put on her jacket in a huff and stood over her desk, steaming red. She stood there for a few seconds grinding her teeth. A few seconds that felt like a whole lot longer and then she sat down and pushed receipts and file folders into her bag. She went the long way back through the office, through the emergency exit into the building stairwell. To not walk past his office. She walked down the stairs, stomping on the concrete, going as fast as she could manage. Around and around, past keycard-locked doors that led into law offices and engineering firms, or whatever it was all the men in the suits looking at their cellphones in the elevator did. She stomped down eighteen flights of stairs and then stood outside on the sidewalk in the cold, wheezing a bit to catch her breath. Sweating and wheezing, but at least that's why her face was red now. Eighteen flights of stairs, not because she was angry and hurt and embarrassed.

At home she sat on the couch watching cartoons, Shelly in her pyjamas curled up beside her, eyelids droopy, one thumb in her mouth. Her forehead was hot and her face was flushed. Audrey gave her a plastic dropperful of children's Tylenol. They watched animal astronauts explore the surface of the moon. Brave little ducks and pigs and even a llama, each in a bubble astronaut helmet, taking big bounding steps across the cratered moon surface. The llama had a big magnifying glass and bent down with her long neck to peer at moon rocks and craters.

When Shelly was asleep, Audrey went downstairs and spread the receipts out across the kitchen table. She could at least do the sorting tonight, she figured. Uncapped her highlighters. She sat holding a highlighter, staring past it at the jar on top of the refrigerator for a long while before she realized what she was doing.

§

She saw the Skinny Cowboy at the Wholesale Club. While she pushed her cart through the aisles, picking up Joe Wahl's groceries. Shelly sat in the top basket of the cart, swinging her feet and singing to herself. Audrey pulled up in the produce aisle to get a bag of onions and a few bunches of celery and she saw him. He had his back to her: black hat, long jacket. He was picking mushrooms out of the cardboard mushroom box and breaking off the stems before putting the white caps into a brown paper bag. Audrey stood watching him with her mouth a little bit open, and for a moment all she could think of was all the mushroom stems she never ate in her life, weighed out at what, a dollar sixty or so a hundred grams? What does that come to? The Skinny Cowboy put the bag of mushroom caps into his shopping basket and turned around. He had green eyes, and the line of his jaw was lantern-shaped, almost superhero square, with freckles powdering the top of his chest above a low T-shirt neckline, and he wasn't the Skinny Cowboy at all. What are you thinking, Audrey, she asked herself, that's not him at all, not even close.

'Mum Mum Glarpy later magic,' said Shelly.

'Sure, baby,' said Audrey, watching the man who clearly wasn't the Skinny Cowboy as he picked up bags of potatoes, hefting them like he was testing their weight. 'Sure thing, baby, magic later.'

'What if it was him anyway,' she asked herself that night on the couch, staring at the wall just above the eleven o'clock TV news. 'What if it was? You don't owe him anything. "Hey, Skinny Cowboy," you can say to him, "Go haunt some other single mom. I'm not afraid of you."'

I'm not afraid of you, she said to herself, just forming the shapes of the words with her lips. In the kitchen, the refrigerator condenser kicked in, the buzzing rattle cutting through the night.

'You should talk to your landlord about that,' her dad had said, the first time he heard that refrigerator condenser. He'd come down from Canmore with her mother exactly once, for two weeks, when Shelly was born. Audrey had insisted on going home to the mustard-coloured house when she got out of the hospital. Not back with them to Canmore. 'I want to learn how to do it all in the place where I'll be doing it,' she said to her mother.

They brought Shelly home from the hospital to the little mustard-coloured house on 12th Avenue and took turns holding her and changing her. Shelly was a little pink screaming force, a tiny wrinkly face that opened up to screech or coo or suckle. Audrey did her best to feed her every two hours or every three hours or every hour or whenever she cried, which felt like all the time. Her parents took turns holding her when they could. Her mother held Shelly in between feedings and sang her songs, and Audrey tried to learn the lyrics so she'd be able to sing them herself when her mother finally went home, but mostly she was too tired in these between-feeding lulls and slept instead.

Her father held his granddaughter, sitting on Audrey's lumpy old sofa or pacing around the creaking floor.

And they never asked her. Her mother had never asked, not even the first day, when Audrey finally broke down and phoned her, eleven months after disappearing from Moose Leg. 'Mom, I need help,' she told her mother on the phone. And when Madeline Cole arrived at the mustard-coloured house on 12th Avenue behind its ragged caragana hedge and saw her six-months-pregnant daughter for the first time in a year, she didn't ask any questions. She led her back inside and sat down at the kitchen table and Audrey sat down across from her and cried. Cried and cried for a long time, not saying anything, then eventually went upstairs and crawled into bed.

When she came back downstairs, her mother didn't ask. Instead, her mother asked for her doctor's name and number, and how often she'd been to see him, and how many ultrasound appointments she'd been to so far. And then she called and made arrangements for all the appointments that Audrey had blown off or missed or hadn't made yet.

And when her father came down from Canmore the day after they brought Shelly home from the hospital, he didn't ask. He walked around the house poking at the cracked plaster and peering up into the corners of the ceiling at the water damage. He frowned at the hole in the basement door and sucked air in through his closed teeth when he looked at the furnace.

'You should get your landlord to fix that,' he said the first time he heard the refrigerator rattle to life. But he never asked her. Audrey saw her mother give him a look, and he shook his head, and never asked.

'This place is a wreck, Audrey,' said her father before he went back to Canmore.

Her mother stayed longer and eventually she went back to Canmore too, and Audrey spent her first night alone in the house with her daughter, carrying her around between feedings while she whimpered or wailed. Tried to sing her songs that she hadn't learned the lyrics to. Did her best to feed her when she needed feeding, no matter how tired or sore or raw or confused she was. Terrified, alone in the dark. She sat on a chair gently coaxing burps out of her tiny daughter, tapping her back with a flat palm, and her heart raced and raced. She tapped and Shelly wouldn't burp and instead she squirmed and screeched, and Audrey, heart racing, alone in the suddenly-way-too-big house, couldn't imagine not being scared and exhausted ever again.

Her mother came back a few days later with more baby clothes, more diapers, more muslin blankets and wipes and little cloths for cleaning up the spit-up, for wiping milk off chins. She brought a little countertop sterilizer for bottles and a rented pump to help Audrey's milk come in.

She brought a year's worth of mail, which she left on the counter. Audrey waited until she was alone in the kitchen to go through it all. Pay stubs from Moose Leg, and then an employment termination letter. Bank statements. And then the letter from the insurance company. She read the letter from the insurance company that explained her new premiums following the accident involving her Honda Civic. She set this face down on the table and cried, as quietly as she could, alone in the kitchen.

They never asked, and after a few months had gone by, Audrey realized they never would. She'd never have to tell them the story. She'd never have to tell anyone the story, she realized. Her mother came for a few weeks at a time and gradually her trips back home to Canmore got longer and longer, and Audrey sat alone in the dark, burping her daughter, and she wasn't scared anymore, just tired.

§

In the Frequently Asked Questions section of their website, West Majestic Developments outlined the various provincial regulations for walleye fishing in Two Reel Lake and explained that it was the responsibility of individual property owners to secure fishing licences. Audrey sat at her desk at lunch and looked at artist renderings and floor plans. Sixteen two-bedroom condominium units, and twelve one-bedroom units, as well as eight two-storey main-floor town homes. Quartz countertops, steam showers, wide-plank hardwood floors. The townhouses had real wood fireplaces.

There was a digital illustration: a huge red-brick building in a sun-washed, idyllic valley. In the foreground, a family of four sat in a boat, fishing. All of them blond and apple-cheeked. A red-brick building that was just part of a larger, sprawling complex – reflective glass in black steel frames, stainless-steel balconies, red cedar patios with colourful sun umbrellas. You could make out the small shapes of people in swimsuits sunning themselves on their cedar decks or drinking from martini glasses around gas barbecues.

She tried googling:

Crash Palace Closes

Alex Main Arrested

Two Reel Lake Drug Bust

... but didn't find anything. The *Calgary Herald* and *Red Deer Advocate* stories hadn't made it to their digital archives.

She went back to the West Majestic FAQ page. 'Construction begins Spring 2010!' it told her. She stared at the illustrated building. Tried to imagine the Crash Palace underneath all the new wood and glass and steel.

'They should just knock it down,' she muttered at the computer. 'Knock it all down and start over. If they haven't already.'

'But they probably haven't,' she said to herself that night, standing over the sink doing dishes while Shelly played with her train blocks in front of the TV.

It's probably just sitting there empty in whatever shape he left it in. She hadn't been able to find more, so her imagination just had that original paragraph in the story about his death to go off. A few words and phrases: 'fined,' 'unlicenced hotel and bar,' 'known to police,' 'ongoing problems.'

She imagined the building, alone and empty, in the cold. She wondered what state it was in. Had they known? Did they have time to pack everything up and clear out? Or were they surprised? Had the RCMP rolled in while the party was in full swing, music blasting, hundreds of kids dancing upstairs in the ballroom, Gurt Markstrom somewhere in the crowd whispering in people's ears and making tallies on his little notepad?

'Choo choo choo,' sang Shelly in the living room, knocking blocks together.

You know who wasn't surprised? The goddamn Skinny Cowboy. No one caught him at anything. No one ever had and no one ever would.

Heck, Audrey didn't even know his name. The goddamn Skinny Cowboy. He'd found her, but if she ever wanted to find him, she didn't even have a name to go by.

Hey, Skinny Cowboy, she couldn't phone him up to say. *Leave me alone 'cause I don't owe you anything, but first tell me about the night the RCMP came and tell me how it all went down and what's even up there still and what kind of shape is the place going to be in when the bulldozers finally show up in spring 2010?*

She stacked the dishes on the counter, propped on a tea towel to dry. Dried her hands and poured herself a glass of water.

'Mom mom come see,' hollered Shelly from the living room.

She drank a glass of water, looking up at the jar on top of the refrigerator.

He'd found her but she wouldn't even know where to look for him.

'Mooooooommmmmeeeeee come seeeeeeeeeeeee,' whined Shelly.

'Coming, baby,' she said. She drank her water and put the glass into the sink. She went to the living room and Shelly showed her the train course she'd made. Audrey sat on the floor with her daughter and listened while Shelly pushed the train along the plastic track, singing a little made-up song that was mainly snatches of 'Row Row Row Your Boat' with train sounds instead of words. She sat on the floor watching and sometimes she looked up, over her singing daughter, into the kitchen.

§

At work she placed the cut-out photograph of the Skinny Cowboy from the newspaper down on the copier. Closed the lid and hunted through the menu, then found the option to Enlarge 200%. The result was grainy and pixellated, but you could get the general idea looking at it.

She'd printed out the words HAVE YOU SEEN THIS MAN? in a large font across the top of another page. She carefully positioned the two sheets together on the copier and ran off a page combining them. Now the image quality was even worse.

Anyone who knows him would recognize him from a worse photo than this, she thought.

At her desk she turned the page ninety degrees and carefully wrote an email address across the bottom, over and over, in a series of vertical tabs: haveyouseentheskinnycowboy@rocketmail.com. She made twenty copies. Then she sat with a pair of scissors and cut around each of the email tabs, to make tearaway flaps.

When Shelly was in bed, Audrey went out into the night, down the block to the wall around the hole. She was careful not to cover any of Marnie's posters. Marnie would pull down anything that had been put overtop of one of her own. She'd pull them down and crumple them up and leave the crumpled paper there on the sidewalk. Audrey stapled her posters to the wall in a strip a few feet to either side of Marnie's block of nightclub and theatre bills. Stapled them up and then spent a minute pulling off a few of the tearaway address tabs from every fourth poster.

Make it seem like there's some action, she thought. Get the ball rolling.

The hole behind the plywood wall hummed. There was a pump down at the bottom. They'd dug below the water table, Audrey figured. Water was pumped into a firehose that wound up the four storeys through a concrete stairwell that protruded upward like a stalagmite, then out into the alley on the other side of the block. Even after they'd stopped working, after they'd packed up all their tools and taken down the crane and left the hole, the water kept pumping. The pump ran around the clock, all year long, the electric hum and gurgle of water pumping out of the hole and into the drain in the alley.

§

Audrey didn't own a computer. Her cellphone was an old flip-top with a black-and-white screen, not one of the new smart phones with a web browser that the men in suits riding the elevator at work stared into between floors. If she needed to send an email or fill out an online form, she did it at work, on her lunch break.

She sat at her desk eating reheated rice out of a Tupperware container and opened her email. There was a reply. Her heart jumped in her chest. A reply from a garbled address made up of random letters and numbers at a domain she didn't recognize. She opened the email and there was a URL, which she clicked without thinking.

Dozens of browser windows immediately opened, all of them pornography. The volume on her computer was up and groaning slapping panting grunting poured out of the speakers.

'Cole, what the hell are you doing?' asked Harold, standing behind her.

'Sorry sorry sorry,' she said, doing her best to close the windows. She clicked the little 'close browser' buttons as quickly as she could and more windows opened – harshly lit naked men and women fucking on couches, in showers, on kitchen tables. She tried to close the windows and her hands shook.

Harold reached across and turned off the power of her computer. 'Jesus, Cole, be a little smarter. Don't click email links. Don't make me get some internet safety consultant in here.'

'Sorry, Harold. Sorry.'

When he was gone, she went to the bathroom and sat in the stall, her heart racing, and she wanted to cry, but goddammit if she was going to cry at work.

§

She dressed Shelly up for daycare on a Thursday morning. Mittens, jacket, toque, boots.

'Mum, I wanna stay. No daycare.'

'Come on, kiddo. Let's go see all your friends. Let's go see all your teachers.'

Shelly sat down heavily on the floor and pulled off her mitts. 'Mum, I don't wanna!'

'Shelly, come on.'

The little girl stretched out on the floor crying. Audrey stood above her waiting.

She stood above her crying daughter and then she stepped over her and walked into the kitchen. Audrey reached up above the fridge and pulled down the mason jar. Dropped the key into her hand and slid it into her pocket. She put the jar back on the fridge top.

She phoned Harold.

'I can't make it, Harold,' she told him. 'It's a stomach thing. You don't want me around.'

She listened to him for a while and when he was done she said, 'Sure thing, Harold. I'll see you tomorrow.'

She went back to her crying daughter.

'Come on, kiddo,' she said. She reached down and pulled Shelly up by the armpits. Shelly flopped back down on the floor. She picked her up again and held her this time, kneeling down so her face was level with her daughter's. Found a tissue in her pocket and wiped Shelly's face and nose.

'Come on,' she said, holding Shelly's face tightly against her shoulder, 'let's go to daycare.'

Later she pulled Joe's van into a gas station in Inglewood just off Blackfoot Trail. Filled the van's tank and paid with her own credit card. She watched the dollar counter climb and climb on the pump. Winced inside thinking about the number. She imagined all of the next month's bills spread out on the table in front of her, with eighty extra dollars on the credit card balance.

'We'll make it work,' she said to herself, topping up the gas and twisting the fuel cap back into place with a click. 'We'll make eighty bucks work.'

She sat in the idling van, staring at the traffic up ahead on Blackfoot Trail. She put a hand in the pocket of her jeans. Pulled out the single key with the blackened tab of masking tape.

That's Blackfoot Trail right there and then you take the second exit to get Deerfoot northbound. And then Deerfoot Trail takes you right out of the city. Turns into Highway 2 going north. It'll be busy with midweek traffic but not so bad and just stick to the right-hand slow lane and let everyone pass you. Joe's van will be fine. Full tank of gas. Stick to the slow lane and then turn off at Red Deer. Turn off and head west, past Nordegg, and find that Two Reel Lake road. You'll remember the turnoff when you see it.

You'll be up there in three hours. You can get out and have a look. And then you can come straight back. You'll be back to pick Shelly up from daycare just like always. It will just be like you'd spent the day at work. No one will ever know you were gone.

'I just want to see it one last time before they tear it down,' she said to herself, sitting in the van. 'If I can see it, then I'll stop thinking about it. See it one last time and then they'll knock it down and I'll never have to think about it again.'

Her cellphone rang.

She pulled out her little flip-top cellphone and looked at the tiny display screen. The 12th Avenue United Church number. Sometimes Joe Wahl would call her when she had the van if he remembered something extra he needed: pads of paper from the office supply store, or maybe he'd put the wrong quantity of coffee on the list. 'Hey, Audrey, see if you can pick up some fresh fruit,' he might ask.

When he called though, he called from his office, which was a different number. This was the number the Misses from the daycare used.

It rang a few times and she stared at the screen. It vibrated in her hand while it rang. She sat in the idling van, listening to the phone ring and vibrate in her hand.

Then she answered it.

'Miss Cole, Miss Cole. So glad we caught you. It's Shelly, Miss Cole. She is pretty sick again. Throwing up, diarrhea. Like the other day, Miss Cole. Needs to go home. Needs to go home and get better.'

Audrey said, 'Of course, I'll come get her. I'll come get her right now.'

She sat in the idling van for a while, staring out the window, not really looking at anything. After a while she drove out of the parking lot. Headed downtown, toward 12th Avenue, where her daughter was.

§

On Friday, when Shelly was feeling better, Audrey took her to Mirko's. The street in front of the grocery store was full of big suvs parked in the no-parking zone with their hazard lights blinking, people inside lined up for their black kalmata olives and Macedonian sheep feta in brine. Glen sat in his chair with his papers. People came out of Mirko's with their grocery bags and Glen looked expectantly at them, holding up the stack so they could read the masthead.

'Glarpy,' asked Shelly, 'how magic work?'

Glen took a deep breath and puffed out his cheeks. 'That, little miss, is a very serious question for a very little girl. You must be a very serious little girl, yes?'

'How, Glarpy?'

'Shelly, you don't ask how the magic works,' said Audrey. 'That's part of the magic.'

'Well, my serious little girl, the truth is there are different kinds of magic, and they work different ways.' He held up his long yellow fingers and counted on them as he spoke. 'There is the deceptive magic that comes from fairy land like a cold wind and fools people into thinking that things are other than they are, and a clever magician can harness this magic and confuse the senses of people. There is the hungry magic that makes people and things disappear. And there is the cruel magic that transforms people into things other than they used to be.'

'And you do all three?' asked Audrey.

'Your humble practitioner makes small trinkets appear and disappear for the pleasure of his audience.'

He reached out quickly and snatched the knit toque off Shelly's head. Turned the floppy white-and-pink hat over in his hands. There was a kitten face knitted in brown wool on the front, and little wool ears pointed out from the sides. He turned it inside out and held it toward Shelly. A delicate, intricately folded origami rose sat on the wool, made of green and red paper.

'Thank you, Glarpy.'

'Go show Mirko,' said Audrey.

When Shelly was inside, Audrey gave him five dollars.

'Is magic that transforms people into other things always cruel?' she asked.

He took the money and put it in his jacket, then looked at her with an eyebrow cocked. Rooted inside the pocket and gave her a tiny slip of paper – a little photocopied flap that said haveyouseentheskinnycowboy @rocketmail.com. He winked at her and touched the side of his nose.

She took the paper, looking at him cautiously.

'Well?' she asked eventually.

'Miss Cole, although I scrutinized the photograph carefully, I can't say that I recognize the individual depicted.'

'Not someone you've seen around the neighbourhood?'

He shook his head.

'Well,' she said, 'if you see the individual depicted, let me know.'

The bell above Mirko's door rang as people pushed in and out. Couples with plastic bags full of pita bread and olives, of hummus and dried figs. They opened the hatchbacks of their big SUVs with a push-button fob. Loaded up and pulled out onto 12th Avenue. They pulled out, and more SUVs pulled into the just-opened spots. Put on their hazard lights and rushed inside. Glen sat in his chair, holding up his papers, watching them go, not saying anything.

'Most missing people end up in the same place,' Glen said to Audrey.

'Is that so?'

He shrugged. 'Sure, a fair number of unlucky people may just have scored bad dope behind the Cecil Hotel or run afoul of ill-intentioned predators at the 8th and 8th train platform. But taken as a sample and allowing for the proper margin of error, most missing people are on the moon. On the moon against their will.'

Inside she could see Shelly leaning on the glass of the back cooler at the end of an aisle. Mirko Lasko reached into the cooler and pulled out an octopus. Shook it for the little girl, making the tentacles waggle. Shelly put her hands on her face and Audrey could hear her squeal through the closed door.

'The moon,' said Audrey.

'The technology to get to the moon is hundreds of years old. A rocket is a diving bell and a firecracker. Plus trigonometry, and the metallurgical wherewithal to anticipate stresses from pressure and temperature changes minus an atmosphere. Greeks knew the distance to the moon within a few hundred miles centuries before Christ.'

'Missing Greeks are on the moon?'

'The first would-be lunar pilgrim was Averroes. He developed the science of extraterrestrial rocket travel after this insight: the blank moon was a canvas, with an audience of everyone on earth. Writing on it was strictly an engineering problem – there needed to be so many holes and they needed to be placed here and here. Everything else was just scale. He was going to use the moon surface to dispute al-Ghazali on the value of syllogism, but as far as I know never completed the journey.

'Unfortunately for us though, he was not the last would-be moon man to take to this idea. Others with more malicious intentions seized on the concept.' Glen pulled a packet of cigarettes out of his jacket. Lit one up and blew smoke up into the night. 'There are sects with long genealogies devoted to secrets, that pass down esoteric knowledge like so many safety deposit box keys through generations. Some of these traditions keep heresies alive and some protect dead practices through indifferent and hostile times. Some schools teach Latin and some men's clubs pass down the real dimensions of the foundation footings of Solomon's Temple in figures transposable across ages or changing ideas of measurement. But there is an old, evil practice that dwarfs other conspiratorial ambitions.

'There are men who kidnap lost individuals and send them rocket-ways to work camps on the moon, where they will drive backhoes digging trenches to carve a megalithic secret script. The slave-labour inscription of a terrible secret message that stares down at us out of the sky every night.'

Shelly held up her little origami rose and Mirko bent forward over the cooler to examine it. Raised his glasses and nodded appreciatively.

'Disfiguring the entire face of the moon would be a massive undertaking for plate tectonics and interstellar projectiles requiring geological time: attributing these works to human hands seems preposterous. But there is no task that cruelty and time can't achieve together. The Sea of Tranquility and Crater Tycho were dug and raised by forced labour. Generations of lost individuals spirited to our geosynchronous satellite. Given pickaxes and shovels, then dynamite, then steam shovels, and worked to death inscribing designs they could not see or understand into the stone.

'These messages radiate down upon us in the night, reflected by the sun's ambiance and invading our minds like single-frame suggestions in advertising footage. We, uninitiates, do not know the secret moon language. But they allow us to know it in pieces, a word snuck into our attention here, a phrase here, until looking at the moon we unknowingly absorb its message like an unheard dog whistle. The atoms vibrate in waves: the dog hears it and so do we, even if the bones in our ears don't vibrate properly.'

'What does the moon say, Glen?' asked Audrey Cole.

Glen Aarpy tugged his jacket tightly around his shoulders, his cigarette held between his teeth. Rocking in his creaky chair to get more comfortable. Shuffling his boots on the folded panels of cardboard he kept underneath him on the ground, to insulate his feet a little bit from the cold concrete. 'They take us out of the alleys when we're alone. When we're lost and helpless. Out of bus shelters in the night between stops. From stairwells and fire escapes. Phone booths and garages. Then,' and he snapped his fingers loudly, 'bang and upward.' He blew cigarette smoke up into the sky.

12

She grew up in Canmore, high up the Bow River, inside the first ranges of the Rocky Mountains. When her mother baked an angel food cake or a tray of cupcakes, she always adjusted the recipe, changing the baking times according to a faded pencil chart on an index card she kept taped to the inside of a cupboard door.

'The altitude,' she told Audrey. 'They write these recipes at sea level. Things change 4,500 feet farther up in the air.'

She remembered mornings growing up when the sky dropped down. White puffs of cloud pulled themselves down and roamed low in front of the mountains. White puffs floating past the green pine trees, their wispy edges made real by the contrast.

Some mornings the mountains vanished altogether. The sky dropped and the town and the mountains surrounding it disappeared in white.

Audrey looked out a window at the Crash Palace into a white Sunday morning. The sky had dropped and taken everything away. Somewhere east the sun must have risen, east of Red Deer, east of Alberta. Outside her window, a little of the light that the rising sun made found its way into the dropped sky and the snow inside it. She watched the flakes swirl in the wind one way and another. White snow to join the thick white sheath skinning Two Reel Lake, the valley around it, the stones and trees inside. She was inside the sky now. The earlier snows had been only the open mouth and teeth, inverted, widening around her. This was the interior, through and down the throat. Inside the white belly of the sky.

§

She pressed buttons on her phone and it didn't say anything because the battery was dead. She sat folded over on the mattress, forearms resting on her knees, looking unfocusedly at the dead phone.

'Kitten,' she said. 'Kitten, it's Sunday morning and I left home Friday night and it's still snowing.'

Her head hurt. A full sinus-choked hurt that ran from the back of her throat outward and up. She felt her glands. She pinched the bridge of her nose. Her neck ran sore from the base of her skull down into either side, the linkages between each set of muscles strained and wrong. Where her head had snap-stopped by the Audi seat belt. Under her arms and shoulder blades where she fit improperly on the couch.

Her nose was too clogged to tell but she knew she must stink. Woodsmoke and sleeping in the same clothes. Hard work and no baths. Her hair was thickened and tangled and stood out sideways when she ran her hands into it.

The rack beside the cold fireplace was empty, all of the wood turned into ash and smoke. The cold now all the way inside the room, radiating from the floors and windows, out of the chimney flue, oblivious to her dead-sometime-in-the-night fire.

Someone must have noticed all the smoke, she thought. Surely they'd see the smoke, and when they did their plow route they'd come to have a look.

They'll call to make sure everybody's all right and we'll tell them that we'll be all right.

She put the Dungeons & Dragons books into the fireplace and lit a fire. Muscled barbarians with longswords, floating disembodied eyes, women with black Vampirella hair in slinky dresses, holding green-and-blue flames in their hands. Caught quickly and the pages burnt and curled. She opened a can of chickpeas and ate it watching the little fire. The books burned fast, too thin to keep a flame, curling and twisting into ashes. Smoked and went out before she could finish her cold breakfast.

'Kitten,' she called out into the empty room. 'Here, Kitten. We've still got a fire here. Still got a fire. Come on out, Kitten.'

She went upstairs and looked into rooms, remembering her tour yesterday. Found a dirty old quilt and a fuzzy Hudson's Bay blanket. She found a balled-up University of Alberta sweater and pulled it over her head. Then she came back downstairs and tore up the other paperbacks, feeding the cheap paper into the fire. Blew at the embers to try and save a match until they caught.

'The snow can't last all day, Kitten. We'll stay here, stay warm, wait for the weather to break.'

She tried to remember if there was a restaurant in the village. They'd sell hot coffee in the gas station. Plastic-wrapped submarine sandwiches: egg salad, ham and Swiss. They'd let her make a phone call.

How'd you get out here anyway without a vehicle? they'd ask. She tested answers in her head, chewing cold chickpeas.

She picked up one of the wooden chairs. Not too heavy. She carried it up the stairs to the second floor. She lifted it onto the railing. Balanced it for a moment, then let it fall over the side. The chair fell and crashed into splinters on the hard floor.

She turned the chair wreckage into a fire. Sat feeding the flames and watching the wood blacken and slowly turn to cherry-red coals.

Audrey watched the fire, thinking about when she'd need to break up another chair.

'Kitten, the cold is in here with us but you've already lived through worse, right? The cold is in our blood and it's making me slow and stupid. But you've survived and so will I, right? I'm going to get confused and slow as I get colder, Kitten. That's what happens. But we can't make that walk in this snow. We'll get you to Shelly and she'll be so happy to see you. But we can't leave yet. Not until the wind dies down. So we'll just keep the fire burning. Right, Kitten?'

She got on her hands and knees and looked under the couch for the little reflective eyes.

'I thought I saw the Skinny Cowboy, Kitten, who is a shitty junkie who reminds me of this other shitty junkie and that got me thinking about other shitty people I've met and all those step-by-steps that make up life and you mostly just coast downhill in neutral not thinking about these things, Kitten, because what happens if you do? You coast downhill not thinking too much about any of it and any given time there's enough happening out the window to keep your mind away from it all. Most of the time.

'I'll get home and I'll tell Mom all about it. She never asked but I'll finally tell her all about it when I get home.'

She turned around and sat on the cold floor with her back against the couch. Reached into her pocket and took out the key. She held the front-door key of the Crash Palace in her cupped-together hands. Just an old key with a smudged-black square of masking tape on it that someone left for her in an envelope. Came to her house and gave to her mother. Came to give to her.

'I know, Kitten,' she said. 'What did I think was going to happen?' She put the key back into her pocket. 'We'll just keep the fire going until the wind stops, Kitten. Then we'll start walking. Then we'll get you home to Shelly, Kitten.'

§

She went upstairs then to the fifth floor, down the other hall to the bedroom. Opened the door and stood in the doorway, leaning on the jamb. A big room, much bigger than the little rooms on the third and fourth floors. Big windows looking out westward across the valley. On a clear day up here you could see the easternmost tips of the Rockies poking up above the pine-covered ridges of the high foothills. Today they were inside the white belly of the sky though. Just white snow blowing across the frozen white lake top.

There was just an old king-sized bed frame and a couple of wooden chairs. Everything else – even the mattress – gone. No dresser, no mattress, no bedsheets. No lamp, no clothes, no books on the bookshelf, no bookshelf. No flowerpots, with no dried-up little stick remains of the plants she'd brought up from around the building over the six months she'd lived here. She turned around and closed the door.

She brought down all the paper from Alex's office. Mostly it was loose in cardboard filing boxes. She burned all the paper in the fireplace.

At first she read while she burned. Receipts for liquor, groceries. Case of vodka, six 750 millilitre bottles at $18.99 per. Six 700 millilitre bottles of blended Scotch at $24.99 per. Twelve cases of twenty-four beer bottles. Invoices for boxes of soda syrup and invoices for the bottled gas to blend and deliver it. Lemons, limes, oranges. Four-inch straws, eight-inch straws, square napkins, kraft paper napkins. Contractor bills for painting, dropped-ceiling installation, plumbing.

Audrey sat there with paper in either hand. It was just boring. She hadn't expected that it would all just be boring.

She opened a box and it was full of little notepads. She knew right away: the exact size and shape. She took one out and opened it. A little graph-paper notepad. Each page the same five columns: a date; initials; a column of letters – c, h, cm, mdma; then a quantity in grams or milligrams; and then a dollar amount. Anywhere from twenty to a few hundred dollars for each item. All crammed in the same tight, messy pencil printing.

There were dozens of little graph-paper notebooks, all the same. The earliest date she found was in 2001 and the latest she could find was for 2007.

She looked for names. But they weren't that stupid. No names, not Alex's name, not Gurt's name. Certainly not any name that might have been the Skinny Cowboy's. Just quantities, grams and milligrams.

She stopped reading and just fed the notepads into the fire. She burned all the notepads and then started burning all the other paper, staff schedules, band-booking calendars, pages of phone numbers, lists of email addresses. The paper crumpled and burned quickly and the thin ash it made blew up the flue and piled in the hearth.

Her fire smoked up the chimney, and outside the smoke disappeared into the snow.

'Kitten,' she said into the empty room. 'Kitten, it's all boring and it must have always been boring and everything it turned into is boring and I'm dying of hypothermia a long way from my daughter. My daughter doesn't know where I am, Kitten.'

The kitten wasn't around and Audrey cried for a few minutes, sitting on the cold floor. She cried softly sitting there, sniffling, and felt the cold climb up into her legs and feet. Then she hauled her tired body up off the ground and stood in front of the fire that was already dying down.

She dropped another chair from the top floor.

13

She found him on the stairs in the morning. Rodney lay face down on the stairs with his wrist under his forehead, his other hand reached up and hung on the lip of the next step. She came down the stairs and saw him below her just around the last landing. Audrey put her hand on his neck and he was cold. She stood and wrapped her hands around her shoulders. Her chest surged with the need to do quick, sudden things, to run and yell and move as quickly as she could, and her mind tamped these feelings down and she sat down and tried to catch her breath. She checked his neck again to make sure she was right and she was. Clammy and cold. His skin felt dense, the blood behind it already thick and stiff.

His wrist under his skull maybe to protect it from the stone, if he had fallen, or maybe she thought it looked more like he'd lowered himself, lowered and carefully arranged himself for what little comfort there was to be had on the cold stone steps when he knew he couldn't climb any more of them.

'Rodney, you did a lot of hard things in your life, and staying alive should have been the least of them,' she said to him.

Koop found her on the steps, sitting with her arms wrapped around her knees. He put his box of juice bottles down and touched Rodney's neck in the same place she had.

'How long?' he asked her.

'Me, probably ten minutes. But him, I don't know. How long does it take to get cold like that?'

Koop sat down on the step beside her. He pulled a package of cigarettes out of his chest pocket and tapped the bottom with two tight fingers to pop one free. He lit a match. Blew a thick cloud of blue smoke into the white morning air. The match burned down to his fingertips and out, and he held it pinched while he smoked. 'It'll get loud. Loud and complicated. Right away. Really loud and really complicated.'

Audrey nodded. 'I know. I wanted a bit of time before that started.'

'Sure,' said Koop. He was stretched on the steps under the first landing, not far from the main floor, and people came down the stairs in the morning as they woke and found Audrey and Koop. Koop stood and directed people, moving most of them down the stairs, taking the elbows or shoulders of people who wanted to stand and stare or who asked questions or displayed emotions, moved them down the steps and away, before they could perform a question or put their hands in their hair. He prevented a crowd from forming on the landing as best he could. Hector Highwater sat down on the step beside Audrey, and Wrists leaned against the wall, looking anywhere but at people's faces – out the window or up into the ceiling – and everyone smoked and the air thickened with cigarettes, a cloud that hung in the crowd and got in eyes and throats.

Alex Main came downstairs and sat cross-legged beside Rodney. Put his hand in the same place on the throat. Two fingers like Koop used to pop his cigarettes out of the packet.

Koop moved the crowd away except for some allowed-to-be-there people, and this allowed-to-be-there group grew until they blocked the landing, and people coming down stopped on the stairs above them, backed up like traffic behind an accident on a bridge.

'We have to call the police.'

'Oh, man.'

'Get an ambulance up here.'

'Now hold on.'

'The fuck? Hold on, Alex.'

'I don't want the police here.'

'He's dead, Alex. A cold corpse.'

'They can't get an ambulance up here in any kind of time.'

'They'll send a plow if there's an emergency.'

'What does he need an ambulance for?'

'Because he's dead.'

'They'll send the police with a plow.'

'Alex,' said the big man in the black leather vest, 'no police. No ambulances. Nothing with a siren.'

He'd appeared on the landing and stood with his arms crossed over his chest, staring at Alex. Then he turned and stared at Wrists.

Wrists scrunched his face, swallowing something he meant to say. Then he did a funny thing. He spread his fingers wide at the big man and said, 'Poof.'

Wrists turned to Alex and said, 'We don't need an ambulance.'

'What are you going to do,' asked Alex, 'pack him in the van? Up on top of the drum hardware? Where are you delivering him to?'

'It's Rodney Levermann,' Wrists said. 'What's he going back to?'

Wrists walked down the stairs. People in the crowd tried to ask or start conversations or begin questions and he pushed past them with his shoulder and walked out the door.

'Where's he going? Hey, somebody go talk to him.'

'I'm getting the phone.'

'Nobody's phoning anybody. Everybody, just chill out. I've got to think.'

'For Christ's sake, Alex. Rodney is dead. He's dead and all you can think about –'

'No one is phoning anybody until we get this figured out,' said Alex Main.

Audrey sat against the wall with her arms wrapped around her knees, and beside her Hector Highwater smoked a cigarette down to the filter and lit another. His forehead lay on his wrist where he'd landed or placed it, she thought. He put it there for softness on the cold step. The cigarette smoke made her mouth dry and phlegmy and she wanted to hack and spit.

She looked around for the skinny silver-haired man in the cowboy hat she'd talked to the night before. She felt like he'd know what they ought to do. But she didn't see him anywhere.

Downstairs, the door opened and Wrists came inside. He walked up the stairs carrying a steel toolbox in one hand and a crowbar in the other.

He must have gone out to the shed, thought Audrey. He walked past the knot of people standing around Rodney's body.

'Hey, Wrists,' said Alex. 'Wrists, hold on.'

He pushed through the crowd up the stairs and they watched Wrists walk to the top of the landing, then to the double ballroom doors. He pushed the door open with a shoulder.

'Hey, Wrists,' shouted Alex. 'Shit.' He ran up the stairs, two steps at a time. They all followed him. Audrey stood and followed the crowd up the steps to the open ballroom door.

In the ballroom, Wrists stood on top of the stage. He knelt and opened the toolbox. He had a framing hammer and the crowbar. He put his weight on a bent knee and set the crowbar tooth on the floor at the seam of two boards.

'Hey, Wrists, come on, we've got to figure out what we're going to do. Don't fuck around, it's a distraction,' said Alex Main.

'You're the one doesn't want any cops,' said Wrists. 'Doesn't want any cops or ambulances.'

'Wrists, what are you doing?'

'Well, Alex, I apologize, but I'm going to pull up a lot of these floor-boards.'

'The hell you are. Why on earth?'

Wrists raised the hammer and Alex took a first two running steps toward him. He ran and Audrey jumped, tackled him in the midsection like he was a running back, and the two of them sprawled onto the ground. Alex threw her off, startled, and got to his feet, but she was up first, and she reached and bunched her hand in his shirt, and before he knew what was happening she hit him in the face with a closed fist. She'd never hit anyone, and the jolt of his solid cheek shocked her arm up to the shoulder. His head snapped back and he staggered to the ground. Her hand throbbed in hot pain right to her collarbone and someone grabbed her from behind and pulled her arms around behind her.

'What the hell?' muttered Alex from the ground, holding his cheek.

She meant to say something but had no words. Someone else worked their arms behind her and separated her from whoever had held her originally, and she stepped away, her hand pulsing in bright pain. She didn't turn to see who either of these people were.

Alex looked up at her from the ground, eyebrows up in bafflement. 'I just need a second to think is all,' he said.

'Like I say, I apologize,' said Wrists. He lifted the hammer and hit the crowbar's tooth into the stage, one swing. Stood and, leaning, pried up one of the floorboards. He pried it up at one end, then further into the middle of the board, then further until he could bring it up whole. He stood holding the long pine floorboard, painted black on top, bright pine on the sides and underneath, staring at the floor, thinking.

'Dick,' he said, 'I need you to go to the shed out there. There are a couple of sawhorses. Bring those up here. The sawhorses and the circular saw. It's up on one of the shelves, and there's an extension cord hanging on the pegboard, I think I saw.'

'Sure thing, Dallas,' said Dick Move.

By the time Dick brought the saw and sawhorses, Wrists had pulled up several armfuls of narrow floorboards, exposing the thicker blond two-by-ten floor joists underneath. He plugged the saw into the orange extension cord and Dick ran it over into the wall. The blade whirled up, loud, and Wrists cut into the joist, spitting sawdust out behind him, sawed out a two-foot length of wood. Dick brought the sawhorses up onto the stage and they laid a long thin floorboard across them. People smoked and stood or sat quietly, and Audrey wanted to sit down on the floor but didn't. Koop went to the bar and picked out a bottle of whisky.

Wrists laid floorboards across the sawhorses and cut. He cut them into seven-foot lengths, eyeballing as best he could without a tape measure, which he laid down on the stage. Koop brought the bottle through the crowd and people drank from the mouth while they watched Wrists work. When the bottle was empty, he went back for another. The air filled up with sawdust, the smell and the dust up in their noses and settling on people's shoulders and heads like snow.

He laid four of the cut floorboards flush together and three of the thicker joist lengths perpendicular across these. Made a pencil mark on either side of each joist and then cut these with the saw to the width of his four floorboards. Laid them back across at rib intervals, then found short nails in the toolbox and started to nail it all together.

'What do you want for runners?' asked Dick.

'Let's cut some longer stretches of the floor joists,' Wrists said, and Dick nodded.

They pulled up more floorboards and people watched, taking the bottle from Koop when he brought it around. Alex Main sat on the floor watching and took the bottle from Koop for a long pull. His cheek already turned red. Audrey didn't sit down on the floor like she wanted to, and she took the bottle from Koop and the whisky was hot and made her mouth water.

They cut longer lengths of joist from the floor, two six-foot pieces, and laid these flat-ways on either side of their project, then hammered them into the ribs. They each took an end and flipped it over, the runners on the bottom now, sitting on the sawhorses. A simple sledge, with high sides. Or a coffin on sled runners. The same thing, Audrey supposed.

'Dick, Hector. Let's go get some firewood out there on the lake.'

'Sure thing, Dallas,' said Hector.

§

The sun went down at six and they carried chairs down to the beach while the last blue light pulled back behind the easternmost black peaks. Chairs and stools from the mezzanine and ballroom. Folding chairs from the third and fourth floors, a couple of rolling desk chairs from Alex's office, wooden dining chairs. Two teenagers carried a loveseat from the parlour. They sat in their chairs wrapped in sweaters and blankets.

Wrists pulled the sledge by a length of rope looped around the front-most slat. He walked forward across the ice while everyone on the shore stayed quiet. He leaned forward, pulling the sledge, leaving a flat, wide wake pressed into the snow behind him. The lean and the wake showed them the weight, wrapped up in white bedsheets, bound up with grey gaffer tape, at the shoulders, waist, hips, knees. He must have done the wrapping alone, away from everyone: no one had seen him at this task.

In the middle of the lake the pyre waited, a dark mound against the grey surface. Wrists and Dick and Hector had carried wood from the shed out before the sun went down, back and forth, each with an armful stacked up chin-high, and then they laid out a bed of split logs and cross-hatched the top with kindling and stuffed the seams with splinters. Now Wrists was there and he knelt and struggled the sledge with its burden up onto the pyre. There was a red jerry can, which he uncapped and lifted, splashing everything in gasoline.

'Somebody should say some kind of prayer,' said Dick Move on the shore. 'He'd have wanted a prayer.'

'Rodney was the only guy I knew could find something useful to say in a circumstance like this,' said one of the women with the Bettie Page haircuts.

'Amen,' said Hector.

Wrists backed away from the pyre and crouched. Then a flash: a sparkler candle, spitting sparks. He tossed it forward and white-yellow light burst up ten feet. White and yellow and orange in the deepening blue-grey night. Wrists backed slowly away from the blaze, then crouched, watching. The flames made yellow edges pulse around his black silhouette.

Audrey stood at the lakeside with her arms hugged around her shoulders. She stood shivering and then turned around to see Alex Main carrying a couple of wooden chairs. He set them down close to each, and he had a thick wool blanket that he flapped out and spread over the chairs. His chin was red where she'd hit him. Red like the knuckles she'd hit him with.

He stood beside the chairs, waiting. She looked at the chairs and the quilt and then back out at the fire on the ice.

'Fine,' said Alex Main. 'Freeze standing there.'

She sat down and he sat down next to her. Pulled the blanket over her shoulders. She could feel the heat of him underneath the itchy fabric.

The fire burned and burned and the people on the shore watched the flames or stared up into the sky or spoke in hushed voices to the closest person until a crash raised everyone's attention, when the ice, softened from the heat, gave way under wood and body weight, and the pyre dropped into the cold water. A huge hiss choked out the flames, and steam and smoke billowed into the grey-and-blue night.

Her breath caught and she choked it and sat up as straight as she could, blinking, not looking at him beside her, even though she felt him staring.

She watched Wrists walking toward them, away from the steaming hole in the ice. He closed the hundred yards and stepped off the ice onto the snow-slick rock beach without breaking stride. He walked past the crowd in their chairs without slowing or looking at anyone. Up the beach and between the arms of the Crash Palace. They sat wrapped in blankets and sweaters and then someone stood up, and they folded or lifted their chairs and followed Wrists into the building.

'I guess Koop will be busy tonight,' she said.

He nodded and the quilt around her moved with his shoulders.

'He'll need a hand,' she said.

'He'll be fine,' Alex said.

They sat together under the blanket, staring out at the steam rising out of the hole in Two Reel Lake.

'This was their last stop,' he said after a while. 'The road gets plowed out, you're going to drive them back to Calgary. Take Dick to work. Take Wrists back to his ex-wife and his daughter. What then?'

She didn't know, she realized. She imagined standing somewhere in Calgary, handing the van keys back to Wrists. Her Honda Civic somewhere in the airport parking lot still, covered in snow. Her unopened termination letter from Moose Leg at her parents' house in Canmore.

She thought about the drive up Highway 11 to Two Reel Lake. About all the side roads she'd passed on the way. A whole alternate series of overlay worlds, little gravel-covered portals like from science-fiction or comic books, trap doors into secret places. All she'd need to do was get the Honda Civic up here. She'd already learned how to make Caesars and Manhattans. Get her baby up here and make Caesars and Manhattans to keep the tank filled.

'I don't know,' she said. 'I hadn't thought that far.'

'Well, don't think about it now.'

'Okay,' she said, and didn't.

14

Yellow eyes watched her through the window. The little kitten sat outside in the night, on its haunches on top of the rain barrel, watching Audrey through the glass.

'Kitten. What are you doing back out there? How'd you manage that? Come inside. Come on.'

She walked slowly toward the glass, made each step as gradual as possible. The kitten stiffened and stood. Audrey stopped and waited. The kitten looked over its shoulder, then back at her. It padded across the barrel lid to the window. Audrey reached out and touched her index finger to the cold smooth surface. The kitten swung up a paw. It bumped the tiny grey pad against the glass and could not close the last distance to Audrey's fingertip.

Audrey tapped her finger and the kitten mirrored her movement. 'Hold on right there and I'll go get the door. We'll get you back inside.'

A coyote walked into the circle of window light and stopped a few feet behind the rain barrel. Rusty brown fur shot and mottled grey, its tongue hanging out of long, scruffy jaws. Audrey stared, stiff, her finger still pointed into the windowpane at the little kitten. The coyote leaned into its feet and walked toward the window. Audrey smacked both of her palms loudly on the glass. The kitten scampered backward. The coyote lifted itself up to the barrel top on its front paws, opened its mouth, and shut its jaws around the back of the kitten's neck. It turned around with the kitten dangling from its teeth and walked back across the snow, out of the window light into the dark. Audrey stood with her palms flat on the cold glass, her mouth open, watching the bushy tail disappear into the night.

She pulled herself up the stairs two at a time, grabbing the brass bannister for another limb of force in each step. Around and up each landing into the dark top of the building.

The case at the back of Alex Main's office was locked. She jiggled it back and forth. She turned and shoved paper off the desktop. Found a brass letter opener. She dug at the lock with the tip and nothing happened.

She wrapped her hands around the office chair and lifted, hoisted it up by the arms. She put it on the desk for balance and got a better grip around the stem between the seat and legs. Lifted it and took a breath. She bent her knees and then threw the chair up out of a lunge and it did not fly like she wanted, but it hit the window hard enough and the glass shattered. The pane cracked and split and the chair and long sharp glass shards fell down on the ground. She squeezed her eyes shut at the impact and didn't flinch, still forward in the momentum of her throw. Stood and waited a moment after the crash had finished and she was not cut. No shards stuck in her arms, no shrapnel cut her cheek or forehead.

She took a leather-bound ledger off the desk and used the spine to smash out the teeth of glass still standing in the cabinet walls.

The rifles were not locked or chained, and she took the longest from the centre. Heavy and solid, smooth wood and cold to the touch. Too heavy. She put it back and took a slimmer one, a shorter barrel, less mass in the stock and body. She raised it up into her shoulder. Shut an eye and looked down the barrel. Felt the trigger. She pulled back the bolt and the chamber was empty. She leaned the rifle and looked in the cabinet. She opened drawers in Alex's desk where she knew she'd seen them, and found a cardboard box of bullets. She loaded three brass rifle rounds into the magazine.

Outside on the ice, snow blew into her face, lifted up off the lake, and flung into her cheeks and eyes. The thick low sky screened and limited the moonlight and she squinted into the dark. No details, only shapes: where the far shore stood above the lake, where the sky zippered in and out of the treetops. She carried the heavy rifle forty-five degrees across her chest like an oar. Her feet sank into drifts as she walked out across the lake. The sharp snow crust bit her ankles and calves when she lifted her feet out of the snow. She stared ahead into grey and paler grey shapes. She watched for the eyes. Was there enough light for them to reflect? If she were incapacitated they would know. A wrong step and a twisted ankle. If she fell or sank, they would understand, no matter how far off they were. They'd slip out of the dark and pour down and over in a flash. Oily fur and strong stringy muscles, bright teeth, sudden in the dark.

She knelt on the ice and laid the rifle across her thighs. The cold shot up from the ice into the balls of her feet and knees and into and through her. She held the cold wood and metal tightly against her chest and shivered.

It walked into her peripheral vision from behind. Strolling twenty yards to her left. She lifted up off the ice, the muscles in her thighs shaking. She shook from the cold and the size of the world behind her. Just the one. It just rolled right up to the window and closed its jaws. A mother might pick up her baby by the little scruff where the coyote had bitten. Audrey raised the rifle and she was shaking and had to lower it back down for the longest, deepest breaths she could manage. The coyote stopped and looked back over its shoulder at her. She raised the rifle up to her cheek.

Squeezed the trigger and the barrel jerked, stock kicking back into her shoulder socket. Yellow light sudden in the dark, and the *bang crack* burst and whipped back from the hillsides. Straight back into the ball of her shoulder, yellow light flashing through the backs of her eyes, and her feet slid out from under her. She fell hard on the ice, the yellow thunderclap and burst of pain all the same sensation. The coyote bolted and she heard yelps behind and the sound of paws running in the snow. She turned, ears ringing white after light splashed on her eyes, and they were running in different directions. Three four five. From behind her. Paw prints in the snow, scattered where they'd wheeled and turned ten feet behind her. The crack-back echo in her ears. The coyotes howled and she lifted herself onto her knees. She pulled back the bolt and the shell kicked out, flew hot past her cheek. A hard smack in her shoulder, harder on her hip, a bruise blossom throbbing on the bone ball. She shook, and yowling echoed off the valley bowl sides out and back. She stood shaking and coyotes ran across the ice fifty yards from her. She put the stock in her sore hot shoulder and the barrel down her squint sight shook widely in her hands. She followed the running coyotes with the barrel eye squeezed and could not grip the shake tightly enough. *Yowl crack snap* echoing off the hills.

She limped across the ice, stopping at five or eight steps to turn with the rifle at her hip, sweeping the barrel through an arc of lake top and grey shore shape. They howled sometimes and she stopped walking to swing the barrel held at her hip in the direction. Howled there on the lake against the pale grey treetops. Audrey walked ten, thirteen steps and planted her feet. A coyote watched at eighty yards. She pointed the barrel and it howled in the night. Squeezed her hands around the oiled wood and iron. Planted her feet into the snow, and icy water soaked her feet and stung her toe tips and ankle balls. Her pants wet and heavy stuck to her legs halfway up her shins.

A coyote at forty metres moving her way and she pulled the trigger at hip height, the rifle jerking backward in her hands. White light crack and the coyote leaped and ran. The rifle yanked in her hands like a tug-of-war rope. The *bang* hard in her eyes, the smell of burnt powder in her sinuses, lit up in her head with white light flint. The bullet sang and disappeared into the blowing snow like music.

What did you think was going to happen, Audrey?

On the shore she stood and shook, slumped shoulders dragged downward by the rifle weight. Pain throbbed in her ass and back from the hard ice. She turned around to look at the Crash Palace. Two trigger pulls and three rounds in the magazine. She pulled the rifle bolt a third time. Raised the barrel and fired at the building. Through the blast she heard a window break. The noises echoed and she heard glass shards falling into snow. She walked back toward the building through these sounds.

15

On the sidewalk, Marnie was tearing down posters. Someone had covered the entire plywood wall around the hole with a letter-sized black-and-white Xerox handbill. She'd leaned her bicycle and satchel against the No Parking sign and was tearing the papers down two at a time with either hand. Crumpled them up and threw them over the wall into the hole.

Audrey stood and read one of the remaining handbills and it said:

ONE NIGHT ONLY
Marvel at the Magical
SUE FATHER featuring THE FATHERS
with Special Guest
ELLA VAVUE

There was an address and a date: next Friday.

Sue Father. The name rattled around in her head, ringing around memories that wouldn't quite come together. She tore a handbill free from its staples, folded it, and slipped it into her jacket. Up the block, Marnie pulled handfuls of posters down, tearing the paper out of the staples, crumpling and throwing them into the hole.

'Why don't you just cover them over?' Audrey asked.

Marnie stopped and looked at Audrey, a crumpled piece of paper in either hand.

'Got to make an example,' she said. 'Keep other people from getting the same idea.'

§

She stopped for a slice of pizza. Ducked into a little by-the-slice place on First Street, the size of a coat-check alcove. The man behind the counter got her a slice of Hawaiian pizza out from the rotating tray under a hot lamp in a glass box. It was cardboardy and she stood at the counter chewing it.

She took the poster out of her jacket. Double-checked the address. Just a few blocks from here. She finished the pizza and put the poster back into her jacket.

She crossed 9th and 8th Avenue, heading north. Checked the poster again and then walked into an alley, looking around garbage bins and restaurant grease traps, looking for numbers on doors. Doors were propped open and men and women in kitchen whites sat on overturned ice buckets smoking. Steam heat and white light from inside their tile kitchens lit the alley. She walked down the street and a car rumbled past her. A man and woman inside looked right and left for a parking spot.

Ahead of her, a giant came out of a shadow. He stood up from a little folding chair, above a flickering light, and she smelled propane. He was giant height, six foot five, but skinny, all head and neck, and wore a reflective green vest over his black fleece sweater. He leaned down to the car and Audrey heard him say, 'Seven dollars you park all night. Or just dinner five dollars two hours.' He stood and pointed down a ramp incline to an enclosed lot and the car drove around the tight corner.

Audrey unfolded the poster. 'I'm looking for this address,' she told the giant.

He nodded. Reached behind and banged on a steel door. It opened and let red light into the alley.

'Have a good time,' said the giant.

She walked down a concrete staircase into a low-ceilinged room, hot with a crowd. A brick-and-black-plaster basement full of people, sitting in rows of folding chairs, two hundred packed in a space small enough to put all of their chatter and laughter into everyone's ears at once. Teenagers in black with gloves, silver jewellery, and thick mascara, men and women in tailored suits and dresses with silver hair and severe, expensive eyeglasses, old men with lank hair and trench coats, sitting by themselves. A man in wire glasses had a camera on a tripod by the brick wall, tightening and loosening the nuts that controlled the angles. Audrey walked through the crowd and the seats were taken, couples and threes and fours, people chatting over red plastic cups of beer and clear plastic glasses of wine. At the front there was a single seat in the middle of the front row. She sat and was close enough to see the scratches and shoe scuffs in the stage surface. She looked for seams in the floor, for borders or hinges. The stage was empty, no set, just a long straight microphone stand, a black curtain across the back wall. The stage lights had coloured gels, orange and red and purple, and made white light where the cones intersected, white light fringed in purple and red and orange.

The crowd got quiet for the show to start.

Ella Vavue wore a polka-dot bandana tied around her coal-black hair. When she smiled, the stage lights made her red lipstick and cheeks brighter and redder than they may have been off the stage.

Audrey leaned forward and stretched her neck. She tried to see back into the wings, around the side of the curtain. She looked from side to side at the aisles.

A stagehand in head-to-toe black ran out with a decorative tripod table and a brass birdcage, all cast curlicues and leaf details. Set these up for Ella Vavue and then backed quickly off into the wings. Ella Vavue produced a red satin cloth and waggled it in front of the cage, then draped it top to bottom. She spread her fingers and waved her hands. Then pulled the cloth away.

The cage was empty. Surprise registered on Ella's face, and she did nothing for a moment. Then she caught herself. Too late, thought Audrey, we saw. We saw that look. Ella Vavue smiled at the crowd and covered the cage again. Her repeated gestures larger and more exaggerated this time. When she pulled off the cloth, a little sparrow chirped inside. People in the crowd shifted and their chairs creaked. People looked at the screens of their cellphones.

A bushy-bearded man in a black T-shirt came to the microphone when she had finished her routine. 'Ladies and gentlemen, Sue Father and the Fathers will be on shortly.'

Audrey twisted in her seat, looking around the room. You should have brought Glen Aarpy, she thought to herself. He could have grumbled to himself and later explained how all the tricks were done. She looked around to see if he was back there in the crowd somewhere, but of course he wasn't. Just expectant faces watching the stage.

Down the row, a woman stood up. She had hollow cheeks and dark shadows under her eyes and wore a washing-machine grey T-shirt with holes around the neck and hem. She squeezed out of the row, excusing herself, and then she put her hands on the stage and hoisted herself awkwardly up with a grunt.

She walked into the middle of the stage and wrapped her hands around the long straight microphone stand. And now she was tall and sheer and wore a tight black suit, with perfect straight seams, and a skinny black tie over a half-untucked white shirt. Her black leather boot heels clicked loudly on the wooden stage. She had hollow cheeks and dark shadows under her eyes. Audrey shook her head and blinked. She looked back and forth for the other woman, and the people sitting next to her did the same. Then the crowd exhaled and the auditorium broke into loud applause. The woman onstage nodded and adjusted the silver microphone. People clapped and whistled, and in the tight basement the noise crashed and grew until she held up a hand and snapped her fingers, and the crowd was silent.

'Everyone, I'd like you to please meet the band.'

The curtain pulled back and it was not flush against the back wall like Audrey thought but showed an alcove with a raised floor, on which seven men in black suits stood or sat. An upright bass, a piano, an organist with banks of keys on two sides. Two guitarists, a baritone saxophone, a trumpet, and a drum kit. The crowd clapped and the drummer stick-clicked a four count and they rolled into a tight twelve bars, gunslinger accents, flatted suspended chords, tremolo, and they built steam and volume while the crowd clapped until she held up a hand and they cut out.

'I'll start small and work my way up,' she said.

She showed them all a deck of cards. Held up a card and showed the face to the crowd: the four of diamonds. She placed it in the air and let it go and it stayed there, hanging. She stepped away and put the king of clubs in the air beside it. The two of hearts, jack of spades, six of spades, all hanging in the air above the stage. Then she snapped her fingers loudly and they disappeared.

The crowd inhaled sharply and then clapped.

She freed a cloud of butterflies from the inside pocket of her jacket, and it flew around the room making shapes in the air – a heart, a lightning bolt, a star – that flew around the stage where she pointed, and flew back into her pocket.

She found a bottle in her hat and uncorked it and it sang a song in a cherubic mezzo soprano.

She made little flames appear on the tips of her outspread fingers, and they bounced and danced and twirled.

For three-quarters of an hour she did things that seemed simple, that took the audience a few moments to wrap around the impossibility of. She pointed to members of the crowd and they discovered flowers in their pockets. She made a little rainstorm. She pulled an icicle out of a glass of water, then turned it into a sunflower. She commanded their attention with her eyes and hands and drew applause from them exactly when she wanted. The band honked and vamped along, comping along in the lead-ups and ringing big chords and brass flourishes for reveals. The crowd clapped and people stood up and sat down. They flashed photographs with their cellphones. Audrey sat and watched.

Sue Father stepped back and held an arm out for the band, who picked up tempo and volume. The baritone player stepped forward and took an outside solo, honking and strangling, overblowing the notes and picking uncomfortable pitches that made people shift in their seats. The guitar ran through unpleasant tritone scales and people looked at each other in discomfort. They traded off these increasingly dissonant solos for a long time and people gripped their chairs.

Sue Father raised a hand then and the music cut cleanly like she'd pulled a cord. The band stood stock-still, posed where she'd stopped them.

'Ladies and gentlemen, you have been an appreciative crowd,' she said, 'which is all anyone can expect of anyone. That they be generous and appreciative.'

Then she disappeared.

The audience sat as quietly as they could, packed together on folding chairs, too many of them for the basement theatre. They watched the empty space on the stage where she'd disappeared, waiting. Behind, the band stood frozen like mimes. Everyone waited and someone sneezed, loud and stark.

Someone clapped then, and, taking it as permission, they all did.

They applauded for a long time, on their feet. Audrey sat forward with her elbows on her thighs, watching the stage. Around her the applause slowed down. Some people sat down and some people stayed on their feet, clapping, the sound of which grew thin and sporadic. People sat back down or reached back to lift their jackets from chair backs, pulled toques and earmuffs onto their heads, purse straps over shoulders, mitts, gloves. People left in bunches and many people stayed sitting, watching the stage, or whispered to the person in the next seat.

Audrey shifted back and her fold-down seat creaked. She watched the stage, which the band had not left. They still stood where they were, did not pull the instrument cables out of their guitars and wrap them into loops around their elbows. They did not twist the mouthpieces off saxophones, or spin the wing nuts up off each cymbal stand. No one opened a case to put anything back inside. They stood where they had stopped, looking out toward the crowd, orange and yellow stage lights hot on their damp faces. Their faces were wet and none of them had opened their white shirt collars or loosened their black ties. None of them had taken off their black suit jackets.

None of them moved at all, but stayed frozen, like mimes, where she'd made them stop.

A couple in fur-collared ski jackets squeezed past the knees out of their row, up the aisle and out of the theatre. Everyone else stayed sitting, each conversation finished. Everyone watched the men onstage.

'Is she coming back?' someone nearby whispered.

Someone applauded again. A few people clapped and then they all did, the whole theatre, and then the band broke their pose, they smiled and shook out of the tableau, they raised their instruments, turned to one another, shaking hands and joking. The baritone player raised his saxophone up off the strap toward the crowd and people whistled, the guitar player who'd played the key lines and riffs made a big, sweeping bow, rolling his arm forward, and everyone hooted and cheered. Everyone stood again, Audrey with them, clapping, and the band all bowed and then walked offstage into either wing.

She clapped in time with the crowd and felt dizzy, her hands coming together loose and flat. She felt dizzy and found her breath uneven. She slowed her hands, tried to take air in with that rhythm, tried to get air into her lungs to fight back that fuzzy, spinning feeling. Her back, neck, shoulders all clenched and knotted, did not relax, and she stopped clapping and sat back down, breathing, feeling tense, feeling however long a time she'd sat hunched, staring at the stage.

The applause trailed away to silence again. Sue Father did not come back. Then the house lights came on.

The crowd funnelled up a different set of stairs and out into a snow-cut wind, and they weren't in the alley but out on 8th Avenue. The wind broke apart knots of people, rushed goodbyes, pushed them to the taxi stand or either way along the sidewalk to wherever they'd parked, and Audrey stood in the jostle pulling up her collar and her jacket tightly around herself, wishing for gloves and a hat. She walked up 8th and the coming-apart crowd mixed with other coming-apart crowds.

Across the street, in front of the Jack Singer Concert Hall, she saw the Skinny Cowboy.

He was standing with his hands in the pockets of his leather jacket, looking in her direction across 8th Avenue. The black hat pushed back a little bit so that the yellow street light showed his face. Audrey saw him across the street and their eyes met and he saw her and she was sure he saw her and he smiled.

The doors of the Jack Singer opened and people started coming out, a just-finished concert crowd, men in black felt jackets and ladies with white hair and pearls flooding out of the high-ceilinged marble lobby and the noise and bustle and yellow incandescent light spilled into the street. Husbands held up hands for taxi cabs, leaning forward for attention. They spilled all around the Skinny Cowboy and he disappeared.

She was scared but then she wasn't scared. And standing there, the thing she wanted most in the world was to tell him that. 'I'm not scared of you,' she wanted to tell the Skinny Cowboy. 'Why would I be? I don't owe you anything. We don't owe you anything.'

Audrey tried to fight her way through the sudden crowd to the other side of the street. Women cupped hands around cigarette lighters against the wind, some of them jacketless, in red and green cocktail dresses, and men in overcoats and banded hats pressed against them to shield the wind and to be close to the women, and they laughed and had confetti on their shoulders and in their pinned hair, paper squares and glitter on their cheeks and in their eyeliner, sipping champagne flutes smuggled out past red-jacketed valets and busboys. Audrey ducked and pushed through grey flannel shoulders and cashmere scarves, around women in sheer dresses pushing into the jacket fabric of more smartly dressed women and men for warmth. The crowd was becalmed now, no movement or flow up or down the street, and she put her hands on shoulders to steer and pull her way through, one step at a time, through wine breath and hot gin laughs.

She emerged from the crowd at the end of the block and confetti sparkled on the front of her jacket. She opened up her hands and confetti and glitter sparkled in her palms under the street light.

He was down at the end of the block, walking away from her. The silver hair underneath the hat, above the silver-thread roses. He turned south around the corner, south down 1st Street. She hurried after him, walking as quickly as she could. A knot of people stepped in front of her to flag down a taxi and she sidestepped through them. On 1st Street she saw him disappearing under the railroad underpass.

She shouted at him but he was gone.

She waited for the light to change at 12th Avenue. Across the street, music ground out of a dark pub. The door opened and inside she glimpsed a few thin teenagers in black denim vests sitting at a bar. Jean jackets, roughly screened patches sewn on the shoulders with dental floss, unevenly cut hair, dyed and re-dyed. Black eyes and cracked teeth, holding brown bottles or pint glasses. The music stopped, only for a second, and another song started up, ground-glass guitars and rat-a-tat drums. At the bar they hoisted up their drinks and shouted along to the lyrics, the racket all indecipherable, and they clanged glasses and bottles together and shouted.

Audrey reached into her jacket and the folded-up poster was gone. She had set it down somewhere. Or it wasn't there. She looked inside her jacket and confetti glittered on the lining.

'I'm not the one who owes someone something,' she said, out loud on the corner in the night.

The light changed and she should have gone across, west along 12th Avenue. She went the other way, trying to find the Skinny Cowboy.

16

MONDAY

On the moon, the surveyors drive iron stakes into the grey rock according to their map. The surveyors run long silver string lines between the stakes to mark edges. They fly still steel flags from high poles to mark points.

They leave their tents on the moon and take long floating steps toward the work site. Bounding strides that arc across the black moon sky, loaded down with their burdens: food for the day in galvanized lunchboxes, boots and gloves and goggles, picks and shovels. They bring hammer drills to pierce deep into the moon on the points marked by the surveyors. Explosives to feed into drill holes inserted deeply into the moonskin. The explosive carriers lag behind and take more careful strides, each parabolic step more deliberate at the bottom, loose knees cushioning their burden.

'From here to here,' says the foreman, pointing down the line.

They clap gloved hands to the sides of their heads and turn their faces from the noise and shock of each deeply buried explosion. The ground buckles and grey dust puffs out from the shaft. Diffuses out into the moon sky, a dense, free smear against the black behind. The charges break and shatter the rock, free it in tiny pieces to float away from formations hardened into long, long before.

On the moon they cross gloved hands and lean on shovel shafts to look up into the sky. More stars than they'd ever seen wheel above them. Any constellations they may have known in an old life filled and made different by new stars, hidden previously by the fog of atmosphere. Or maybe, someone thinks, they just hadn't looked for so long. There wasn't a lot of time before for looking up at night. They look up and the dust of their detonations doesn't settle back onto their uplifted faces, but floats, finely sifted icing-sugar snow set free in all directions, free of the rock and the air, free from drifting back toward the ground the way snow would, somewhere back below where there are still winters.

§

She went through the rooms looking for clothes. She found five socks in three different colours. A pullover hoodie, a roadrunner with bloodshot eyes embroidered on the chest. A black T-shirt with holes around the hem and in the collar. She found handkerchiefs tied in a long string, as if someone planned to pull them dramatically from a sleeve. A summer dress splashed with dyed flowers. A denim jacket, the breast pocket worn white into a cigarette packet rectangle.

She found a pair of steel-toed workboots and said, *Thank god*. They were big, bigger than her feet. But big was an easier problem.

There were no gloves. She hoped to find gloves.

She went out back to her pile of empty bottles and found three plastic water bottles that still had their caps. She poured water into them, first to rinse and then to fill. She screwed the caps back on.

Oven mitts, she thought.

The kitchen was dark without the flashlight. She propped open the door and waited for her eyes to adjust to that little bit of light. Then walked, hands out, feeling for counter edges. She pulled open drawers and felt inside them carefully. Watch for knife blades, don't get cut or stuck. Drawers and drawers of pot lids, skillets, rolling pins, spatulas, aluminum foil, and plastic wrap, and finally, deep in the kitchen, quilted oven mitts.

She felt for the sink and opened the cupboards underneath. Found crumpled plastic bags, folded for space. She felt her way back toward the light with her mitts and bags.

In the parlour she put on four of the five socks. If you have more socks on one foot you will walk funny. It may matter eventually. So she left off one of the socks. She pulled the topmost up over the cuff of her jeans.

She crumpled some of the plastic bags and squashed them up into the toes of the too-big boots. When she pulled them on and laced them tight, they were heavy and awkward but her feet did not move inside them. Her feet sweated in the heat immediately and she thought, That's good. Bank the heat. Be hot now. She put the T-shirt on top of her own T-shirt and then pulled the dress over her head. It reached down to her ankles but it was large and loose and she could walk freely in it. She lifted her knees up above her waist. Took some practice reaching steps. She put on the hoodie and then the denim jacket. She sweated. She tied a handkerchief around her head, over her ears knotted in the back, and repeated, three handkerchiefs. She pulled the hood over her head and then knotted another handkerchief around that. There were still more handkerchiefs and she wrapped these around the water bottles and put them in her pockets. Then she pulled on the oven mitts.

'I'm sorry, Kitten,' she said.

Then she walked out into the morning snow.

ACKNOWLEDGEMENTS

Excerpts of this novel appeared in *Geist Magazine* issue 116, and in *The Calgary Renaissance*, edited by rob mclennan and derek beaulieu, Chaudiere Books, 2016.

The Tommi Mäkinen dialogue is based on a 2017 video interview from the FIA World Rally Championship.

Thank you to Nicole Kajander, Julia Williams, Samantha Warwick, Tara Scott, Dave Anderson, Sean Dennie, Aaron Booth, Lee Shedden, Eric Kingori, Curtis Marble, and Lorrie Matheson, for being insightful readers, sharing stories (some deliberately and some that I quietly took and stripped for parts), and for answering all my questions and helping me better understand cars, Fort McMurray work camps, crew-driving, rally racing, and rifles.

Over the last twenty-plus years I have been on the road with Aaron Smelski, Joel Nye, Mark Macarthur, Chris Vail, Patrick May, Matt Swann, Lorrie Matheson, and Nicola Cavanagh, none of whom are anything like any of the Lever Men but will probably recognize a few of the bars they played.

The building at Two Reel Lake had a different name in early drafts and we knew we needed to change it. James Lindsay at Coach House suggested 'the Crash Palace' which I really liked, and that became both the building and the novel.

Alana Wilcox was tremendously patient and supportive through the thirteen years it took to write this novel, and was instrumental in bringing Audrey and her story to life. Thank you, Alana.

Thank you most of all, Jennifer Tamura, the most important part of my life and the centre of everything I do, always.

Andrew Wedderburn's debut novel, *The Milk Chicken Bomb*, was a finalist for the Amazon First Novel Award and longlisted for the IMPAC Award. Wedderburn's musical work includes the groups Hot Little Rocket and Night Committee.

Typeset in Albertina and Bourton

Printed at the Coach House on bpNichol Lane in Toronto, Ontario, on Zephyr
Antique Laid paper, which was manufactured, acid-free, in Saint-Jérôme, Quebec,
from second-growth forests. This book was printed with vegetable-based ink on
a 1973 Heidelberg KORD offset litho press. Its pages were folded on a Baumfolder,
gathered by hand, bound on a Sulby Auto-Minabinda, and trimmed on a Polar
single-knife cutter.

Edited and designed by Alana Wilcox
Cover design by Ingrid Paulson
Author photo by Malcolm Overend

Coach House Books
80 bpNichol Lane
Toronto ON M5S 3J4
Canada

416 979 2217
800 367 6360

mail@chbooks.com
www.chbooks.com